GHOST OF THE HEART

What Reviewers Say About Catherine Friend's Work

The Spanish Pearl

"Exciting, thoughtful and told with the right amount of humor and romance, *The Spanish Pearl* is a hit. ...Friend has done a wonderful job..."—*Lambda Literary Review*

"The author does a terrific job with characterization, lush setting, action scenes, and droll commentary. This is one of those well-paced, exciting books that you just can't quite put down. ...This is one of the very best books I've read in many months, so I give it my highest recommendation! Don't miss this one."—*Midwest Fiction Review*

"Catherine Friend is not only a skilled and talented writer, but a wonderful story-teller of a high caliber. With *The Spanish Pearl* she has crafted an engrossing thoroughly enjoyable story that pulls you in from page one, and then? Never lets go till the very end." —*Kissed by Venus*

"This is a great time travel fantasy based on solid history. We rated it five hearts."—*Heartland Reviews*

"This is a rollicking good tale, full of adventure, humor, romance, and high stakes suspense."—*Just About Write*

The Crown of Valencia

"Her storytelling talent is superb and her plot twists continually keep the reader in suspense..."—*Just About Write*

A Pirate's Heart—*Lambda Literary Award Finalist*

"Catherine Friend's freshly-plotted and engaging dual romance knocked my "arrrrghyl socks" off and turned me on to a whole new world of fiction. Friend's fans are well aware of her sharp wit and indelible humor. *A Pirate's Heart* is an engaging page-turner. Throw in two compelling romances, and you have double the fun. Friend delivers the ancient sea lingo spot on and gives details so rich and real that her characters leave a lasting impression. The parallel between present day Minneapolis and The West Indies in 1715 is beautifully crafted and brilliantly tied together."—*Lambda Literary Review*

"Friend masterfully blends past and present to take us on a journey into a historical period filled with thrills, adventure, lore, and love, and adds a dash of modern day exploits, mystery, and romance for good measure. Avast, matey! This book will appeal to the pirate's heart in everyone."—*Just About Write*

The Copper Egg

"*The Copper Egg* by Catherine Friend is a modern day Indiana Jones style adventure. [It] has a bit of everything, adventure, kidnapping, double crossing frenemies and of course a romance. ...Well written and an action-packed adventure of fun."—*Romantic Reader Blog*

Hit By a Farm

"*Hit By a Farm* goes beyond funny, through poignant, sad and angry, to redemptive: all the things that make a farm—and a relationship—successful."—*Lavender Magazine*

"A sweet and funny book in the classic 'Hardy Girls Go Farming' genre, elegantly told, from the first two pages, which are particularly riveting for the male reader, through the astonishing revelation that chickens have belly-buttons and on to the end, which comes much too soon. It has dogs, sheep, a pickup truck, women's underwear, electric fences, the works."—Garrison Keillor

Sheepish: Two Women, Fifty Sheep, and Enough Wool to Save the Planet

"As provocative as her reflections are, it is Friend's acerbic wit that keeps the reader turning pages. A perfect choice for book groups, this is a look at the road not taken with a guide who pokes as much fun at herself as she does at the world around her."—*Booklist*

"Friend details the challenges of balancing a writing career with sheep farming in southeastern Minnesota. ...Her voice is wry and funny; she's self-deprecating and thoughtful, and strikes a balance between teasing and kindness, whether her subject is pregnant sheep, yarn-loving 'fiber freaks,' or spirituality and nature."—*Publishers Weekly*

By the Author

The Spanish Pearl

The Crown of Valencia

A Pirate's Heart

The Copper Egg

Spark

Ghost of the Heart

By DaCapo Press

Hit by a Farm: How I Learned to Stop Worrying
and Love the Barn

Sheepish: Two Women, Fifty Sheep, and Enough Wool
to Save the Planet

GHOST OF THE HEART

by
Catherine Friend

2024

GHOST OF THE HEART

ISBN 13: 978-1-63555-112-9

This Trade Paperback Original Is Published By
Bold Strokes Books, Inc.
P.O. Box 249
Valley Falls, NY 12185

First Edition: November 2024

CREDITS
EDITOR: CINDY CRESAP
PRODUCTION DESIGN: SUSAN RAMUNDO
COVER DESIGN BY INK SPIRAL DESIGN AND SHERI

Acknowledgments

My sister Sandy deserves a special thanks for her help. Seven years ago, when we were standing by the river at St. Augustine's Castillo de San Marcos considering scenes for this novel, a fort volunteer approached us to see if we needed help. "No, thanks," I said. "I'm just plotting a murder and need to figure out how to dispose of the body."

Dead silence.

My sister quickly stepped in. "For a *novel*! Plotting a murder for a *novel*! Disposing of a body for a *novel*!"

"Ahh, I see." The poor man couldn't get away from us fast enough.

Life interrupted my writing for a few years, but last year I picked up the novel again and entirely revamped it, which required another trip to the Castillo with my sister. I found the perfect room for a pivotal scene, but the only entrance was a low, narrow tunnel that required either crawling on your knees or duck-walking in a squat, neither of which my "new" knees will do. Always up for adventure, Sandy duck-walked through the tunnel and took photos for me. So when you reach the BIG scenes in the powder magazine, those were only possible thanks to my sister.

Thanks to everyone at Bold Strokes Books for welcoming me back with kindness and enthusiasm after my six-year absence, and a special thanks to my editor, Cindy Cresap, who always catches my stupid mistakes. Sheri Halal and Ink Spiral created an amazing cover with just the right amount of spookiness.

And I deeply appreciate those friends and family willing to read early drafts: Phyllis Root, Anne Ylvisaker, Mary Casanova, Margi Preus, my supportive wife Melissa, and my mom, Irene Friend. (I love that she was so engrossed in the novel that when it was time for *Jeopardy*, she waved me away. "Gotta keep reading," she said.)

And finally, thanks to all the readers over the years who have read my books and let me know they like what they read. Your words keep me going when the going gets tough.

Dedication

To my sister, Sandy Friend Elbracht

While I do not believe in ghosts, I fear them nonetheless.

—EDITH WHARTON

PROLOGUE

The ghost hovered above the fort, unable or unwilling to leave, it didn't know which. It could move through the rooms, float up the staircase, and brush past people with enough force to make them turn, startled, but it could not do much more than that. It pushed through the wall once but could go no farther. The ghost was trapped by its death, by time, and by the unwavering need...to wait.

The ghost had been waiting so long that its reason for remaining had been lost decades ago. Now, only threads of anxiety and dread held it together as it waited. Would it know when to act? What to do?

Even though the years had jumbled its memories into a soup of confusion, it did know that everything rested on its shoulders. It would either save a life or take one, but which was it supposed to be? And where was the woman? When would she come?

After yet another endless day, the ghost hovered above the fort, exhausted by the eternal wait. Only when it performed its task would the ghost fade from the world, a murdered soul free at last.

CHAPTER ONE

Gwen, November 2

Gwen Tucker flipped through the pages of her drawings and groaned. All of Flagler College's history professors had agreed to the Art Department's challenge: they'd sketch one hundred images in one hundred days, but Gwen wasn't an artist. Her straight lines looked like they'd been drinking. Her faces made cathedral gargoyles look like *Vogue* models in comparison. She could analyze historical events, cross-country ski for hours, and make a killer French onion soup from scratch. But this? She couldn't do this. It was hard to admit, but she needed Billie's help.

When the front door opened, and Billie joined her on the porch swing, Gwen smiled. Perfect timing. Billie kicked off her sandals and tucked her bare feet under Gwen's thigh. "Hi, babe. How's it going?"

Gwen gave Billie her saddest smile. "Not great. My wrist really hurts."

"Really?"

"Arthritis probably."

Billie made a sad face. "Aren't you too young for that?"

Gwen sighed dramatically. "Fifty-four is just about the age when most people develop it. I hate to let the History team down, but I don't know how I'm going to finish this challenge. One hundred sketches?" She held her wrist at an awkward angle for visual effect.

"You poor thing." Billie tried moving Gwen's wrist. "Wow. That's really locked up."

"Yes, I probably need surgery."

Billie took Gwen's hand tenderly into her own. "You do need surgery, but not on your wrist." She flashed her half-grin. "You need *brain* surgery if you think I'm going to do your drawings for you."

Gwen threw up her hands as Billie laughed. "Oh, *c'mon*. Seriously, look at this monstrosity." Gwen showed her the drawing she'd done of a man in a downtown coffee shop. The eyes were at different levels and the poor man's ears were big as plates.

Billie nodded. "I think you're improving."

Gwen growled.

"C'mon, babe, where's your school spirit? Think of all the money your department will get from donors if you win. And you've got it easy. You're making those poor art professors write one hundred essays in one hundred days. That's brutal."

"They are personal histories, which are easy. The day I fell off my bike. My favorite TV show. Pets I've owned. I could write those in my sleep. I could write those in a *coma*." She sighed. "I still can't believe you won't help. *You're* the artist in the family, not me. If you really loved me you'd finish the drawings for me."

Billie squished Gwen's face between her palms and gave her a big kiss. "Guess I don't really love you then."

"I knew it," Gwen said, kissing her back, but bummed that she'd have to continue with the sketches herself, unless she was lucky enough to sprain a wrist or something.

"Movie tonight?"

Gwen groaned. "My choice, not yours." When they first fell in love, the only thing they argued about was movies, but after all these years their list of disagreements and slights and resentments had grown frustratingly long. Gwen hadn't realized it took so much work to stay in a relationship, but she did love Billie. She didn't think *that* had changed.

"What's wrong with my movie choices?" Billie grinned.

"First, ghosts aren't real. I think I've made that clear. Yet you talked me into watching that romance called *Truly, Madly, Deeply*, which turned out to have a *what*?"

"A ghost," Billie said gleefully.

"Second, I've also made a point with you that time travel isn't possible, yet you bring home the DVD—God, DVDs, feels like those were eons ago—for a charming Meg Ryan/Hugh Jackman romance called *Kate & Leopold*. And what happens in *that* movie?"

"Time travel!"

"And finally, aliens do not live among us, yet that old underwater adventure movie we streamed last winter, *The Abyss*, ended up having *what* in it?"

"Underwater aliens!" Billie chortled, throwing her arms into the air.

Gwen shook her head. "Twenty-five years and you still get a kick out of winding me up." She'd enjoyed all three of those movies even though they were based on wildly impossible events, but she wasn't going to tell Billie that.

"Well, I know your 'ghosts aren't real' mantra is how you survived your mom, but it bugs me just a little that you refuse to admit there might be even a *tiny* chance of the supernatural or paranormal existing in our world. What if time travel is possible? And what if aliens do live among us? We don't know for sure."

Gwen sighed. "How have we stayed together so long?"

Billie hugged her. "Because opposites attract, right?"

"Harrumph. Not every day." Gwen returned the hug, squeezing hard. Billie was tall and sturdy, not willowy like some taller women. Her eyes turned from green to hazel to gray depending on what she wore, but no matter the color, they were always bright and intensely focused on life. Billie moved through the world like someone who knew she could fix anything that broke. Get locked out of your house? Billie was the neighbor who'd figure out how to get you back inside without breaking a window. Lose your dog? Billie was the one who'd be out in the dark, as long as it took, driving up and down each block until she found the dog. Snowblower on the fritz? Billie would take it apart for you until she found the wire or part that had gone bad, then replace it. Billie exuded strength and competence, which made the last two years even harder because she'd become anything *but* strong and competent.

Just then, Jeremy Wilkinson pulled up in front of their bright teal bungalow and honked. Gwen rolled her eyes.

Billie pointed to Jeremy. "Seriously, Gwen, *anyone* could be an alien. Take your friend Jeremy out there, all fake tan and big white teeth and obnoxiously expensive watch. For all we know, he could be an alien from Alpha Centauri wearing a Jeremy *suit*."

"Enough," Gwen said as she gathered up her stuff.

Billie got in one final shot. "Careful not to strain that wrist."

With a grunt, Gwen hurried out to Jeremy, another history professor in her department. As she threw her backpack into the back seat, she noticed the creepy neighbor across the street and down one house, Clayton Black, doing what he often did—standing under his carport, staring at their house. With his shaved head and neck tattoos, Clayton looked like the type of young man who'd defend his right to do whatever he damn well pleased on his own property. Usually Gwen admired this trait, because she felt it as well, but it was unnerving that the guy spent so much time staring at their house. Plus, he'd never spoken to them, but just stared, week after week. It freaked them out.

Jeremy leaned over to pop open her door, his high forehead shining from the open sunroof. Jeremy was someone who was hard to picture or even remember when he wasn't standing in front of you. The only feature that made him stand out in a crowd was his massive watch, some ugly thing he'd inherited from his grandfather that was supposedly worth twenty-five thousand dollars.

"Hey, boss," he called. "Ready for another field trip?" Jeremy's insanely strong Axe body spray attacked her senses as she climbed inside. People usually looked themselves over before leaving the house, searching for lint on their pants or food on their mouths; why didn't they take a sniff of themselves as well?

Jeremy was one of those bouncy, happy upbeat people that she liked being around for about twenty minutes, then his cheeriness grated on her so much she wanted to bite his head off. But since she was the new chair of Flagler College's History Department, avoiding carnivorous behavior was probably a good idea. She buckled herself in. "How many drawings have you done so far?"

Jeremy grinned as he pulled out into the street. "I've got sixty-eight," he said. "And you?"

She cleared her throat. "I'm at forty-two." She looked back over her shoulder. Instead of watching her drive away, Clayton still stared at their house. Was he waiting for Billie to come outside?

Jeremy made an unhappy sound in his throat. "Gwen, we've only got four weeks left, and we've already lost three team members. There are only a handful of us left to defend the honor of the History Department." He turned onto Avenida Menendez and drove them around the outside edge of St. Augustine's historic downtown.

Gwen watched the city pass by. She loved the old, worn buildings and narrow streets of St. Augustine, the country's oldest continuously inhabited city. Not much of the original 1565 city remained, but some structures were from the 1600s. Jeremy drove them past the Bridge of Lions, a graceful arch guarded by stone lions that crossed the Matanzas River to Anastasia Island and the ocean beaches. Sailboats bobbed in the marina. She was still amazed at how quiet it was in this small city compared to St. Paul—fewer sirens, less honking, softer road sounds. But it was hot down here, even in November, so she always felt just a little sticky most of the time.

With her window open, she could smell the river, grilled food from an outdoor restaurant at the marina, and the absence of cold. Cold air had a nasty bite that attacked your nostrils, your eyes, and your lungs, but she and Billie lived in Florida now. No snow, no ice, no blizzards.

Gwen had pushed for the move from Minnesota to St. Augustine in a last-ditch effort to save Billie from herself. Yes, Gwen had to make a difficult sacrifice, one that Billie could never learn about, but it was the only option she had. As she passed a long string of palm trees, a shard of homesickness stabbed her. No more freshly fallen snow. No more snowshoeing. No more cuddling up next to a fireplace in the dead of winter. They were Floridians now and had to adjust. At least they'd added to the ranks of rational voters in a state full of MAGA cult members.

But it wasn't just the move that bothered her. Gwen's stepbrother Mason had, over the years, fallen in love four times. Gwen had also fallen in love four times…but with the same woman.

She fell the day she met Billie on the San Francisco streetcar, then again when Billie helped Gwen with *everything* after she'd dislocated her elbow. She fell that moonlit night on their Alaskan cruise, and again when Billie slow winked at her from across the room during her office party.

By now, Mason had likely fallen in love a fifth time, but Gwen was still waiting. She loved Billie, but it'd been five years since the slow wink, and she missed the warm flush that spread through her body like melted honey when she realized—once again—that Billie was The One. Falling in love with the same woman had made Gwen happy, content, and feeling as stable as a continent.

However, five years was a long time to wait for another satisfying *Yes* moment to reinforce the hard work. And staying with the same person for twenty-four years and ten months *was* work, no matter how much they loved each other. She and Billie were only two months away from their twenty-fifth anniversary, but Gwen's emotions felt as flat as the Florida landscape to which they'd just moved, and that worried her. What was wrong with her?

Jeremy parked in the last spot in the fort's narrow parking lot. The fort was a dark structure squatting at the northern edge of the historic downtown. Both the fort and the huge grassy grounds surrounding it were now a US Park Service property. The first time Gwen had seen the fort, built in the 1600s by the Spanish and called the Castillo de San Marcos, she'd proclaimed it a major disappointment. *Castillo* means castle in Spanish, but this building looked nothing like a castle and more like a big old black turtle with the top third of its shell shaved off. There were no turrets, no tall towers, no romantic balconies, no charm. The "castle" was just a two-story dark wall with a few flags flying overhead.

Jeremy locked the car as Gwen shouldered her pack. She and Jeremy had been taking these field trips together to ensure they'd be able to finish this playful competition between the art and history departments. As they started down the long sidewalk, Jeremy swept his arm toward the fort. "You're going to love this place. It's full of amazing stories, like the time the entire city took refuge in the fort when the British attacked. And the time—"

Gwen held up her hand. "Okay, I get it. It's rich with history." She loved history but was too out of sorts to handle a lecture from Jeremy. The guy meant well but was constantly rubbing her the wrong way.

"Yes, and the fort is haunted."

Gwen stopped in her tracks. "What?"

Jeremy nodded as he adjusted his sunglasses. "Ghosts. St. Augustine is full of them. I know you've only been here a few months, but surely, you've seen those ghost tour buses all over the city at night. If you're going to live here, you need to get comfortable with ghosts. C'mon, I'll buy our tickets."

Gwen rolled her eyes. "Jeremy, you're a logical thinker, a brilliant historian. How can you possibly talk about ghosts as if they're real?

"They are real." He frowned. "What's the problem?"

She shook her head. "Ghosts are not real. They are figments of people's imaginations, made up to explain bumps and noises that have causes based in reality."

"You're serious?"

"As a heart attack," she replied. "Here's a little reality check. Ghosts do not exist. Time travel is not possible. Aliens are not living among us."

Jeremy lowered his sunglasses and made a sad face. "You poor thing. Who *hurt* you?"

Gwen sighed and laughed at the same time, which came out sounding like an asthmatic cough. Jeremy's tease tiptoed quite close to the truth. For her entire childhood, her mom had force-fed her the supernatural—ghosts, time travel, aliens, astrology, tarot, séances. It was more than intense. Seriously, what six-year-old wanted a Ouija board for her birthday?

Not Gwen, that was for sure. She'd wanted the Barbie Style Set, a large Barbie head with thick, gorgeous hair you could style and curl and spray with Barbie's exclusive perfumed hair spray, but her parents—read, *her mother*—gave her the Ouija board. She had few memories of her early childhood, but one had stuck with her: When six-year-old Gwen watched her mother use the new Ouija board to "chat" with nearby spirits, she decided then and there to resist her mother's weirdness with all her might.

"Repeat after me, Jeremy. Ghosts do not exist. Time travel is not possible. Aliens are not living among us."

Jeremy shrugged. "Okay, boss, you do you. But just repeating something over and over again doesn't make it true."

Did everyone on this planet believe in ghosts? She inhaled slowly, counting to four, then exhaled to the same count.

"You okay?"

She nodded, feeling a bit of anger start to bubble up again. What was the *matter* with her? She'd felt on edge for weeks and it had been getting worse. "Yeah, I'm fine."

"Good. Now for the fort's layout." He began vigorously pointing toward parts of the fort. "It's built in a square with diamond-shaped extensions on each corner called bastions. The walls between each bastion are called curtains."

"Bastions. Curtains. Will there be a test?"

"Cute. I'm serious. You need to pay attention." More pointing. "The fort's walls are thirty-three feet high and twelve feet thick. The rooms inside are called vaults."

"Bastions. Curtains. Vaults."

"There's an open courtyard in the middle, then stairs leading up to the second level, where you can see those people standing. That second level is called the *terrepleine*, but since you're mocking my extensive knowledge, you can just call it the gun deck."

"Enough, Dr. Wilkinson. Let's get in, draw our great works of art, then get out again."

Jeremy bought the tickets with a college credit card and handed her a brochure. Gwen skimmed the brochure's map as they crossed the wooden bridge over the dry, grassy moat and entered the fort's main level. The entrance to the fort was basically a passageway that led to the outdoor central courtyard ahead. As they walked, Jeremy waved around them. "We are in the sally port, which is basically the fort's entrance. It runs from the main door out into the courtyard." His voice echoed in the empty area.

"Yes, I can see that." Between the lecture on fort architecture, the talk of ghosts, and her subterranean anger, Gwen's patience was spread thinner than tissue paper. They were nearly through the passageway, or sally port, when someone touched her hair.

She whirled, ready to snap at whomever was responsible, but there was no one there. To the left, an open door led into a brightly lit gift shop with two tourists arguing loudly about which fridge magnet to buy. To the right was an open door labeled *Soldier Barracks*. She and Jeremy were alone.

"Very funny," she said.

"Huh?"

The touch came again, so gently that goose bumps raced up her bare arms. "How are you doing that?"

"Doing what? C'mon, let's get out into the courtyard where it's warmer."

Gwen stepped out into the sunshine. The grassy courtyard was ringed by a limestone slab sidewalk, and open doorways led into display rooms—vaults according to Jeremy—all around the courtyard. A small cannon was bolted to a concrete pad in one corner of the grass. She touched the rough wall nearest her, surprised to see tiny, tiny shells buried on the concrete.

Gwen felt someone standing too close behind her, so she turned again to find no one there. Jeremy stood ahead of her, and a woman in a yellow *Fruit Cove Elementary* T-shirt passed by as she herded a small group of noisy school children wearing the same yellow T-shirts, but otherwise, there was no one near enough to have touched her.

She jammed her fists onto her hips, ready to fire Jeremy on the spot, even though he was tenured and couldn't be fired. "I'll ask you one more time. How are you doing this?"

"Doing what?"

"Do you have some sort of feather on a stick or something?" She looked around him to see if he was hiding anything behind his back. Sometimes this guy took his teasing way too far.

"What are you talking about?"

Gwen stepped closer and lowered her voice. "Someone is touching me." She shuddered as the light caress returned, this time along the back of her neck and down one arm.

Jeremy froze. "What do you mean?"

"I mean someone just touched my hair...and now my arm." Gwen swallowed, feeling stupid.

He lowered his sunglasses and looked right at her. "There isn't a breeze here in the courtyard, and no one has come near us." He bounced on the balls of his feet for a second, too excited to stand still. "Oh, my god, oh my god, oh my god. I can't believe this is happening."

"Can't believe *what* is happening?"

He shook his head. "Amazing. It really must like you."

"It?"

"Gwen, I was serious when I said there are ghosts here. Usually they're seen at night, often walking up there, along the gun deck. But I think you are experiencing one in the middle of the freaking day. The SAPS people will go apeshit when they hear this."

"SAPS?"

"St. Augustine Paranormal Society."

Gwen's jaw tightened and she clenched her fists in frustration. Ghosts were not real. Time travel wasn't possible. Aliens were not living among them. That mantra had kept her sane throughout her teens as her mom had fallen so deep into the supernatural well that she wouldn't make a decision without consulting her astrology charts or Ouija board. Her mom, an intelligent, articulate, professional woman, had gone over to the Dark Side, as Billie liked to say, and Gwen had refused to follow.

But now her skin tingled with a fear she'd never felt before. If ghosts were not real, then who, or *what*, had just gently caressed her cheek, and was now running a finger lightly down the side of her throat?

CHAPTER TWO

Billie, November 2

Billie watched Gwen walk toward Jeremy's car, admiring her curves. Gwen was six inches shorter than Billie, which had created in Billie the intense need to protect Gwen, both physically and emotionally, but when Gwen had figured this out their first year together, she'd accused Billie of being "heightist" and told her to knock it off, which had only deepened Billie's desire to protect her. Gwen's peppery personality matched her salt-and-pepper hair, and Billie loved both.

Gwen was so competent and confident that when forced to engage in something she didn't do well, she got ornery. Billie was proud of Gwen, however, for sticking with the art challenge even though she possessed little talent. A weaker woman would have bailed, but Gwen was hanging in there.

As Billie stood at the top of the porch stairs, she clutched a post in each hand and took a deep breath. She could do this. She knew she could leave the house because she'd done it now for two weeks. But this stupid condition was so inconsistent. Some days she could leave, some days she couldn't. Some days she could travel three or four miles from home, other days she broke out into a cold sweat thirty *feet* from home. Her doctor said this was normal, but Billie hated it.

Each day she had to take a leap of faith and step from the porch down onto the ground, not knowing if today would be one of those bad days. She hesitated on the bottom step and ran through her list of truths just as her therapist had taught her: There was no ice in Florida. She was only one mile from work, well within her comfort zone. She didn't have to take unfamiliar streets or walk in unknown neighborhoods. She'd successfully left this new house dozens of times without a panic attack, so she could do it again.

She patted her chest for courage then stepped down onto the grass. One step, then another, then another. Billie blew out a deep breath of relief, then realized their elderly neighbors Earl and Sassy were struggling to unload a box from their trunk, so she crossed the street, pleased she could do so without shaking and feeling dizzy.

Billie loved Earl and Sassy. Clayton, the man next door to them, however, gave her the creeps. "Here, let me help," she said as she reached the couple.

Earl stepped back, flashing a grateful smile. Short and wiry, Earl reminded Billie of an elderly terrier too stubborn to slow down.

"Thank you, dear," Sassy said, moving back like the former dancer she was, fluid and graceful even at eighty. "We believe in giving young people as many opportunities as possible to feel useful."

Billie chuckled as she pulled the small TV box from the trunk and carried it into their living room. After they escorted her back outside, Billie cleared her throat, realizing this was the perfect opportunity. "So, inquiring minds would love to know how you two have successfully reached fifty years together."

Earl and Sassy looked at each other. "Cocaine and pot," Earl said.

"Whiskey and red wine," Sassy added.

"Ear plugs," Earl said.

"Nose plugs."

Laughing, Billie held up both hands. "Okay, okay. I get it. But if there was a couple who'd reached, say, twenty-five years, and were concerned they might not reach, say, twenty-six, what advice would you have?" She paused. "I'm asking for a friend, of course."

Sassy laughed so hard she needed to lean against Earl and have a brief coughing fit. "Of course you are, dear," she finally managed to get out. She looked up at Earl. "Well, we'd probably tell that couple to remember that marriage isn't about committing to the relationship."

"It's not?"

"Nope, it's about *re*committing to the relationship, over and over again."

Billie screwed up her face. "Sounds exhausting," she said.

"It is," Earl said with such a booming laugh that Sassy slapped at him half-heartedly.

Billie tried again. "But plenty of people get divorced somewhere between year one and year fifty and they are fine. How do you know whether to recommit or to bail?"

Sassy, smelling of lemons, gave her a sideways hug,. "You don't."

"I was hoping you'd say that if you love each other enough it's easy to stay married."

The couple looked at each other. "Nope," they said in unison, then with friendly waves headed back inside.

Billie spritzed the next little windowpane and wiped the glass clean enough to squeak. Walt's antique shop was in one of the oldest buildings in downtown, a sweet one-story stucco on Cuna Street, one block off St. George. The ancient slate roof had sprouted grass, so the little building wore a green crown. The windows, while perhaps not original, were still very old, so Billie was careful not to push too hard.

Walt was happily setting up his new digital cash register, exclaiming over each feature as he hummed some unknown tune, his snow-white afro bouncing with whatever beat he was keeping.

Walt had proudly proclaimed that he'd worn his afro ever since protesting the Vietnam War in 1972. During her job interview he'd shown her a photo from that time, and sure enough, his currently white afro matched the young Walt's dark one exactly.

She'd laughed at the photo. "Okay, Brian May," she said, cementing their friendship, and getting the job. Walt loved Queen and knew that the lead guitarist's long curly locks looked exactly the same today as they did in the 80s, only now pure white. "Yup, me and Brian looking hotter than ever." Billie loved working for Walt and enjoyed meeting customers. It was the lowest paying, lowest stress job she'd ever had. She knew some people in her life judged her for no longer working a professional job but screw them. She was able to leave the house, which was more important for an agoraphobic than any "professional" job.

Walt chortled as he rang up a dummy sale. "I love this new thing. Don't you just love technology?"

Billie murmured her agreement, but as she cleaned the smooth glass, she was distracted by what Sassy had said. What did it mean to *re*commit? Had she and Gwen done that by moving from Minnesota to Florida? Why did she feel they were in trouble even though they seemed to be a little closer since the move? Was reconnecting the same as recommitting?

Billie had trusted she and Gwen would always be together, but lately they seemed to have lost their HEA. She now understood that Happily Ever After wasn't a solid place on which you could stand, like, say, Australia. It wasn't a place where, once you'd landed, you could stay as long as you wanted. No, Happily Ever After was a slender wisp of smoke that could slip through your fingers and drift away until it was totally beyond your reach. She missed it.

Couple counseling had helped Billie and Gwen straighten out some of the more crooked, unhelpful ways they'd developed to communicate, but Billie could still feel Gwen holding something back. Since moving to Florida, they'd have a string of good days, then a bad one that erased all the good days. It felt as if Gwen were constantly angry or frustrated.

Billie couldn't blame her. For the last two years, Gwen had been nothing but supportive. When the panic attacks had started, Billie breaking down into a quivering mess whenever she got too far from home, Gwen had found her a doctor to help. *Agoraphobia*, the doctor had proclaimed, and thus started Billie's two years of struggling to leave the house. Most days she failed, but now most days she could go about two miles away without a panic attack.

Finally, Gwen had proclaimed to Billie that it was time to move south. "I have a great job offer," she'd said, "and I found the perfect little house in Lincolnville, a neighborhood on the edge of downtown St. Augustine." They fell in love with the house when their research revealed the neighborhood had been settled by newly freed enslaved people after the Civil War. The quaint homes had tiny front yards, the occasional narrow second-story balcony, and slender palm trees or gnarled live oaks draped with pale Spanish moss. The best part of the neighborhood was the old oak tree growing in the middle of the street two blocks down. The city had obviously left the tree standing and paved around it. Billie thought their house was the prettiest on the block—painted sea foam green with white trim and built on short stilts to allow the air to circulate below and cool the house.

Getting Billie from St. Paul down to this Florida house, however, had been a circus that still made Billie shudder. How were they going to get her over one thousand miles away from home when she had panic attacks whenever she went more than two miles from home? The doctor prescribed a heavy, Valium-sort of drug, then Gwen and their best friends, the Lauras, packed Billie into the back of Laura G.'s panel van along with boxes of books and suitcases full of clothing. Everything else had been stashed in a storage locker.

Gwen and the two Lauras traded off driving the van and Gwen's car while Billie spent the twenty-four hours half-drugged on an air mattress. The Lauras' elderly terrier, Murphy, proved to be the perfect travel companion for her, since his aging, rough coat felt a lot like the teddy bear she'd loved almost to death as a kid. The dog snuggled up against her and slept most of the way, his snoring and snuffling and twitching paws oddly comforting. Even his old-dog breath didn't bother her for it helped ground her in the car so she could ignore the strange cities and states whirling by outside.

They only stopped to let Murphy out to do his business, and, with a Laura on each arm, hurry Billie into and out of the rest room before she had the chance to panic. Billie loved her friends for being so great, but shame at putting them through that trip still haunted her two months later. She no longer had any family alive, other than distant cousins she barely knew, so Gwen and the Lauras formed her family, and she loved them desperately. Gwen's dad, before he died, and her stepmother Faye and stepbrother Mason were also part of her family, although she hadn't seen Mason much since he'd grown up.

Billie jumped when the entry bell jangled right over her head and the door opened. *Damn it!* Billie grimaced. Martha was back. Billie had been silent the last two Mondays Martha had come, but maybe it was time to voice her concerns. Billie, before her troubles, had worked as an insurance investigator for Prudential, investigating suspicious claims, and while she could longer do that job, her suspicion genes could still fire up, which they did when Martha entered.

Walt strode toward the door. "Martha! Let's see what you have for me today." The short woman, dressed in drab slacks and shirt, her black hair pulled back into a messy bun, put her burlap sack up onto the counter. Her pale skin had been reddened by the sun in blotches, so Billie couldn't tell if she was flushed or just sunburned. She watched the woman chew the inside of her cheek and shift from side to side, as if she were a greyhound ready to run, and wondered why Martha was so nervous. Billie hovered nearby, pretending to dust the antique salt and pepper shakers.

"How is your nephew? Raising a teenager can be hard," Walt said as he sorted through the items from Martha's bag.

"Very well, thank you. I bought him his first candy bar. Sneakers like you told me. He loved it." Martha's accent was a thick Southern drawl that Billie couldn't narrow down. Georgia? Alabama?

"Ahh, Snickers. Nothing better." He began making a small pile on the counter.

Billie grimaced. What teenaged kid had never before had a candy bar?

"Thank you for buying from me. When I've saved enough money, I'll bring my nephew here."

There was something about Martha that felt off. Using a burlap bag seemed strange, although certainly more ecofriendly than plastic, but more concerning were the items Walt was swooning over. A set of antique silver spoons, an antique pistol called a pepperbox, and a bag of square-headed nails that Walt proclaimed to be from the 1800s. The items were authentic, but in weirdly great condition, as if untouched by the ravages of time. The spoons looked as if they had never been used.

There was no way these antiques were just "found items" as Martha had claimed during her first visit a few weeks ago. Their condition was just too pristine. Martha had either broken into a museum and stolen them, or she worked in a museum and was able to access the collections after hours. If she was selling stolen goods to Walt, he could lose everything.

As Walt oohed and aahed over the items, Billie did a quick search on her phone for recent museum thefts. She found nothing, but that didn't necessarily mean there hadn't been any, since most museums didn't want to advertise they'd been burgled because this tended to make museum donors of both items and money nervous. If Walt was caught buying stolen items, he could lose his business.

In just a few minutes, Walt placed a stack of bills into Martha's waiting palm. "See you next week," he said, grinning broadly. As Martha nodded and rolled up the empty sack, Billie decided to follow her. This would give Billie more information. In her job as an investigator, she'd followed dozens of people. She could totally do this. She'd moved over one thousand miles to Florida, for God's sake. She should be able to walk behind someone for a few blocks.

The entry bell rang as Martha left. Billie approached the front door and saw through the window that the woman had turned right onto Cuna Street.

"Hey, Walt, gonna take a short break," Billie said, then she was out the door and following Martha down the street. *Just go slow*, she told herself. *Pay attention to everything around you. You can do this. You'll be fine.*

But Martha soon reached Avenida Menendez, a major thoroughfare full of car traffic and bikes and pedestrians that Billie avoided like the plague because the noise felt like an assault. Instead of using the crosswalk, Martha jaywalked, running to avoid a fast-moving CR-V. Jaywalking across a busy street. Who *did* that? It was illegal. It was unsafe. It was something Billie used to do all the time before her "troubles."

Billie stopped at the curb, her arms windmilling to keep her balance. What if she tripped on that pothole in the middle of the street? What if a bike zoomed past and hit her? She could be so focused on Martha that she might get hit by a car or bitten by a rabid dog or she could fall and dislocate something. Then she heard her therapist's voice in her head: *Your agoraphobia is caused by your* algo*phobia, which is your fear of pain. You have all the symptoms: envisioning the worst possible outcome, focusing intensely on the threat of pain, avoiding everything out of fear. But you will get better.*

The world was full of innovative and surprising ways to experience pain, and Billie believed she had the creativity, skill, and shitty luck to encounter them all. Still frozen on the sidewalk, she jammed her hands into her pockets to rub the smooth river stone she kept there, another therapist tactic. But today the stone, warmed by her body, wasn't doing the trick.

She stepped back from the curb and gave up. Once, she would have hated herself for being so frightened, but she'd had enough therapy now that she could look at things more objectively and practice better self-compassion. Instead of hating herself, now she merely considered herself a pathetic loser with the spinal strength of a Republican politician.

Frustrated, Billie watched Martha disappear into the fort's parking lot, then Billie retraced her steps and went weak with relief when she was safely back inside Walt's store. The world was so large and limitless that when out in it, Billie felt small and tight, like a turtle stuck in a too-small shell. But in Walt's cramped store, small enough a claustrophobic person might pause at the threshold, Billie's chest expanded, her breath loosened, and anything felt possible. Now if she could just take that feeling with her everywhere, she'd be fine.

Billie picked up her cleaning rag and began to dust, chuckling quietly. If she could bottle confidence, she'd not only make a billion dollars, but then she could get her life back. God, how she missed it.

CHAPTER THREE

Gwen, November 2

H ey, hey!"
Gwen blinked, wondering why Jeremy was shaking her by the shoulders. "What?" She stepped back, pulling free of his grasp.

"You kind of checked out there for a second. You got all blank-eyed and slack-faced."

"Don't be ridiculous," she snapped, then rubbed her arms, the pressure bringing her back into her body. "I'm fine, I'm fine."

Clearly, Jeremy didn't believe her, but he didn't push. "Let's go up to the gun deck and draw. We'll leave all talk of ghosts down here in the courtyard."

Gwen was tempted to insist that they leave the fort entirely, but Jeremy was right—they only had a few more weeks to meet the challenge. She was fine.

The stone steps, worn down by centuries of climbers, went up one side wall, turned at the corner, and continued up to the gun deck. Gwen trailed one hand against the rough stone wall to keep her balance.

On the upper level, a welcome breeze washed away the sensation of someone touching her. Relieved, Gwen scanned the horizon. The view from the gun deck spread out in a 360-degree panorama. The wall had gun ports built in every ten feet so she could easily see the horizons. To the east was the wide Matanzas River, noisy with speedboats, then beyond that was Anastasia Island, flat but tree covered.

St. Augustine was home to the strangest geographical setup Gwen had ever seen. North of the fort, the Atlantic Ocean threaded itself inland and became the Matanzas River that headed thirty miles south, then turned east and returned to the ocean, thus carving off a chunk of the mainland into Anastasia Island.

To the south, the small, compact buildings of downtown rose up over the trees and she recognized Flagler College's bell tower at the far edge of the old city. To the west, the Ripley's Believe It or Not building peeked out from behind a stand of live oak trees. St. Augustine was a surprising mix of rich history, ridiculous claims of ghosts, and kitschy tourist traps.

"So the dry moat below us is about forty feet wide. This short wall that we're standing next to is called the parapet and has openings for sixty-four guns. That small structure down there, outside the fort, between the fort and the sea wall, is a hot shot oven, built in the 1830s to make ammunition."

Gwen put her hands over her ears and began to hum.

Jeremy laughed. "Okay, okay, enough." He led them to a bench full of kids pushing each other. "Hey, kids! Adults want your bench. Get lost." The kids scattered like startled rabbits and Gwen slid onto the smooth stone, grateful to sit.

Jeremy plopped down beside her. "I wish my kid was still that age, all silly games and laughing."

"Cameron's in middle school, right?"

"He's bored. Hates it here. Wants to move to someplace 'cool,' but I won't. He says I'm afraid, but I'm not. It's that I've lived here all my life. I'm rooted here, committed to the city, to the college, to the river, to Florida. My son doesn't understand being so deeply connected to a place that the thought of leaving is incomprehensible."

Gwen nodded, once again relieved that she and Billie had chosen to remain child-free.

"Sorry, didn't mean to bitch about my kid. I love him, but even if the only job I can find in this city is picking up cigarette butts, we're staying." He pointed toward the river. "Okay, let's draw the guard tower over there, at the end of the bastion." The tall, skinny domed "room" was barely large enough for the three kids who'd just crammed themselves inside, giggling hysterically.

Gwen grimaced. "It looks like a penis."

Jeremy chuckled. "Sorry. Not your thing. You can choose the next one; we just need to get started."

As Jeremy sharpened his pencil, Gwen looked around the gun deck. She knew most of this fort's history, more than she let on with Jeremy. She could feel the history rising in waves from its 400-year-old bones. She could imagine the pain of its many battles, the sadness of all the death, and the despair of its imprisoned Native Americans, held here in the country's push to move the Natives farther west. For many people in the past, this fort had been a very unpleasant place, and she could sense this even with the bright sunshine and laughing school children. Sighing with the weight of her thoughts, Gwen opened her sketchbook just as Jeremy's phone rang.

"Yes, this is he...What? He did *what*? Yes, I'll be right there." He jammed his phone into his back pocket, voice tight with disgust. "Cameron hit another kid. I gotta go deal."

"I'll come with—"

"No, we need drawings. Please keep going." Before she could pack up and follow, Jeremy was already halfway down the stairs.

Anger bubbled up. Was he really leaving or was he going to hide and pretend to be a ghost to freak her out? She hurried to the wall and looked down toward the wooden bridge, the only access to the fort entrance. In just a few seconds, Jeremy hurried from the fort, phone to his ear, index finger jabbing the air as he likely yelled at his son. Gwen watched long enough to make sure he didn't double back, then returned to her bench. She glared at the guard tower, which had narrow slits to protect soldiers while firing at the enemy and began to draw the top of the dome.

But her hand slipped and made marks lower on the page. Startled, she tried moving her hand back up, but it wouldn't budge even as she continued to draw. What the hell? She squeezed the pencil so hard that her hand spasmed, sending sharp pains all the way up to her shoulder. Frightened now, she tried using her left hand to stop her right, but then her left spasmed as well. She tried releasing the pencil, but that didn't work either. Her hand just kept drawing.

As she fought against whatever was controlling her hand, she tried calling for help but couldn't open her mouth. The sounds around her faded to a thick, unnatural silence. All she could hear was her own distressed breathing. Minutes later, tears of frustration streamed down her cheeks. How could she call 911 if she couldn't move?

Then her calves tightened into horrible cramps that would have made her cry out if she could have. *Stop, stop,* she moaned in her head as every muscle in her body tightened like rubber bands stretched nearly to the point of breaking.

Her hand flew across the page, but her vision was too blurry to see a thing. *Billie, Billie, help,* she silently pleaded through the pain.

Her skin suddenly felt too tight for her body and her spine throbbed. Then everything went limp and all the cramps disappeared. The pain was gone but she was almost too weak to hold up her head. "Holy shit," she managed to say, just to make sure her voice still worked. She dropped the pencil and shook out her hands and arms, then wiped at her eyes. What the hell had just happened? A stroke? Some sort of seizure?

But then Gwen's gaze dropped down to her sketchbook. "*What?*" The drawing she'd made was of a beautiful man with high cheekbones and long black braids, obviously a Native American. But what took her breath away was that the skill necessary to draw such a detailed and expressive face was *way* beyond her ability. This was no ugly gargoyle. The man slouched in an ornate wooden armchair with one leg arrogantly draped over one of the arms. His face, hair, and a single feather hanging down one braid were the only Native things about him, for his costume was straight out of Hamlet—short, puffy pants and a tight velvety jacket with split sleeves. How had she drawn the fabric so well that she had no doubt it was velvet? And who *was* this guy?

Gwen looked around. Was she going crazy? Seeing things? Other than every muscle in her body aching, she seemed to be okay. She smelled the fishy river, suntan lotion, and a man's aftershave. More *Fruit Cove Elementary* kids ran by screaming something about a cannon, a nearby park ranger guide lectured a small group about the crushed shell material called coquina used to build the fort, and a park ranger invited tourists to gather at the far bastion where she would soon fire off two cannons. No one was paying any attention to Gwen or had any idea she'd been in distress. Was this a joke? Had someone drawn this while she was seizing? But Gwen had never released the pencil. Her hand had moved across the paper the entire time.

She did a quick search on her phone and found a neurological condition called "alien hand." She snorted. Apparently, aliens did live among them. With this condition, people often could not control one of their hands. Every time one poor woman with "alien hand" swore, her left hand would haul off and slap her, hard. Okay, well. Alien hand was usually caused by some sort of brain damage. Had she fallen? This diagnosis explained why she was unable to control her hand, but not how she'd been able to draw such a detailed and beautiful image of this man, and only in a few minutes. Maybe she should call 911. At the very least she should call Billie. There was clearly something wrong with her.

Suddenly, she turned to a fresh page, picked up the pencil, still slippery with sweat, and began to draw again, but not by choice.

Gwen resisted as before, using every ounce of strength she had to stop her hand, to lift it, to stand, to scream, but failed at all of it, trapped inside a body she did not control. Pain pounded her brain and then everything stopped. She didn't know if she'd been struggling for a few seconds or a few hours, but she finally regained control of her hand.

Gwen managed to wipe away enough tears to see what she'd drawn. *What the heck?* She'd just drawn what appeared to be her fifty-fifth birthday party, with a decorated cake that said, *Happy 55th Gwen*! Their best friends, the Lauras, sat beside her, but the three of them did not look happy. How could she have drawn the three of them well enough to not only recognize the faces but the emotions as well? And where was Billie? Most importantly, however, Gwen wouldn't turn fifty-five for another six months.

Sitting there, the air felt thick around her, as if she were breathing through layers and layers of N-95 masks. The fort now felt like a predator watching for another opportunity to torment her. Unsure what had just happened, Gwen shook with a fear she'd never felt before.

As the new chair of Flagler College's History Department, Gwen had immediately felt the pressure to reduce her budget. That's why, when a Flagler alumni donated ten thousand dollars to the winner of a History vs. Art Department competition, she'd leapt at the opportunity. But now? Suddenly, ten thousand dollars didn't feel worth whatever *this* was. So Gwen stood and threw the pencil over the exterior wall, nearly clipping a man's ear on the way past. Then she grabbed her stuff and dashed down the steps and out of the fort.

She jogged a block then finally had to stop, out of breath. She didn't want to order an Uber and have to make small talk. She didn't want to hop aboard one of the trolley trams and be nice to tourists. She just wanted to be home. She just wanted Billie.

It took her an hour, but by the time she reached their front porch, she'd resolved two things: 1) she was going to open a bottle of wine and drink the whole thing, and 2) no one, not even Billie, would ever see those drawings. They were impossible to explain.

CHAPTER FOUR

Billie, November 2–7

B etween work and Zooming with the Lauras, Billie's week passed quickly. She had tried to find the courage to bike down the block and back but was only able to sit on the seat for five minutes, then relock the bike to the patio railing. *Pathetic.* She'd distracted herself by cleaning their little house, which was compact, but felt larger because of the huge front porch and a back patio. The instant she and Gwen had walked in, they'd felt as if this was their place, near to the action but removed enough to be quiet and quaint. All the rooms were painted light turquoise or sea foam green or peach, which reminded them they were living in the tropics now.

Early in the week, after Gwen and Jeremy had visited the fort, Gwen had gotten so sick she'd asked her TA to take her classes so she could stay home. All week, Billie brought her hot chicken soup and texted her encouraging words. Late Friday afternoon, after a busy day of selling antiques with Walt, Billie entered through the back door and noticed a mug of tea on the kitchen table, still steaming. Huh. Gwen never drank tea when she was sick. And why leave it here?

Billie poked her head into the bedroom. "You feeling better?"

"No," came the weak reply from deep within the covers. The window blind knocked gently against the window as if it had just been closed, which meant it had been open. When she was sick

Gwen only wanted total darkness. Suspicion bloomed as Billie considered the clues.

Shaking her head, Billie reached for the covers and yanked them off the bed. "I knew it. You're goldbricking!" Gwen was fully dressed in hot pink capris and sandals.

Gwen shot up. "Go away. I'm sick."

Billie dumped the covers on the nearest chair. "No, you aren't. If you were sick, you'd be wearing your yellow ducky sweats, which you clearly are not wearing. What's going on?"

Gwen swung her feet to the floor. "Nothing. I'm going to finish my tea."

Billie followed her into the kitchen. "You haven't gone to work since you got home Monday from the fort. In fact, you haven't gone anywhere, yet you clearly aren't sick." Billie grabbed an apple off the table and began cutting it into thin slices for them to share.

Gwen plopped down onto a chair, arms wrapped around herself, mouth hardened into a grim line. "Wow, there's a shocker. Refusing to leave the house even though you're not sick. Where have I heard *that* one before?"

Billie felt her eyes widen, stunned that Gwen would throw this back in her face. "Seriously? You're going there? What happened to *Don't worry, Billie, take all the time you need to recover.*" She could feel her anger building like a gathering storm, ripe with black clouds and destructive winds. "What happened to *We'll do whatever you need to get better*? After two years, you're coming after me now?"

Billie placed the knife in the sink, flung the uneaten apple onto the counter, then forced herself to sit down, shocked at Gwen's hurtful words. "It's not like I planned to stop leaving the house. It's not like I have *fun* being afraid." She fought back sudden tears.

Gwen hunched over the table. "Then back off. If you don't like what happens when you push me, don't push me."

Billie forced herself to breathe slowly through her nostrils to give her brain time to calm down. They couldn't both go nasty in the same fight. "Did something happen at the fort? Did Jeremy do or say something that has ruined your week?"

"Nothing happened."

Billie tried but couldn't stop pushing. "I don't think you're being honest with me." When Gwen's spine straightened with indignation, Billie was transported back to St. Paul, immersed in one of their so-often-they-were-almost-scripted fights. How could two people who loved each other fight so much?

"You think I'm lying."

"I think something has really upset you and you're lashing out at me. It's almost as if you're hiding here in the house, with the windows shut up tight. It's crazy stuffy in here."

"I like stuffy."

"No, you don't. It's like you're trying to keep out the world, or at least some part of it. But that's *my gig,* not yours. You don't hide, *ever.* Maybe we could go for a walk or something since I manage to do that now most days."

Gwen just frowned. "Where is that stack of brochures we collected when we first moved here?"

Billie nodded toward the small pantry. "Bottom shelf." Gwen's attack still stung, especially since she'd been so patient and supportive as Billie's fear of falling on the ice yet again and breaking some body part yet again had begun to interfere with their life together. Billie had become less and less willing to venture out into the winter, fearing that nothing but pain awaited her. Her therapist helped her realize that her joy of being active was battling with her fear of pain. Unfortunately, in this battle Fear was kicking Joy's butt. Change a few letters of algophobia, the intense fear of pain, and you had agoraphobia.

"What you said a few minutes ago was incredibly mean," Billie said.

Gwen couldn't meet her eyes. "Yes, it was. I'm sorry." Her voice had softened but her mouth was still severe with something Billie didn't recognize. Gwen flipped through the brochures. "You are right. We should go do something." She pulled out a black brochure with lime green lettering and dropped it onto the table in front of Billie.

Billie laughed. "Ghostly Trolley Tour? You want to go on a cheesy tour meant to thrill little kids and bore their parents?"

"Yeah, why not?"

"Because—what's your mantra? Ghosts aren't real. Time travel—"

"Okay, okay, I know." Gwen jammed her hands under her arms. "Maybe we need a good laugh."

Billie read the brochure. That Gwen was interested in this was very odd, but maybe poking fun at fake ghosts would relieve the tension. She grabbed her phone and punched a few keys. "Okay, we have tickets for the seven p.m. tour tonight."

"Billie."

She looked up. Gwen's eyes were moist. "I'm sorry. That was a shitty thing to say…what I said earlier about you not leaving the house. I haven't…I haven't been myself for a few days."

Billie nodded. "I am getting better, you know. It *has* helped to move out of winter. I can walk to work. I can walk home. I'm not terrified of getting hurt all the time." She hadn't told Gwen about her setback the other day when she'd tried to follow Martha. Partners were supposed to tell each other everything, but Billie had decided this "rule" needed to be ignored now and then. She wanted Gwen to relax and stop protecting her, to stop putting Billie's needs before her own. She wanted their lives to be the way they were before, when both were strong and independent and things felt in balance.

Gwen lightly touched her arm. "I'm glad you're doing better, really. I'm going to change into my ghost hunting clothes." Gwen's small smile gave Billie hope as Gwen left the room.

Billie sat quietly in the kitchen, marveling that life with Gwen had begun to feel like a roller coaster, and not in a good way. She folded her arms on the table and burrowed her face into her arms' comforting darkness. When had being in love gotten so exhausting?

And when had life itself turned so sour? Billie's face flamed with shame even though she was alone. When her problems had all started, things just kept spiraling. The more she had worried about pain, the stronger her algophobia. The more she had worried about falling, the more she stayed home. Her winter algophobia had hung around through spring, summer, and fall, which meant her algophobia turned into one neat package called agoraphobia. She had gone from outgoing to never going out. Two years of her life, up in smoke.

Billie sighed, still cocooned in the warm shelter of her tabled arms, and remembered a time when life used to be so clear. She'd been so certain about so many aspects of life, even the unknown aspects. She smiled when she remembered her "Movie Theater Theory of Time Travel." When she'd been in high school, she and Laura B used to start in the Cineplex theater of the movie they'd paid for, watch for twenty minutes, then sneak into another movie. They'd go from a western to a legal drama to a romantic comedy to aliens destroying the planet, then back to the western. Talk about mind-blowing. They felt like time travelers.

That's why they, after too many beers one Friday night, developed the theory that if a person was able to travel through time, this meant that all time periods were occurring simultaneously, like all movies in the Cineplex played at the same time. You could move through time just like you could move from theater to theater. The movie in one theater didn't stop while you were in another—all moved forward in time. If you *couldn't* travel through time, you'd be stuck in the same movie, unable to leave, or skip ahead, or go back. To non-time-travelers, life was linear, lived one moment after the other.

Billie finally sat up and stretched her back, ready to experience this silly ghost tour one moment after the other. She had faith in her ideas and beliefs, like the "Movie Theater Theory of Time Travel," but nothing else felt as certain. She studied the brochure. Luckily the tour stayed within the old section of St. Augustine, the downtown, so hopefully there'd be no embarrassing panic attacks. She had no idea how long it would take to be free of agoraphobia or algophobia—if ever. She didn't understand this tension with Gwen. And now they were going in search of the ghosts of St. Augustine at *Gwen's* suggestion. The world had begun tipping enough that Billie worried about sliding off.

Chapter Five

Gwen, November 7

The wooden trolley car, converted to a street vehicle, quickly filled up with mostly young families excited about the ghost tour, the kids squealing at the fake spider webs and plastic skeletons hanging from the ceiling. The trolley was open to the air, so Gwen sat next to the window, needing a breeze to keep her connected to reality. Billie's comforting presence warmed her side. Thank God Billie seemed to have forgiven Gwen for her earlier attack. *Christ. What was I thinking?*

Gwen squeezed her eyes shut in shame. What a horrible thing to say, and she'd almost blurted out the truth about their move. She'd begun to realize that secrets between spouses were sometimes necessary. All she'd done for two years was take care of Billie, protecting her, and now, every day, she had to push down the anger that felt like a live power line, fatal if touched. *Get a grip, Gwen.*

"I learned something about our unfriendly neighbor from Sassy the other day," Gwen said for a distraction.

"That he hates gays?"

"He might, given the way he glares at us, but Sassy said she thinks Clayton might have made an offer on our house, but we got it instead. Maybe that's why he doesn't like us."

A young man in black-and-white-striped "prison-garb" hopped onto the bus with such energy it rocked on its wheels. He flipped on his microphone and turned on the charm. "Hi, folks. Welcome to Ghostly Trolley Adventures. I'm Todd, and tonight I'm going to drive you to an early grave." Everyone on the bus groaned as he gave a practiced smile and plopped down into the driver's seat.

He continued with his annoying, pun-filled script as he drove the trolley car onto Pacific Avenue. Gwen and Billie rolled their eyes at every pun as Gwen struggled to hide her anxiety. She needed answers. She knew ghosts were not real, but she needed confirmation. For years, her mom had told her ghost stories that she insisted had really happened, which was why Gwen suffered from insomnia from age five until she left home for college. Every creak of the floor, every tap on the roof, every tingle of her skin, Mom would insist was a ghost and Gwen could barely breathe for the fear of what could be there that she couldn't see.

Mom refused to acknowledge that Gwen didn't share her passion. She had tried to calm Gwen's fears by explaining that ghosts were merely a person's transition from the living to the dead, and that sometimes departed souls lingered too long as spirits. Gwen remembered asking how to make them go away, and her mom's answer only made things worse. "People called 'mediums' communicate with the spirits and encourage them to leave. They're like magicians that way because they make the souls disappear."

From that day forward Gwen hated magic shows, imagining hundreds of spirits hovering above the audience just waiting for the "magic" to happen. When she turned thirteen, being a teenager gave Gwen the strength she'd needed to opt out of all the crazy. "Mom," she'd finally said, "ghosts aren't real, time travel isn't possible, and aliens don't live among us." Her mom, stunned, spent the next few years arguing with her, but Gwen was immovable.

First stop on the ghost tour was a combination old drugstore display and wax museum with dusty apothecary displays and Todd's spookily voiced tales of ghosts seen in the building. Badly constructed dummies of a pharmacist and his customer were arranged along the counter.

"This is worse than I thought it'd be," Billie whispered into her ear. Gwen agreed.

They then filed through the dark wax museum, its figures covered in white sheets.

"Are these supposed to be ghosts?" one man asked with a disgusted snort.

"No, sorry," Todd said. "Your ticket price doesn't actually cover viewing the wax figures."

People laughed at that ridiculous answer, then Todd led them out the back of the building to a fenced cemetery. Palm fronds rattled overhead, and the sound of traffic just a block away was oddly reassuring. Gwen was relieved they could spread out now as this group of tourists smelled like coffee and body odor. She moved up to the iron fence separating them from the cemetery.

Todd made his voice even more theatrically spooky. "No one's allowed inside Tolomoto Cemetery so as not to disturb the spirits who walk here every night. Keep your eyes open for eerie apparitions and glowing orbs." As he described how some people had seen the ghost of a young boy named James jumping around in the trees, something caught Gwen's attention out of the corner of her eye. A man, dressed in baggy pants and tunic, stood inside the fence.

Gwen nudged Billie and nodded toward the man. "I guess *some* people are allowed inside.

Billie looked in that direction, then frowned. "What?"

"That guy over there," Gwen said. The man wore brown pants and some sort of loose tunic. Black beard, receding hairline. Few things bothered Gwen more than people not obeying the rules, which was why she used to stop Billie every time she started to jaywalk. Gwen gripped the cold iron bars. "Why can this man enter the cemetery and we can't?"

Todd stopped his story about glowing orbs and everyone turned toward her, then looked at each other in confusion A few guys ran to join her. "What man? Where? Is it a ghost?" one asked breathlessly.

"It's not a ghost," Gwen said. She pointed. "It's a man. Hey, you! You're not supposed to be inside the fence."

At that same moment, the man looked directly at Gwen. Goose bumps skittered down her arms as she realized something was very wrong. The man's eyes were blank and dead. The man slowly raised his arm and pointed off into the dark.

"Babe, what do you see?" Billie's touch on her arm was gentle.

Gwen struggled to breathe normally but instead could only take in shallow gasps. "Man in the shadows, staring right at me."

"I see him, Mommy," said a young girl standing at the edge of the group. "I don't like him. He looks weird." The mother bent over the girl, horrified.

Gwen's heart nearly stopped. Only she and the little girl saw the man.

A wave of something unbidden and unexpected rose up inside her. No, no, no. Mom could *not* have been right. This odd man would not pierce the wall of reason Gwen had built around herself as armor against her mom's ideas.

She shook the fence. "You're not allowed in there."

Billie moved closer and put a hand on Gwen's shoulder. "I don't see anything, but that doesn't mean I don't believe you."

The girl's mother turned to Gwen. "Please, stop this. You're only encouraging Ashley to pretend she's seeing something."

But then a slight breeze came through and the man literally disappeared into thin air.

"Where did the man go?" Ashley began to cry, and Todd struggled to regain control of the situation.

"Let's all return to the trolley, shall we?"

Shaken, Gwen followed Billie. What a stupid idea it'd been to go on a ghost tour. When she climbed on board the trolley, she muttered a weak apology to the others. Some glared at her with obvious skepticism, others in frustration since they were sure there'd been a ghost standing right in front of them and they hadn't been able to see it. Ashley's parents shot Gwen dead with their furious glares.

The next stop was the Old Jail, a two-story cream-colored stucco building. "Henry Flagler built the jail to blend into the neighborhood," Todd said. "The prisoners were kept in iron cells in the very center of the building so residents couldn't hear or see them. This is one of the most haunted buildings in the city. People hear chains rattling, smell terrible odors, and have felt something tugging at their hair, or blowing on their cheeks." The crowd chortled happily, having recovered from Gwen's outburst. Everyone still wanted to see a ghost.

At the entrance, Todd stopped and grew strangely quiet, seemingly unwilling to continue the scripted patter. "Every Ghostly Trolley guide has started this job thinking our ghost stories were created for you tourists. But then every one of us has seen or heard or felt things in this building that have made believers of us all. Please stay close together as we go through the building. If you get separated, you need to find your own way out. I'm not coming back to get you." He looked right at Gwen.

The crowd laughed nervously, but Todd didn't crack a smile. The kid had clearly been traumatized by something.

The jail cells formed a two-story central column, with an inclined walkway circling the jail cells for the guards to walk. As a solemn Todd described the inhumane conditions and agonizing deaths that took place here, Gwen felt an oppressive sadness pushing at her from all sides. The black iron bars and floors sucked up what little light there was. If there'd been a smell to pain, it would have been this sad scent of decay and hot metal. The silence was so complete it almost hurt, and the hair on the back of her neck bristled. Todd was right. There was something here. Even the children lowered their voices to a whisper. No one saw flashes of light or heard chains rattling, but the rooms felt crowded with souls they couldn't see. Clearly relieved, Todd led the disappointed group down the exterior wooden stairway to the Hanging Tree.

Once outside, Gwen wandered to the edge of the group, eager to get back on the bus as Todd described a pirate's hanging. When something brushed against the top of her head, she turned around. A shimmering white figure of a woman in a shapeless dress stood at the top of the staircase they'd just come down. When the woman flickered on and off like a faulty light bulb, Gwen searched the area for a projector.

But then the woman looked right down at Gwen, raised a wispy arm, and pointed off into the dark. "God damn it, not again," Gwen muttered.

She began shivering. These—what would you call them? Apparitions? Why were they appearing to her? And the pointing. What was that about?

"Mommy, who's that lady?" Ashley pointed up the stairs toward the woman.

The whole group turned to look in that direction. "Damn it," one man cursed. "I want to see ghosts. Why can't I see the ghosts?"

"Ashley, there's no one there. You're making that up," her dad snapped.

"No, she's not," Gwen said loudly enough that the entire tour could hear her. People began murmuring nervously to each other, and one woman began reciting the Lord's Prayer.

Billie stepped to her side. "Again?"

She nodded. "Woman at the top of the stairs."

"Todd, this woman needs to stop," Ashley's mother pleaded, her voice high and pinched with fear.

Ignoring the others, Billie took Gwen's hand. "It's a little creepy that you're seeing what are probably ghosts, especially since ghosts aren't real, right?"

Gwen nodded, then gasped as the woman fluttered like laundry in a strong breeze and drifted apart.

"The lady went away," Ashley said. Her parents, now as pale as the woman at the top of the stairs, hustled her back to the trolley.

While Todd drove them to the last stop, Billie did some research on her phone. "It says here that if a human somehow pierces the wall, or curtain, separating the living from the dead, then that person has more access to the spirits, and—" she stopped.

"And what?"

"And the spirits have more access to the person."

Gwen's pulse raced. "Interesting."

"Gwen, have you recently somehow pierced the wall separating the living from the dead?"

Gwen looked out the window, focusing on a passing group of bikers with their tires and bike frames lit by colorful LED lights, their black-clad bodies barely visible in the dark. The combination of lights and black clothing created the illusion that the bikes had no riders. *Great. That's all I need. Ghost riders.*

Billie let out a slow exhale. "Gwen, answer me. Have you pierced this curtain somehow?"

"How would anyone even do that?" Gwen snapped, tense and deathly afraid to admit to Billie what had happened at the fort.

"Last stop. Here we are at the military hospital," Todd announced. "Everyone out."

Gwen said nothing as they filed off the bus and stood outside the one-story building.

Todd motioned for the group to gather around closer as he stood under the single streetlight. "Welcome to the site of the hospital used by Spanish, British, and American military, depending upon who controlled the Castillo de San Marcos." He smiled brightly. "Because the museum is closed, we'll just chat for a bit outside here."

As Todd babbled on about the city's history, Gwen felt the air shift around her. Something had changed. Cold air pooled at her ankles and then began moving upward. When it passed her shoulders, then her face, then the top of her head, she knew what she was supposed to do.

Something wanted her to look up.

Cold dread spread through her, the opposite of a hot flash, but she wasn't going to look up.

"Mommy, what are those things floating over us? I don't like them."

Gwen's heart rate quickened, but she clutched Billie's arm and waited.

"Mommy, they are scary. Make them go away."

"Ashley, that's it. I'm done with your lying."

Gwen shuddered. Damn it. To prove little Ashley wasn't crazy, Gwen would have to look up.

Taking a deep, wavering breath, she turned her back to the streetlight and lifted her gaze toward the stars. A small whimper escaped her lips. Floating overhead, rotating slowly, mingling and drifting apart, were limbs, ghostly limbs—legs, feet, arms, and hands performing a ghastly, ghostly ballet. And of course, all the hands were pointing in the same direction.

Gwen's stomach churned.

Billie leaned in "What do you see?'

"You don't want to know," Gwen whispered.

The girl began to cry. "Where are the rest of those people? Where are their bodies?"

The parents now turned to Gwen in desperation. Todd ceased his lecture and looked like he was going to be sick. "What does the kid see?" he asked her.

"Ghostly limbs," Gwen finally said, jaw tightened in anger. "Legs, feet, arms, and hands. About two feet over our heads."

The whole group ducked. Todd pushed his way through the group to Gwen's side. "You see them?"

She nodded.

"Holy motherfucking *shit*storm," Todd yelled. He bent over, hands on his knees and moaned. "I have *got* to find another job. I cannot *take* this shit anymore." He straightened and looked at Gwen. "We don't mention the ghost limbs on the tour. The only way to really know they are there…is to see them."

"Todd, why is Ashley seeing body parts?" her mother asked as she cuddled the frightened child against her side.

Todd rubbed his face and looked almost ghostly himself under the harsh light. "Army medicine was crude and often ineffective," he said, "but the doctors did the best they could. Hundreds and hundreds of amputations were performed here—legs, feet, arms, hands." A collective moan rose up from the group. "A number of years ago the city dug up the street you are standing on in order to install new sewer and water." He paused to make sure he had everyone's attention.

"The city found hundreds and hundreds of bones—legs, feet, arms, hands." Everyone gasped, including Gwen and Billie. Wind hummed high up in the trees lining both sides of the street. "After each amputation, the doctors tossed the limbs into piles that were eventually buried. When the city discovered that where we're standing was a cemetery of sorts, it rerouted the sewer and paved over the bones. They will never be disturbed again."

Todd cleared his throat. "I don't know about the rest of you, but I've had enough for one night. I need to drive you back to the tour office, then I'm gonna quit." The jolly *Drive you to an early grave* Todd had been replaced by a frightened young man.

Gwen found the courage to look up one more time. Nothing but faint stars.

Back on the trolley, Gwen turned to Billie. "Okay, I need to tell you something. But first, I need your help. Could you open your city map?" Gwen shivered at what she was about to do. Were the pointing fingers connected in any way? Three pointing figures (or hands) meant three lines.

As Billie held open the glossy map, Gwen located the cemetery. "Could you draw a line from the cemetery pointing this way?" she asked. Then the jail and the military hospital. She showed Billie which direction to draw the second and third lines.

Billie's three light pencil lines converged at a single point: the entrance to the Castillo de San Marcos.

Gwen heaved a deep sigh. Of course. Why should she be surprised? "Billie, I'm sorry I didn't tell you, but...but something is trying to send me a message."

"Some*thing*?"

It was time to finally say this out loud. "I think..." She exhaled slowly. "I think there is a ghost at the fort...and it wants me back."

CHAPTER SIX

Billie, November 7–8

Gwen had refused to say more when they'd gotten home, but had just changed into pjs, crawled into bed, and fell into such a deep sleep that she didn't respond when Billie said her name several times.

Frustrated, Billie changed into her T-shirt and pink plaid boxers then crawled into bed, gently rearranging Gwen's limbs to make room for herself. Some people thought long-term relationships were boring, but Billie sighed with the comfort that came from curling up next to a familiar back. She wasn't bored with Gwen, but they'd both become as prickly as a pair of cactuses.

Sleep refused to come. First, there was the astonishing statement from Gwen that ghosts were real. She chewed on that for a while, a little excited, actually, to see a tiny crack in that anti-supernatural wall of hers. But without knowing anything more, Billie's mind began its usual return to pain. Flashbacks of her dislocated elbow and knee replacement and broken ribs and everything else kept her staring at the ceiling, watching the palm tree shadows flicker as cars quietly passed through the night. She could feel the eye-watering pain, the sense that she'd never be whole again, the belief that she'd aged ten years in about ten months. She rolled over and tried to get her brain off its fruitless track. *Always take a minute to check the facts*, her therapist had said.

Fact: The pain she'd felt in the past had been real and all-consuming.

Fact: Some people's nerve synapses are so sensitive that they feel pain more intensely than most people, and Billie had joined their ranks.

Fact: Here, now, in Florida, she did not have pain. She was safe from ice and blizzards.

But Gwen and her strange behavior? *Fact*: This was something to worry about, so Billie pulled the covers up higher against the cool night air and worried.

❖

When Billie woke up, she rolled over to find Gwen awake, blue eyes still soft with sleep. "Morning," Billie said.

"I guess we should talk about what I said last night...about a ghost."

"No, that's fine. I much prefer to be kept in the dark. Worrying about the unknown is much more satisfying than knowing what's going on, so you just go back to sleep."

Gwen snorted. "You're in fine form this morning. Gotta get my sketchbook."

When she returned, she opened the book to an amazing drawing of a Native man dressed in soft velvet, and began to explain.

Billie listened with one half of her brain, while the other half screamed *Ghosts can't do that*. Unlike Gwen, Billie believed that ghosts were real, but not real enough to actually touch someone or control them. That was fictional Ghostbusters material, not reality.

Gwen turned the page. "This was the second drawing."

Gwen and the Lauras appeared to be celebrating Gwen's fifty-fifth, which wouldn't happen for another six months. "Where am I?" Billie asked. "Is this your way of telling me you don't want...that we are not..."

Gwen waved her off. "No, but look at these faces. I can't draw that well, which means that while I held the pencil, it was...it was something *else* that drew them."

Billie sighed. "Some sort of spirit or force or *something*, took possession of your hand and forced you to draw these images?"

Gwen huffed through her nose like a cornered animal. "I know it sounds crazy." She told Billie about "alien hand," but they both agreed she'd had no neurological triggering event for that wacky condition, so it wasn't a likely explanation. However, for a second Billie wished that Republican lawmakers would come down with "alien hand" and uncontrollably slap themselves every time they lied. That'd be fun.

Billie flipped back through the sketchbook, examining the drawings Gwen had done *before* her visit to the fort. While Gwen's skills had certainly improved, she was nowhere close to achieving the detail, the energy, the soul of the drawings she'd done at the fort. Billie returned to the drawing of the Native man. "Did you contact the SAPS that Jeremy mentioned?"

Gwen shook her head. "Too freaked out to tell anyone."

Billie gently closed the book. "Well, as I see it, there's only one thing to do."

"And that is?"

"You and I are going to the fort, right now, with your pencil and this sketchbook. We are going to see if this happens again."

Gwen moaned and collapsed sideways onto the bed. "No, I can't."

"Yes, you can," Billie said, dropping down on the bed beside her. "You're going to get up and get dressed." She wrapped her arms around Gwen. "We are quite the power couple, aren't we? One of us is paralyzed by fear, the other by a ghost."

"Ha. Funny."

As they both rose and dressed, the irony was not lost on Billie that the tables had turned, and she was now the one helping Gwen leave the house. While Gwen made coffee, Billie found the website for the St. Augustine Paranormal Society. *We are committed to finding the truth, whatever that truth may be. SAPS works to prove and disprove the reality of any supernatural activity, approaching your situation with an open mind. Our goal is to shed light on the dark shadows where many fear to tread.*

Billie composed a short email, then took a deep breath and hit Send.

❖

Today was proving to be one of Billie's hard days, so she kept her eyes closed while Gwen drove them to the fort. She opened them only as Gwen pulled into the fort's parking lot. Billie's head hurt a little, but no cold sweats or pounding heart. She could do this.

Gwen turned off the car. "You okay? Maybe I should take you home."

Billie shook her head carefully so the headache wouldn't worsen. "Nice try. You aren't getting out of this that easily. I'll be fine."

Just then Gwen's phone chimed with a text. "Mason again," she said, tapping *No*.

"Why are you avoiding him?"

"Just don't have the energy to deal with *his* energy." Billie couldn't blame her. Gwen's stepbrother could be too much some days, often complaining and whining about his life. When Gwen's dad had married Faye fifteen years ago, Mason had been only fifteen and actually thought she and Gwen were cool. They took him to the Minnesota State Fair and watched a calf being born, which Mason pronounced the grossest thing he'd ever witnessed. They took him to Valleyfair and rode the rides with him until they were all a little dizzy.

The guy was gifted in an odd way: he could see patterns, see solutions to puzzles, see how unrelated events fit together. Billie called him a visual savant and urged him to go into cryptography, while Gwen had pushed for some sort of legal or investigative work, but he lacked the discipline for any of that. For a year, he attended Carleton College in Northfield, a short drive from the Twin Cities, so they'd drive down and take him out for dinner, canoeing the Cannon River, or finding corn mazes to visit every fall. But then Mason dropped out, saying school wasn't his "bag," and he eventually grew up, grew apart, and she and Gwen were no longer "cool."

Gwen bought tickets and they entered the fort, which bustled with weekend tourists even though charcoal gray clouds hung low over the city. Two cannons fired up on the gun deck and the crowd cheered.

"Where did this…this *thing* happen?" Billie asked, relieved she felt better.

Gwen motioned to the stairs. "Up on the gun deck." They climbed the stairs, Gwen reluctantly, Billie energized by the desire to figure out what was going on. Was it a fluke? Was it insanity? Was it a ghost?

The horizon stretched out for miles when they stepped onto the second level, and Billie could feel the tug of the beaches waiting for her just on the other side of Anastasia Island. She hadn't yet been there, for the ocean was outside of her comfort zone, but one day soon she was going to try. As Gwen sat down on the end of a bench occupied by an elderly couple, Billie checked her phone. Nothing yet from SAPS. Billie hoped they would clarify that ghosts couldn't take possession of a living person.

"Oh, oh," Gwen said. "Here we go." And she was drawing, her pencil moving faster than any normal person would draw.

Billie ran to her side, then stopped. Holy shit. Gwen's eyes were black as oil, both the whites and the irises. "Gwen, oh my god." Billie grabbed Gwen's drawing hand with both of her own and tried to stop the pencil. She grunted with the effort, but as strong as she was, Billie was unable to stop Gwen's rock-hard hand. When Billie bent down to get better leverage, she suddenly flew back, landing on her backside with a surprised grunt. "Gwen, did you just push me?"

Gwen couldn't respond, grimacing in pain, so Billie got to her feet and tried again. This time a force knocked her sideways so hard that she stumbled into the elderly couple.

"What are you doing?" the woman cried. They both stood and gave Billie dirty looks as they stalked away.

Gwen's hand finally stopped moving and she sort of collapsed into a human puddle on the bench. "Honey, are you okay?" Billie cried. "Jesus, but that was intense. And did you see what happened?

Twice something knocked me back." She massaged Gwen's arms and checked her eyes, relieved to see blue instead of bottomless black.

"God, it hurts."

"Don't fight it!" someone shouted. Billie turned to see a woman wearing a long dress constructed entirely of men's ties run toward them, followed by a lanky teenage boy with shaggy brown hair.

The woman, her cropped hair dyed in rainbow colors with eye shadow to match, crouched in front of Gwen. Her features were small and dainty, almost pixie-like, but she moved like a woman who took up more space and was used to getting her way.

"I witnessed the last of your experience as I came up the stairs."

"Who are you?" Gwen managed to sputter.

"Oh, sorry. I'm Kylie Miller. St. Augustine Paranormal Society. SAPS. Your wife reached out to us." She waved toward the boy behind her. "And this is my nephew, Austin. He's our expert on the fort." The tall kid wore heavy black eyeliner, mascara, and one of his ears was lined with silver studs that matched the ones in his nostrils. He wore baggy black shorts, a white T-shirt, and that typical teenager face, disinterested and bored with the world. His eyes, however, gave him away, snapping with energy and reacting to what was said around him. Billie instantly felt connected to the kid.

While shaking their hands, Billie caught the angry glare Gwen shot her for contacting SAPS.

Gwen cleared her throat. "I really don't need—"

"You need to stop fighting the possession. It will hurt less that way. Yielding allows the spirit to take control without causing you pain."

Billie's heart sank. The woman clearly believed ghosts could inhabit humans. Was she right?

Kylie sat down on the concrete and rested both hands on Gwen's knees. "I cannot tell you how exciting this is to have a fort ghost active during the day. And an actual *possession.* Usually we investigate ghost sightings or strange noises." She leaned forward. "Now remember, *yield.* It may feel strange at first but stop fighting for control and let the spirit guide your hand."

Gwen's face had gone pale. "You really think I'm being possessed? Oh, shit, here I go again." She flipped to a fresh page and began to draw.

"Gwen," Kylie said soothingly. "Relax. Don't fight it."

Gwen's neck and forearms were rigid, but at Kylie's words the tension seemed to lessen. "Let the spirit communicate with you through your hand, through your pencil. Welcome the spirit. Thank it. *Love* it." Billie pressed her lips together to suppress a snort. *Love* a ghost? Poor Gwen—Kylie was just like Gwen's mom only in a younger body and many more men's ties.

They had begun to attract a small crowd, curious men, women, and a few kids, all watching from a safe distance, as if Gwen might explode. But as Gwen drew, the murmurs began to sound more alarmed than curious. Billie paced in a tight circle, desperate to help but unsure how.

She stopped pacing. "Her *eyes*," Billie whispered. Gwen's eyes were black again.

"That's normal," Austin said.

Billie looked at the kid, stunned. In what kind of wacky world were entirely black eyes normal?

She desperately wanted to rescue Gwen, but there was little she could do. As Kylie continued to reassure Gwen, Billie took a few steps to the inner edge of the gun deck and looked down into the courtyard just as two men in Park Ranger uniforms began pounding up the steps two at a time. Rangers in a *big* hurry.

After another ten seconds and a huge sigh, Gwen stopped drawing. Billie leapt forward to grab the sketchbook as it slipped off her lap. Kylie moved up onto the bench and put her arms around Gwen. "Was that easier?"

Gwen nodded as the two rangers pushed through the crowd and reached them, one ranger with shirt buttons strained at his belly, the other with buttons strained at the chest. "Ms. Miller," said the muscular one. "I thought we agreed you would not conduct this sort of…of activity within the fort."

Billie stepped forward. "We're sorry for the disturbance. We don't mean to be alarming your visitors, but we needed Kylie's help figuring out—"

The plump one held up both hands and stopped Billie. "Not interested in anyone's imagined fantasies. We must ask the four of you to leave, including Pretty Boy here."

Billie hated bullies, whether in a uniform or out. She clenched her teeth. "You ever heard of Elvis?" she snapped. "He wore mascara."

As Billie and Kylie helped Gwen stand, Austin gave Billie a grateful smile. She nodded in return.

"Whatever," the guard said. "We are escorting you out. Now."

Billie stepped closer to the nearest ranger. "We paid to be here just like everyone else."

"No refunds for crazies who scare the normal folks." He reached a meaty hand toward Billie's arm, as if to take hold of her.

Her nostrils flared. "I wouldn't do that if I were you."

He scowled at Billie but lowered his arm. "Let's go. All of you."

Standing up to him did nothing to reduce Billie's shame of being ejected. Her face flushed hot as the rangers led them to the top of the stairs. She'd never in her life been thrown out of anything.

They hurried down the stone steps, expecting the rangers to follow, but too many tourists crowded around them demanding to know if there really were ghosts at the fort.

As Billie and the others headed through the passageway toward the entrance, Kylie stopped them. "We need to stay inside the fort and try again. Follow me." She led them into a long, narrow room and closed the door, wincing as it creaked. A small sign identified the room as *Soldier Barracks*. "The rangers never come in here." The room was lined on either side with wooden platforms covered with thin mattresses. Shelves and hooks ran along the wall and a stone fireplace at the end of the room was cold. "Billie, could you give the sketchbook back to Gwen? Let's see if the spirit has more to say today."

They waited silently, watching Gwen's face, for five minutes. Nothing. "Okay, I guess it's done for the day. I would imagine it takes a lot of a ghost's resources to possess a live human."

"A ghost has resources?" Billie asked. Could this situation *get* any weirder?

"Some. Let's see your drawings."

Gwen seemed exhausted so Billie took the sketchbook and showed them Gwen's earlier drawings, first the Native man, then the birthday party that hadn't happened yet.

Billie turned the page. "This is the first one from today." The drawing showed two men huddled behind the bars of a jail, a guard outside the cell wearing some sort of period military uniform. The imprisoned men were gaunt and unhappy, staring bleakly toward the viewer. "Is this the fort?" Billie asked. "It could be any jail."

Austin leaned forward and pointed to the delicate detail on one part of the wall. "Bits of shells. The fort is made of coquina, which are tiny, crushed shells dug out of Anastasia Island and cut into blocks. Coquina hardens into a sort of concrete when exposed to the air."

"The men look sick," Gwen said.

Kylie pointed to the men's hair, black and chopped straight across just above their shoulders. She made a sound of disgust. "During the 1800s the fort was used as a prison to house the Seminoles whom the government was trying to bring under control. These must have been some of those men. The first thing the Army officers did was cut off the men's long braids."

"That's cruel," Gwen whispered.

"What's the second drawing?" Kylie asked.

Billie turned the page, and stared, unwilling to process what was on the page. "Oh, my god," she breathed, then turned the book so everyone could see.

Drawn from a higher perspective, the viewer looked down on three people. One person, looking up, with her six-sided wire glasses and salt-and-pepper curls, was clearly Gwen. The other two figures, likely men from their broad shoulders, stood directly below the viewer, faces not visible, heads covered, wearing jackets. What *was* visible, however, was the handgun each man held.

Handguns pointed directly at Gwen.

"What the hell?" Gwen said. "Why did I draw *this*?"

"And *where* is it?" Billie growled.

Austin leaned closer. "Look, more coquina. Based on the angle of this wall, I think it's outside the fort, by one of the bastions, as if the person drawing it was standing on top of the fort wall looking down."

Kylie scowled at the drawing. "Gwen, have you ever been in this situation? Has the spirit drawn something from your past?"

"No."

"Hmm, well. Clearly, the ghost is trying to warn you. It believes you are in danger."

Billie made a face. This was getting too weird, even for her, who believed in ghosts *and* time travel *and* the existence of aliens. "How could a dead person—or the remnants of a dead person—draw something that may or may not be in Gwen's future?" she asked. All she wanted to do was get home and tuck up on the porch swing and Facetime with the Lauras…anything to distract her from the idea of possession.

Kylie frowned. "We need some time to puzzle through this. Let's meet tomorrow at our office and we'll figure it out."

As Billie took Gwen's hand and pulled her to her feet, she realized that a new, sharper sort of pain was piercing her heart, a heavier, unfamiliar fear.

It wasn't fear for herself.

It was fear for Gwen.

CHAPTER SEVEN

Gwen, November 9

The next morning Gwen forced herself to get out of bed, but it was a struggle. She needed to get back to work, but knowing that the spirit of a dead person could take possession of her body and control her movements left Gwen so depressed, helpless, and hopeless that she even considered abandoning both Florida and Billie—if necessary—to run home to Minnesota. That plan lasted about three seconds, then she realized that since ghosts appeared to actually exist, there could be Minnesota ghosts awaiting her. This Castillo ghost made her draw against her will, but what if another ghost forced her to dance or strip in public or even harm another person?

After downing a cup of coffee and two slices of toast almost burned, the way she liked it, her phone chimed. Jeremy.

Reluctantly, she answered.

"Hey, boss, you feeling any better?" Jeremy's perky voice was particularly grating this morning.

"Ahh, a little." There was no way she'd ever tell Jeremy what was happening to her.

"Good, 'cause our drawing numbers are in the toilet. We need you back in the saddle, so to speak."

She sighed. "Actually, I have been drawing."

"Brilliant! I'm happy to continue acting as Chair until you return, but everyone wants you back."

Gwen rubbed her forehead. She didn't remember appointing anyone as acting chair, but her ghostly possession had been taking up all her available bandwidth, so it was very possible she'd done that. Or had Jeremy just stepped up on his own?

She ended the call with a heavy sigh. She wanted to like Jeremy, but it was hard. She wanted to like Flagler College because it was such a cool place. Professors often held classes outdoors. The grounds were lush and welcoming, most of the buildings preserved historical gems. But even before all this "ghostly possession" stuff, she had struggled to feel comfortable. As she put her dishes in the dishwasher, she shook her head. She knew why she didn't feel comfortable here: because she wanted to be back home in St. Paul, doing the job she'd always wanted to do.

When her phone chimed with another call, Gwen grimaced at the ID. What a morning she was having. If she didn't answer, her stepbrother Mason would just keep calling. She slid to green.

"Hey, Gwen, how's the easy life?"

"I'm still working, Mase."

"Yeah, but in Florida how hard does anyone really work, right?"

When Gwen's father had married Faye fifteen years ago, she'd acquired a stepmom and a fifteen-year-old stepbrother. Dad had died four years ago, leaving them to struggle on without him as a family.. Faye was great, but some days Mason was like a grain of sand in her shoe, irritating and hard to get rid of. He was crazy smart when it came to puzzles, but normal, everyday life? Not so much, and she blamed herself for not motivating him enough to finish college. "What's up?" she asked. "Faye okay?"

"Yeah, she's fine. But listen, she's updating her will and wants me to run the changes by you. I thought I could bop on down for a quick visit and get me some beach time."

Gwen grimaced and did the *talk-talk-talk* hand gesture as Billie entered the kitchen.

"Ah, Mason," Billie said with a smile.

"Mase, you don't have to come down. We could certainly do this via email. Besides, your mom can make any changes she wants. It's her money."

Actually, most of Faye's money had originally been Dad's, but his will left it all to Faye with the understanding that she would pass it on equally to both Gwen and Mason. "Does she want to make you sole heir?" That was fine with her, since Mason had always been a little frantic about money and kept losing anything he'd saved through "sure thing" online investments. Besides, Dad had never made much money so half of not much was still not much.

"No, no, God, no. The attorney said that her current will was a little ambivalent, so she's fixing that to make it clear it's a fifty/fifty split."

"Faye's in good health, so I wouldn't start counting those pennies just yet. Besides, Dad didn't leave her much."

"Ah, yeah, that's what Mom thought. But she's been going through his records and found two brokerage accounts she'd known nothing about. Turns out our shared Papa had way more moolah than we knew. I'm talking way, *way* more."

"Wow." Gwen raised her eyebrows in surprise, although Dad had always been so frugal it actually wasn't *that* odd to learn he'd squirreled more money away. "Well, your mom has many years left, so I don't think we should count our chickens before…you know. And Faye doesn't need my help with her will."

Mason had what Billie called "selective hearing," and chose to engage that particular superpower now. "Mom hates doing anything online, so she'd rather pay for my trip down to visit. I see there's some sort of lights festival, Nights of Lights, coming up in your fair city on November eighteenth. That could be fun, and I could stay for Thanksgiving. What say you?"

Gwen covered the phone. "Mason wants to visit."

"Great. I'm busy then."

"You don't even know when—"

"Still busy."

Gwen found it hard to scowl and laugh at the same time, so she gave up on the scowl. "That would be fine, Mase. It'll be good to see you. Billie's looking forward to it." She ducked at the wadded-up napkin Billie threw at her. "We don't have a guest room, so it's either our sofa or a hotel."

"Hotel it is. Mom can afford it. I'll text you the deets. See you on the eighteenth."

Gwen disconnected. "Mase is going to text me the *deets* for his visit."

"Still busy." Billie checked the time and stood. "Speaking of busy, time for us to go."

When Billie hesitated, Gwen stopped moving toward the door. If Billie felt pushed or hurried, a panic attack often followed. But not today.

The SAPS office was located not in historic downtown, where all the ghosts apparently lived, but farther north on US 1 in a sad strip mall that had seen better days. The space's two front plate glass windows were covered with black-and-white SAPS posters: *We Are After the Truth.* A single, handwritten poster on the door listed previous SAPS investigation sites: Castillo de San Marcos, Tolomoto Cemetery, St. Augustine Lighthouse, the St. Francis Inn, The Casablanca Inn, the Ponce de Leon Hotel, Warehouse 31, Fort Matanzas National Park, Harry's Seafood Bar and Grille, St. Augustine City Gates. The extensive list gave Gwen a little more confidence in the paranormal group.

Kylie welcomed them in, explaining that this former retail space was far cheaper than anything downtown. She gave them a quick tour of the office, which used to be a Middle Eastern restaurant so it still smelled of spices and hot oil. The space was so large that their voices echoed; the only items to absorb the sound were a few banged up desks, some overstuff chairs, and an industrial shelf unit in the back corner that Kylie called Tech Central. "Here we've got all the equipment we use to track and measure paranormal activity, like digital voice recorders, an EMF recorder to measure electromagnetic fields, and REM pods designed to find radiating electromagnetism."

Gwen leaned closer, impressed. "Are we going to use any of that at the fort?"

"Don't need to. That you lose control is proof. That Billie tried to stop your hand but *couldn't*, is proof. That she was thrown sideways into those tourists, a movement that is hard to fake, is proof."

The three of them settled into a group of faded stuffed chairs, the arms feeling to Gwen as if they'd been used as scratching posts.

"Where's Austin?" Billie asked.

"School."

"That's where I should be," Gwen said unhappily. "This whole experience has really disrupted my life. I just don't understand how it's been able to...to get inside me."

"We don't really understand the mechanisms ourselves but be glad it's a simple and temporary possession. Some spirits can literally attach themselves to a person, sort of like a lamprey eel grabs onto a shark and lives off its blood. In the case of a ghostly attachment, the ghost feeds on energy and drains the person of the will to live."

"That sounds nasty." Billie looked worried.

"But what about the possession?" Gwen asked. "What sort of physical repercussions might there be? Anything harmful?"

"While you won't be physically harmed, it's unlikely you will emerge totally unscathed. You may begin to feel, well, ungrounded, as if you are less attached to the earth. You may find yourself restless, unable to focus, more forgetful, and possibly depressed."

Gwen ticked off her fingers. "Yes, yes, yes, yes, and yes."

Billie groaned. "Jesus, Gwen, why didn't you tell me?"

Gwen shot her a look of apology. Talking about this stuff made her experiences feel too real. She still wasn't ready for real.

"Any nightmares, feeling a sense of impending doom?"

"Yes, and yes." It felt good to finally put names to all the emotions swirling through her.

Billie glared at Kylie. "What about her eyes? They were black when she was drawing."

"Physical changes may occur. Black eyes, dark as bottomless pits, are normal. Superhuman strength—Gwen's drawing hand being stronger than you applying the weight of your entire body. Foul odors sometimes accompany possession."

Gwen opened her mouth to ask, but Billie jumped in. "You smell fine." Having black eyes was bad enough, but to reek on top of that? At the moment, however, Gwen was less concerned about *what* had happened than the *why*.

"Why has this happened only at the fort? Why not at work or at home?"

"Ghosts tend to haunt the same area. A teenage girl named Elizabeth died of yellow fever in the 1800s and is always seen waving to people at the City Gate on the north end of St. George Street. And have you heard about the little boy ghost on the Flagler campus?"

Gwen shook her head. It might have been mentioned, but she would have discounted it as a silly story.

"A ten-year-old boy fell off a balcony and died, and he haunts that area, mostly pinching girls' thighs and trying to kiss them."

"Creepy," Billie said.

"Students are confused when they wake up to find bruises on their thighs, but it's just the boy. Ghosts can haunt where they died, where they lived, or any place that brings them comfort. It's different with a murder victim, however, as they are often trapped in the area or structure in which they were murdered."

"But why me?" Gwen pushed. Did her mom's paranormal activity plant some sort of marker in her, a marker a ghost would recognize? "Am I somehow weaker or defective in some way so it was able to…to find its way in?"

"No, not at all. I'm guessing that this particular spirit or entity has a message just for you." Kylie leaned forward and flipped through the photocopies of the drawings they'd made on their way to the SAPS office. "I struggle to connect these images into a cohesive story, but this one is the key." She put, on top, the drawing of the two men pointing guns at Gwen.

Gwen stared at the drawing, willing the men to look up so she could identify them, but of course, their heads remained down. "I suppose so, but here's what I don't get. The spirit has access to my pencil. Why doesn't it just *write* what it wants me to know? *Someone's going to point a gun at you on this day at this time.*"

Kylie flung herself back into her chair with the look of someone who's been puzzling the same thing for a while now. "Best question *ever*. Think about the ghost's existence. It has no voice, hasn't spoken in who knows how long---a few months? Years? Decades? *Centuries*? It hasn't written anything or read anything in all that time, so wouldn't it make sense that it has lost its language?"

"So it only has images with which to communicate," Gwen said. "But if there is a connection between all these drawings, we can't see it. Why not draw them in the right order so it's clear?"

"Another brilliant question, one I wish I had a definitive answer for. I'm guessing that not only has it lost its language, but time has befuddled its thoughts. It doesn't really have a brain, right? It's just a whisper, a remnant of a human's soul, so it either doesn't have control over the order, or doesn't know the correct order anymore."

Gwen sat up straighter and caught Billie's eye. "I guess the only thing to do is keep going back to the fort. That's the only way the… the spirit can give us more clues. But I lie awake at night wondering, *who* is the ghost? I mean, who *was* the ghost? Someone I knew?"

Kylie shook her head. "That's the confusing part. We don't know how ghosts move through their existence. Are they able to move through time? There's just no way of knowing. The one thing I do know is that anything is possible."

"Why do you do this work?" Gwen asked. She couldn't imagine devoting your days to something as offbeat and nebulous as ghost-hunting.

Kylie's face softened. "Truthfully, some days I wonder what I'm doing here, especially lately. I'm always trying to prove that spirits exist, that when we die it's not the end, but hard proof is rarely there." She grinned at Gwen. "Until now."

Clearly uncomfortable with personal topics, Kylie stood and reshuffled the images until she reached the one of the Native man wearing the Hamlet costume. "This was the first one you drew, right? If you could figure out who he is, that might give us a place to start deciphering the others."

"Hey, maybe Walt could help." Billie leaned forward, struggling out of the saggy chair. "He knows everything about St. Augustine history."

Gwen's chest warmed with relief that Billie was supporting this crazy quest instead of doubting her. "Let's go."

They stood and Kylie handed back the copies. "Once you have more drawings, let me know."

❖

The closest place to park was in the massive municipal parking ramp at the north end of St. George Street, which Gwen had driven by at least three times her first month there. She'd been looking for a parking ramp, so never considered that the attractive stucco building with a red tile roof and arched openings on every floor was actually a parking ramp. It looked more like a Spanish museum than a place to park.

Walt grinned when Billie and Gwen entered. "Today is my lucky day! I get to see you both." He put down the brass lantern he was polishing and opened his arms in welcome. Gwen stepped into his warm embrace, hoping some of his positive energy might rub off onto her. She patted his soft shirt. "Flannel in Florida?"

"Pretty cool, huh? Now what might I do for you two fine ladies today?"

Billie leaned against the counter. "We have a history mystery we're hoping you can solve."

He rubbed his palms together. "Ladies, you have come to the right place. After garlic shrimp grilled to perfection and dipped in butter, a history mystery is my favorite thing."

Gwen handed him the drawing of the two imprisoned men. "What's going on here, do you know?"

"Hmm. Wait. Did you draw these?" He spoke to Gwen, but shot a look at Billie, eyebrows raised.

"Long story," Gwen replied. "Do you know these men?"

Walt brought the drawing closer to his face. "I know what's happening here, but not when it's happening. Native Americans were imprisoned in the fort throughout the nineteeth century, Seminoles in the first half of the 1800s, then people from more distant tribes later in the century, like the Cheyenne, Arapaho, and Comanche." He shook his head. "Poor bastards."

That was the thing about Walt. His ancestors had been enslaved during the same time period, yet he was concerned about the Natives. Walt tapped the drawing. "Because these Natives are wearing nondescript clothing, it'll be hard to place them in time. But based on the guard's uniform, I'd say this is early to mid 1800s."

Billie gave a low whistle. "Two hundred years ago."

Gwen handed him the drawing of the man in velvet. "This is the other one." She left the drawing of the men and their guns in her bag. No use alarming him.

Walt broke out laughing. "Oh, my gosh, it's him. What an amazing rendering. You did this?"

"Once again, long story. You know who this is?"

"Not from the face, child, but from his clothing. He was the Seminole whom Americans called 'Wild Cat,' and the Mexicans called 'Gato del Monte,' but his given name was Coacoochee." He wrote the name lightly on the photocopy so they could see the spelling.

Billie and Gwen both tried out the name, confused by all the vowels. "Co-ahh-coo-chee," Walt repeated the name several times. "In 1830, President Jackson signed the Indian Removal Act, requiring that the Seminoles relocate from Florida to the Oklahoma Territory. Not surprisingly, the Seminoles fought back. Despite this, almost four thousand Seminoles were forced to move to what would one day become Oklahoma."

"Wait," Billie interrupted him. "The Seminoles from here ended up in Oklahoma? What part?"

"I'd have to double-check, but I think they settled in the area that eventually became Oklahoma City."

"Gwen was born in Oklahoma City," Billie said. "Maybe that's the connection."

"But we moved to Minnesota when I was two. I have no memory of Oklahoma."

Like a dog anticipating a bone, Billie leaned in. "But what if you have some Seminole in your ancestry? What if that's enough to attract the ghost? Maybe the ghost is, I mean was, a Seminole."

When they both looked at Walt, he shrugged. "All I know is that President Jackson's decree started the bloody Seminole Indian Wars, three of them, almost one right after the other. The Natives put up quite a fight, let me tell you, and Coacoochee was one of their leaders. Damn, those were some bloody times. For every two Indians forced to relocate to Oklahoma, the Seminoles killed a soldier. About five hundred Seminoles, let by Coacoochee, escaped into the Florida swamps where they led soldiers on fruitless searches in the wet and mud. Finally in 1842, the US gave up, making the Seminoles the only Indian tribe to never surrender to the US."

"What's the story behind the Hamlet outfit?" Billie asked.

"Coacoochee hated white men, for good reason since they were invading his land and killing his people. In 1840 he attacked a troupe of traveling actors who performed lots of Shakespeare plays. Coacoochee and his men murdered most of the actors and stole their costumes." He tapped the drawing. "He loved showing up to meetings wearing something outlandish."

Gwen looked closer at Coacoochee's face and now could see both disdain and hatred in the man's expression. "But do these two images connect in any way?"

"Hmm. Just a minute. Let me check something." He pulled a fort history book off the shelf, dropped it with a thud onto the counter, and flipped to a specific page. "Ah, yes." Then he put the drawings of the jailed men and Coacoochee side by side and leaned closer. "Look at the face of this man behind the bars, the one on the left. Could it be Coacoochee?"

Gwen started. How had she missed that? "Oh, my god. He's a thinner, sicker version, but yes, that's him."

Walt nodded, pleased. "Yup. I knew it. Didn't I tell you I love me a mystery? Now, according to the fort history, a group of Seminoles, including Coacoochee, were lured into a trap by American soldiers flying a white flag of truce—a nasty piece of deception if you ask me—and imprisoned at the fort in 1837."

"He must have been released if he was able to attack the acting troupe in 1840," Billie said.

"Not released. He escaped. It's quite a story, almost hard to believe. He and his cell mates ate as little as possible in order to get as thin as possible, for there was a small, barred window high in the outer wall of their cell. One night they managed to climb up to the window, squeeze through the bars, slide down the side of the fort, and slip away into the night."

"How do we know all this?"

"Coacoochee wrote an account of his escape years later. I've seen that window and it's small and used to have bars across it, so I suspect he stretched the truth a bit to prove he was smarter than his white captors. Someone probably just forgot to lock the cell and the Seminoles simply snuck out the front entrance."

"When did he escape?" Billie asked.

Walt checked his book. "November 22, 1837."

Gwen frowned, struggling to catch Billie's train of thought. "Is that significant?"

"No idea," she replied, "but look." She pointed to the *Visit St. Augustine* calendar on the wall. "The anniversary of his escape is just two weeks from now."

Gwen felt a sense of purpose settle over her. She had a name: Coacoochee. She had his motive: almost his entire tribe being ripped from their lush land and forced westward. History was full of secrets that never came to light. All she needed to do was uncover the one secret that would help her understand what was happening to her.

And Billie's idea that Gwen might have Seminole blood—maybe even Coacoochee's—running through her veins? That was the first place she'd start.

CHAPTER EIGHT

Billie, November 10

A s Billie toweled off after her morning shower, she felt edgy, almost itchy with a discomfort she couldn't identify. Gwen needed someone strong and fearless to help her through this, and all she had was Billie, still struggling with her fears. Their first month in Florida Billie wouldn't leave home, too afraid of pain to fully engage with the world. She was better now, but how could Gwen continue to love someone who had become such a huge disappointment?

By the time she'd finished dressing, Billie resolved to step up and give Gwen whatever support she needed, no matter how scared Billie was. And she would be there for Walt, protecting him from a certain legal danger by figuring out what Martha was up to.

Gwen was filling the dishwasher as Billie entered the kitchen. "I need you to gather up your water glasses," Gwen snapped, "since you've left one on every flat surface in every room of this tiny house. I don't have time to track them down."

"You're snarly this morning."

"No, I'm not. I have two staff meetings, two classes to teach, and Jennifer's tenure materials to review and forward. No more staying at home."

"But you need to return to the fort."

"I need to return to work." Her voice rose into the Angry Zone.

"I was just hoping we could talk this morning. We still haven't really addressed that whole recommitment thing that Earl and Sassy talked about."

Gwen thrust the upper rack back in place so hard the glasses clinked together. "Why do we need to talk about commitment? I'm committed."

Billie pulled out the rack and added more dirty glasses. "Well, how would I know that? We never talk."

"We talk all the time!" Now Gwen slammed the lower rack in.

"Not about important stuff. We—"

"You want to talk about important stuff? How about the fact that a ghost can wear me like a Halloween costume?"

Billie stepped back. This was not going to be a productive conversation. "It's good you can joke about it."

Gwen's face flushed with fury. "Well, I can't. And haven't I shown commitment? For two years you couldn't leave the house, so I did almost all the errands, all the yard work, all the shopping."

"I know, and I feel guilty about that. I couldn't have made it without your help. But I mowed the lawn. I could do that."

But Gwen was on a fevered roll that did not involve listening. "I don't need to prove anything, to do some recommit bullshit. I took a job that wasn't—" She slammed the dishwasher door shut and pushed *Start*.

"A job that wasn't what?" Billie narrowed her eyes. Now they were getting somewhere. She knew Gwen had been hiding something from her.

"Forget it. I have to go."

"Gwen, *wait*. A job that wasn't *what*?"

Gwen snatched up her leather case and keys and let the kitchen screen door bang shut behind her.

Billie was so angry all she could do was pace through the house shaking her hands to shed some of the negativity. What had Gwen done? A job that wasn't *what*? Wasn't what she'd wanted? Wasn't what she enjoyed? Wasn't enough money? Wasn't enough of a challenge? She'd applied for three jobs but had only gotten one offer, the one from Flagler College. What was Billie missing?

Billie clenched her jaw at the idea that she'd been so out of it, so algophobic, so agoraphobic, that Gwen had obviously made some sort of compromise in her job search and Billie had no idea what it had been.

She stood on the front porch, unsure what to do with her feelings, so she thought going to work might help, since today was a Martha day. Once Martha showed up around one p.m., then Billie was going to follow her on foot or on a trolley car or with an Uber if she had to. She would do whatever it took to protect Walt.

Clayton Black stood under his carport staring at their house. Could he see her standing on the porch? What was this guy's problem? One of these days she was going to march over there and demand an explanation. Was the guy angry that two women lived across the street? This was Florida, after all, where the Republicans had made it cool once again to harass members of the LGBTQ+ community.

She went through her list of facts—no ice, no falling, no pain would come to her, then she stomped down the porch steps, wanting to flip Clayton off, but Minnesota Nice was still too much a part of her DNA so she set aside thoughts of Clayton Black and instead focused on the long walk to work. To keep her mind busy, she thought up memes she'd make some day, like *Agoraphobia: Don't leave home without it.*

Billie's walking route to work kept to the side streets, areas of low traffic and low danger. In fifteen minutes, she'd left Lincolnville and passed Gwen's Flagler College, the ornate red and yellow main building originally a hotel for wealthy friends of Clayton Flagler. She wished she dared stop into Gwen's office and talk, but Gwen's day was too busy for that. As Billie walked, she marveled at how far she'd come. At first, her algophobia had been limited to winter— falling on ice, getting in a car accident during a blizzard—but then she'd tripped on an uneven sidewalk one sunny spring day and broke both wrists trying to break her fall. But here she was—walking on an old sidewalk, full of cracks and heaves. She never lifted her eyes from the pavement because of that, but at least she was walking. She still wasn't comfortable going much more than a few miles from home, but one day she'd make it to St. Augustine Beach.

At least she'd stopped overreaching for solutions that hadn't helped: head massage, reflexology, vitamin cocktails, herbs, essential oils, reiki, acupuncture, acupressure, hypnotherapy, aromatherapy. While she understood these techniques worked for many people and many conditions, none of them touched her fears. The only thing that had worked had been her therapist's exposure therapy, taking her farther from her house each session. *Do what frightens you.* The technique was exhausting but effective.

Billie eventually crossed King Street, a noisy artery of downtown, then sighed with relief to be on the southern end of St. George, a six-block pedestrian street that formed the heart of old St. Augustine. The only danger on that street was being lured by the scent of warm chocolate into one of the many fudge shops. Walt's store was tucked into a side street on the north end of St. George, an area that usually had the best buskers, so Billie tried to drop a dollar in every jar the days she worked. The guitarists, usually playing folk or blues, made St. George feel like a party, another reason she loved going to work at Walt's.

A block from the antique store, Billie dropped down onto a ceramic-tiled bench and texted Gwen. *Sorry we fought.*

During the quiet moments at work, Billie paged through a few of Walt's history books. It turns out the fort had been passed around like an unpopular white elephant at a holiday party. The fort was built by the Spanish in the mid-1600s. The British attacked it multiple times but couldn't put a dent in the coquina with their cannonballs. Instead of shattering like rock, coquina absorbed the energy of the artillery without breaking.

Through treaties, the Spanish gave the fort to the British in 1763, then the British gave it back to the Spanish in 1783 in exchange for Gibraltar, then in 1821, the Spanish gave it to the United States in exchange for Cuba. Billie wasn't sure any of this information would help, but she had to start some place. And if she could find some connection between Gwen and the Seminoles, perhaps that might explain why this ghost—possibly a native?—might be communicating with her.

Martha only had three items for Walt today: an old glass bottle, a repaired blue and black majolica bowl, and a Spanish olive jar, so the stack of bills Walt handed her was smaller. When Martha was distracted, Billie took her photo. Five seconds after the door closed behind Martha, Billie sent a silent plea for safety to the Universe, then followed.

Martha didn't appear distracted by any of the storefronts or loud groups of tourists. Looking straight ahead, she turned off St. George onto Hypolita, a much quieter side street used mostly by delivery trucks. She showed no interest in her surroundings, and clearly didn't suspect Billie was thirty feet behind her.

Martha stepped into a small, pricey grocery store that served those downtown residents with no transportation to the Winn Dixie up US 1. Billie stepped into a narrow doorway and waited, heart pounding. She was *doing* this, really doing it. Walking on unfamiliar streets past unknown dangers. She reveled in her success as a truck's backup alarm beeped. Not even that bothered her today.

As she waited, Billie checked her phone. Nothing from Gwen. Ten minutes later, Martha reappeared with two plastic bags of groceries, not even looking in Billie's direction, and continued down the block. Billie managed to keep up and joined the crowd of tourists waiting for the light in order to cross Castillo Drive, Martha at the front of the pack. Where was the woman going? There was nothing on the other side of the street but the fort and its grassy grounds.

Billie hurried through the pack, concerned about losing sight of Martha, but as the tourists crossed at different speeds, she managed to work her way closer. Martha walked straight down the sidewalk toward the fort. She stood in line at the ticket building as Billie caught up and hid behind a family studying a map.

Martha paid cash, then took the ticket across to the fort entrance and disappeared inside.

Weird, so weird. Billie scanned the area and found a comfortable wooden bench on which to sit. Since there was only one way out of the fort, all Billie had to do was wait. She texted Walt and he suggested she take the rest of the afternoon off since business was slow.

Every ten minutes, she checked her phone. Still no answering text from Gwen. That same edgy feeling returned. How could they possibly last if they kept fighting? Had those last two years in Minnesota irreparably harmed their relationship? She just couldn't get Gwen to talk about anything.

Boat traffic on the river was heavy that afternoon as speed boats and a few Jet Skis zoomed by, followed by two towering yachts, and a handful of silent sailboats. The slight smell of fish and gasoline reached her. With the light reflecting off the river, she found herself starting to relax.

All the activity reminded Billie of the day she'd met Gwen. They'd both been in San Francisco for work conferences and had ended up sitting next to each other on a streetcar descending Powell Street. They'd hit it off immediately, amazed to have run into another Minnesotan so many miles from home. Billie had been drawn to Gwen's strength, her certainly in everything, and Gwen later said she'd fallen for Billie's sense of humor. But that day, when the streetcar had deposited them at the end of the line, they'd smiled at each other, exchanged "Nice to meet you," then Billie had turned left and Gwen had turned right.

A block later, panic had gripped Billie. What was she thinking? She'd just walked away from a woman who was interesting and articulate and could have been *The One* without even getting her contact information. She whirled around and ran back to the streetcar stop, arriving out of breath just as Gwen had arrived, also out of breath.

Gasping, they'd smiled at each other, then took a few minutes to recover. Finally, Billie stuck out her hand. "Billie Norton."

"Gwendolyn Tucker."

Billie held Gwen's firm handshake longer than normal, then finally let go. "I panicked when I realized I didn't get your contact information."

"I did the same. I don't know what I was thinking to just walk away," Gwen said. "But look—we both *ran* back here. What does that mean?"

"It means we need to find a place to sit and talk. Today will either turn into us having a nice time then going on with our lives… or it will be the best *meet-cute* ever, one of those that almost didn't happen."

The sudden date at the nearest coffeehouse turned into dinner the next two nights, then getting together back in St. Paul, then spending so much time together that Billie's best friend Laura and her wife, also Laura, insisted on giving Gwen and Billie a "couple" name. They tried *Bwen*, then *Gillie*, then *Bilwen*, then finally the winner, *Gwillie*. The four of them became *Gwillie* and *the Lauras*.

Getting bored on her bench outside the fort, Billie checked the time. Martha had been inside for an hour; the fort closed in an hour. Was the woman sightseeing? With bags of groceries? Maybe she was bringing a snack for the park rangers. She could be distracting them with food while she stole things from the various displays.

All Billie knew was that when Martha exited the fort, Billie would confront her. She couldn't figure out what was going on with Gwen and her ghost, but she could certainly get to the bottom of the mystery of Martha's "antiques." By now, dozens of tourists had passed Billie on their way into the fort, and then on their way out. She researched more about the fort to keep herself busy.

That got old quickly—Gwen was the historian, not Billie—so she did some research on DNA testing and Native heritage. While some of the DNA testing companies claimed to be able to verify Native ancestry, an article in a recent scientific journal—so detailed in its dizzying descriptions of tests and markers that Billie had to skip most of it—concluded that DNA testing could not specify tribal affiliation with any level of statistical confidence. She texted the bad news to Gwen that taking a DNA test wasn't going to help establish a connection to Coacoochee.

Gwen's responding text came quickly. *Thanks for DNA info... and I'm sorry too.*

Feeling a weight had just been lifted off her chest, Billie settled back into the task at hand, scrutinizing every person who passed by as they left the fort, just in case Martha had donned a disguise. But no one had the same shape or gait.

Five o'clock arrived and the rangers in the ticket building closed it up, chatting about having a few beers before heading home. She heard the slam of the fort's massive wooden door, then three park rangers strolled across the wooden bridge into view.

"Excuse me," she said, rising to her feet. "I'm afraid you still have someone in inside. I've been waiting, watching very carefully, and she never came out."

The three looked at each other, and the oldest, judging by the graying beard, turned to his colleagues, "You followed all the protocols?"

They nodded.

"Checked all the blind spots and hiding places?"

They nodded again, but now were more interested in their phones than in the idea of someone still locked up in the fort.

"Could you check again?" Billie asked.

"Ma'am, we've been doing this for years," the bearded man said. "There are very few places where an adult could hide from us. Trust me, the last thing we want is for someone to get trapped inside. The fort can be a spooky place at night. We'd not only lose our jobs, but we'd likely be sued for emotional distress or PTSD or something like that. Your friend is not inside. We're closed now so you'll need to leave the grounds."

Heaving a sigh, recognizing that she'd lost this battle, Billie nodded and headed down the sidewalk to Castillo Street. She had a long walk home. She was tired, discouraged, and thirsty. At least she had something to take her mind off Gwen. If Martha hadn't left, and wasn't still inside, then where the hell was she?

CHAPTER NINE
Gwen, November 10

When Gwen managed to catch the bartender's eye, she lifted her empty glass and sent a look that said, *Refill please*. God, what a day she'd had. The bartender, covered in tattoos so intricate Gwen gave up trying to decipher them, nodded and made another Harvey Wallbanger, shaking his head. When she'd first ordered the drink, he'd winced and had to look it up on his phone, which made her feel old. But when the drink came and the sharp smell of tequila rose from the glass, she didn't care. The tangy sweet taste of her college years reassured her that she was still Gwen, the same Gwen from 1987 who drank Wallbangers even after they'd already faded in popularity. *That* Gwen believed firmly that ghosts were not real. But *this* Gwen was being forced to accept that they might be.

She hadn't been entirely honest with Billie that morning. Yes, she had lots to do at work, but before work she stopped at the fort for what she called a "quickie," a phrase that gave her a fair amount of discomfort since it was starting to feel good, alarmingly good, when the ghost possessed her. And just when she'd thought life couldn't get any weirder.

That early in the day, the fort tourists were scarce, still tracking down coffee and planning their days. There weren't many park rangers visible, so Gwen took her sketchbook to the far bastion on the gun deck and sat on the floor against the wall, hopefully out of view.

The first drawing was over so quickly that Gwen almost regretted when her hand stopped moving. She felt warm and calm. The second drawing left her feeling the same way, but when Gwen took a few minutes to look at the drawings, she sighed. Why couldn't she find a way to tie these images together?

The first was a night scene of St. Augustine—she recognized the Bridge of Lions arching over the river. The bridge was lit with thousands of tiny white lights, as were all the boats passing beneath it. The ghost's drawing was masterful, presenting a night image in black and white that almost seemed to glow yellow with the warmth of all the lights.

The second drawing was from the same perspective as the "gun" drawing, from atop the fort's outer wall. Two men below were exchanging money and once again, neither face was visible. At least they weren't pointing guns at anyone.

Gwen was preparing to get up off the hard concrete when her hand began to draw again. She leaned back against the rough coquina wall and let the ghost do its thing.

"Hey!"

Gwen's eyes flew open as the ghost, perhaps as startled as Gwen, actually released its hold on her hand and left an unfinished drawing. Above her loomed the pot-bellied ranger from the other day.

"Several patrons have reported a woman who was drawing amazing images with her eyes closed, as if channeling a..." He curled his lip. "...a ghost. I thought it might be you. Nice trick, but the show's over. Up."

Gwen stood quickly to avoid being physically dragged from her spot.

The man pulled out his phone. "I need a photo for the ticket booth. Hold still."

Before she could fully process his words, he'd taken her photo. "We said last time that we didn't want to see you here again, and we meant it. After I post your photo at the ticket booth, no one will ever sell you a ticket here again. You and your silly ghost act are finished."

Gwen sent a silent plea to her ghost. *If you can control me, you can control others. Make this guy slap himself, or stomp on his own phone.* But no luck. It made her a little sad that their connection was so one-sided. The ghost could reach out to her, but she couldn't call it or summon it.

Gwen picked up her stuff, seized with sudden panic. How was she going to figure out the ghost's message if she was banned from the fort?

"I don't think you understand how important—"

"I don't want to understand. C'mon, I'm escorting you out." And this time he did, taking her all the way out of the fort and across the wooden bridge, his heavy footsteps thudding behind her.

Back at the bar, Gwen took another sip of her Wallbanger, shuddering at the memory of the ranger's attitude. He acted exactly as she would have just a few weeks ago, irritated and angered by the idea that ghosts existed. The whole experience had been beyond humiliating, and the day had just gotten worse from there. On her drive to work Mason had texted his flight information with the hope that she'd pick him up a week from now at the Jacksonville Airport, a good two hours north of St. Augustine. And she'd tried to research Coacoochee but hadn't found much more than what Walt had told them.

Before Gwen had left home that morning, she'd texted her administrative assistant to shift the faculty meeting later in the morning. Yet when she arrived after her fort visit and passed the small conference room, she could see the meeting was already in progress.

"Hey, boss, hope it's okay. I went ahead and started us off because there's so much on the agenda today."

Glaring at Jeremy, Gwen accepted a copy of the agenda from her embarrassed assistant and sat in the only empty chair.

"So next on the agenda—" Jeremy started.

"Jer, I'm here now and perfectly capable of running the meeting myself. I don't need any help crossing the street or cutting up my meat either, okay?"

Hands up in mock self-defense, Jeremy grinned. "Got it."

The meeting took forever, then just before her first class, which the TA had planned to cover, the TA broke out in an impressive sweat and threw up, leaving Gwen to teach both classes herself, something she had come to hate.

She wasn't sure when it had happened, but a few years ago at Hamline University as she'd faced an auditorium full of *Introduction to US History 1877 to Present* students shifting in their seats and setting up their laptops, it hit her: she felt *done* when it came to teaching. It wasn't the fault of the students or the college. Something in her just snapped and she realized she'd run out of energy. She didn't want to keep doing something she no longer loved, but how could she stop? Politicians were working hard, and succeeding, at cutting history classes from high schools and colleges to ensure no one knew any history. This, conveniently, would enable them to repeat it, so the profession needed to fight back. But she just felt done. After this revelation, she'd passed on to her TAs as many classes as she could.

Normally, she would never have taken this position at Flagler because teaching was required, but Billie had needed help getting away from winter. The job Gwen had really wanted, and *could* have had, involved no teaching whatsoever. Still, Flagler was a happy place. Professors and students alike seemed to thrive in this environment. Maybe five years ago she would have embraced the college, but now she just felt separate and tense. What sort of person sees a rainbow and turns grumpy? *Why can't I just decide to be happy?*

Struggling back to the present, Gwen drained the last of her Harvey Wallbanger and lifted her glass for yet another refill, feeling pleasantly woozy. Even though their house was only about ten blocks away, she was going to have to leave the car and walk home. She had hoped that the alcohol would banish the bundle of niggling thoughts from her mind, but it hadn't: what was the ghost going to do now that Gwen could no longer be its conduit? What sort of life had he or she led before dying? Did it remember its old life? Could it feel anything, like anxiety or fear or pain? Happiness or love? Did a ghost even think? What would it be like to be trapped in one place for possibly centuries, unable to eat or drink or talk or sleep... or leave?

Gwen surprised herself by chuckling out loud. Somehow, she'd gone from believing ghosts weren't real to actually empathizing with one.

The other bad news in an already difficult day was Billie's text that DNA testing would be unlikely to connect her to the Florida Seminole tribe and Coacoochee, which meant she needed to turn to her stepmother Faye. She checked her watch. Back in Minnesota, Faye would still be up.

"Gwen, dear, it's so good to hear your voice. It feels as if you've moved to the other side of the world. I miss you both."

"We miss you too." They chatted for a while, then Gwen got to the point. "Do you remember that shoebox of Dad's that you wanted to give me but I was too overwhelmed by our upcoming move that I declined?"

"The box of family stuff?"

"Yes. I never paid much attention, but now I'm interested. Aunt Ruthie had given me lots of notes about bits and pieces of the family tree and I'd tossed them into Dad's box."

"I know just where it is, so I'll put it in the mail tomorrow."

"That would be great. Mason could bring it with him when he comes, but that won't be until next week, and as bad as things have gotten at the US Post Office, I think it'll still beat Mason."

"Mason's visiting you next week?"

Gwen frowned. "Yeah, he said you wanted him to explain in person the changes to your will."

She could hear Faye's small sound of surprise. "Well, that's odd. I'm just clarifying the split as fifty/fifty. Nothing major, and certainly not worth having Mason fly all the way down there to explain something I just explained to you in about three seconds."

"Hmmm. Maybe I misunderstood him, but he said he'd be here on the eighteenth."

"He left today and told me he was visiting a college friend in Atlanta." She tsked twice. "What is that boy up to?"

Gwen had no answer to that. "You can mail me the material?"

"I'll box it up right now."

After saying good-bye and ending the call, Gwen tried to puzzle out why Mason had lied about the reason for his visit but gave up. Her open-book stepbrother had slammed shut over the years so she no longer knew what he was thinking.

Gwen ordered another Harvey Wallbanger, then made designs in the wet condensation on the glass. The long bar at the Well cleared as the last group of noisy patrons were taken to their table. Only then did she see who sat alone at the far end, nursing a beer. Sighing, Gwen picked up her drink and sauntered down the bar. "Excuse me, but you're kind of cute. Want to come home with me?"

Eyebrows arched in surprise, Billie gave her the same smile that had charmed Gwen all those years ago. "*Kind of* cute? Hmm. Well, I'm not usually so easy to pick up, but yes, I'd love to go home with you."

Gwen settled both their bills. "However, we have to walk home, in the dark, because I've had a little too much." She waited, wondering if Billie would finally be ready to get behind the wheel again and offer to drive them home, but Billie just nodded.

Steadying each other, they stepped out into the luscious warm air and linked arms.

"Today I lost track of someone I was tailing," Billie said. "First time I've ever lost someone."

"I'm sorry. That had to be hard. But look at you, walking random streets as if you didn't have a problem." Billie beamed. "However," Gwen continued, "not to one-up you, but I had my photo posted at the fort's ticket booth and have been banned for life."

Billie winced. "Okay, you win."

As they walked through a dark broken only by the occasional streetlight, Gwen helped Billie avoid potholes and uneven sidewalks and abandoned Big Wheels. And even though she didn't know it, Billie helped Gwen finally feel good about at least the end of her day. But Gwen had to wonder: Was this normal? At eight a.m. that morning she'd been furious with her, and twelve hours later she was bumping shoulders companionably and considering seducing her when they reached home.

Gwen wished she knew what she wanted.

CHAPTER TEN
Billie, November 11

Sex had always been a great connector for Gwen and Billie, and last night was no different. Humming with the afterglow of their "connection," Billie opened her laptop. Time to find out if Walt was Martha's only victim. The search yielded several St. Augustine antique stores grouped together on the western edge of the city. What Billie really wanted to do was try making it to the beach and get lost in the sounds of waves and seagulls, but she had to solve the Martha Mystery.

Since the antique stores were within her comfort zone she ordered an Uber to take her west instead of east.

"Hey, Minnesota," called the driver. "Climb aboard."

"Chuck," Billie cried. "So glad it's you. I'm gonna need you for four stops and a few hours, if that's okay."

"My time is your money. Or is it your money is my time?" The guy shrugged and tapped his phone. "Okay, let's get started."

At the first antique shop, Billie showed the employee her photo of Martha.

"Yeah, she comes in here maybe once a week?"

"What day?"

"Couldn't tell you."

The story was the same at the second shop. At the third, the employee squinted at the photo. "I recognize her. Yeah, every

Wednesday? Thursday? Can't remember, but she has some bitchin' goods to sell."

Billie leaned across the counter. "Which is it? Wednesday or Thursday?"

The man turned and hollered toward the back of the store. "Pete! That chick with the burlap bag? When she come in?"

"Tuesdays," came the returning yell.

Billie's heart sped up. "Today is Tuesday. Has she been here?"

The yelling relay continued until Billie determined that Martha had been there, but Pete hadn't paid any attention to time.

As Chuck drove Billie to the last shop, she looked at the photos she'd taken of the drawings Gwen had made yesterday. One was of the same two men, seen from above, but instead of pointing guns at Gwen they were exchanging money. And the second was a lovely night scene of St. Augustine aglow with tiny lights. Was this Nights of Lights? Billie had barely looked at the third drawing because it was unfinished.

"Hey, Chuck," Billie said. "I've been seeing posters about this Nights of Lights thing coming up. What's that all about?"

Chuck turned onto San Marco Avenue. "Nights of Lights turns St. Augustine into the prettiest city in the world for the holidays. The first night they make a big deal out of turning the lights on all at once. Thousands come downtown to the Plaza."

"That long, skinny park on King?"

"The very one. There's usually music and food, then someone flips a switch and the whole city lights up—buildings, bushes, trees, the bridge, the lighthouse on Anastasia. It's awesome." He parked in front of the last antique shop.

Billie showed Chuck the photo she'd taken of the night scene drawing. "Does it look anything like this?"

"That's it exactly. City's so bright I'll bet you could see it from the moon."

Billie's finger slipped and the photo of Martha appeared.

Chuck turned to look at Billie. "You know her?"

"Why?"

"Weirdest passenger ever. Had her at least three times. I pick her up at the fort, take her to the same shops you've gone to today. Then we go to Winn Dixie and I wait until she comes out with a bag of groceries in each hand, then I drop her off back at the fort."

"Was that last Tuesday?"

He checked his phone. "Yup."

Weird, weird, weird. "Okay, Chuck, this is the last store, then I think we're done. I'll be right back."

She recognized the owner as a friend of Walt's who'd stopped at his shop a few times. Billie introduced herself, explained her concerns, then showed the woman Martha's photo.

"Oh, yeah, she's been coming regularly for a month or two. She brings in the loveliest antique lace. In fact, you just missed her."

"What?"

"She left maybe fifteen minutes ago."

"Holy shit. Thanks." Billie flew out the door. Would she have time to get to the fort while Martha shopped? "Chuck, to the fort, ASAP!"

Chuck threw the car into reverse and squealed out of the parking lot. "Who are we chasing?"

She explained while Chuck focused on his driving. "If she follows the pattern you described, we might be able to make it to the fort while she's buying groceries." As he reached downtown, Billie leaned forward, straining to see through the windshield.

"Chuck, you gotta clean your windshield."

"Yeah, lost some stars 'cause of that. But look, there she is." He pointed about two blocks ahead.

Sure enough, Martha was exiting her Uber with a Winn Dixie bag in each hand.

"Shoot, shoot. I can't lose her."

Chuck looked at the traffic, then pulled a U-turn that caused some honks but enabled him to pull into the fort's parking lot. "Go!"

"Thanks. You're the best," Billie shouted as she leapt from the car.

"I know!"

Billie half-walked, half-ran down the sidewalk digging out her wallet. She had to detour around a group of school kids blocking the way but got to the ticket booth as Martha was walking away from it. She passed so closely Billie could have reached out and touched her, but then she'd never learn why Martha was so obsessed with the fort.

Billie bought her ticket then ran across the bridge and pushed past another clog of kids. What was *with* people? It was like a population explosion at the fort.

A third school group stood just inside the courtyard with Martha's black hair barely visible on the other side of them. Billie pushed through the crowd, apologizing, horrified she was being rude to kids. She finally fought her way through the courtyard.

But where was Martha?

Billie whirled in a circle, scanning everyone. No Martha.

Billie started with the room to the left of the restrooms, but it was locked and marked "Staff Only." The next door led to a series of three nested rooms, one after the other. The last was a room marked "Powder Magazine" that was only accessible through a four-foot-high tunnel, so Billie dropped into a crouch and scuttled into the powder magazine. It was an odd little room with such a low curved ceiling that Billie felt as if she were inside a barrel…an empty barrel.

Billie returned to the courtyard then quickly searched every room, ending with the soldiers' barracks Kylie had taken them to after the encounter with the rangers. Nothing. No Martha. Not even an empty Winn Dixie bag.

Hot and confused, Billie popped into the gift shop and bought a bottle of water to hydrate, then searched the entire fort again, both levels. The rangers she'd talked to that first time she'd followed Martha were right—there weren't many places for an adult to hide.

Too tired to walk home, she ordered another Uber and spent the rest of the afternoon on the porch swing, stewing about Martha, who kept disappearing, and about drawings of guns and Seminoles dressed as Hamlet and Gwen's fifty-fifth birthday party, *without* Billie.

The mail came and it included a thick overnight envelope from Faye, which Billie signed for. The ancestry information. Gwen had given Billie permission to open it and start combing through the material. The photos had notes on their backs, but Billie didn't recognize any of the names. Gwen's mom had been adopted so that branch of the family tree was as bare as an oak in January; Gwen's father was the one with roots in Oklahoma.

Billie finally found the notes Aunt Ruthie had made. It took Billie an hour to decipher the elderly woman's cramped writing, but she was able to re-create the information on a fresh sheet of paper. Starting with Gwen's father William and his sister Ruthie, the Tucker family records stretched back to Gwen's great-great-grandfather Anthony Tucker and a woman identified only as "Mary." Tucker had been born in St. Augustine in 1820, which certainly connected Gwen with this city, if not the fort. "Mary" was less helpful. Billie realized she was getting nowhere. Would they ever figure out *who* the ghost had been before it became a ghost? Man? Woman? Child? Native? Immigrant?

She had no answers, which circled her back to Gwen's refusal to answer Billie's question about the move and Gwen's job offers. How would they survive as a couple if Gwen kept treating her like someone too broken to be able to handle the truth? Their lives had felt out of balance for so long that Billie struggled to recall what "normal" had felt like. She'd never been so stuck, so unable to feel optimistic about the future. Gwen made everything worse by refusing to be honest with her. How would they get unstuck if nothing ever changed? A mix of emotions began bubbling through her.

By the time Gwen arrived home from work, Billie overflowed with emotions hard to name and fueled by things she didn't understand. Anger? Love? Frustration? Hurt? She didn't know if she wanted to scream or cry.

"I want to talk about us," Billie announced the second Gwen stepped into the house.

"First, not a good time. I'm exhausted. Second, what's there to talk about? You were fine not talking last night." Gwen's eyes sported dark circles, and her shoulders slumped forward.

"Do you resent me? Do you resent the move?"

Gwen slowly lowered herself onto a chair and pulled out her sketchbook and flipped it open to the unfinished sketch. "I don't want to talk about the move. I want to know why the ghost has targeted me. I want to know if I'm in danger or if some twisted evil spirit is having fun with me." She tossed the sketchbook, open to the unfinished drawing, onto the table. "This one is really bugging me. I hate anything unfinished, but when the guard yelled at me, the ghost released my hand and left." She closed her eyes and dropped her head back. "I'm not going to talk about the move."

Billie clenched her jaw and struggled to stay calm. Gwen just kept adding brick after brick to the wall between them, so to avoid exploding Billie left Gwen to her sketchbook and returned to the porch, now in shadows because it was so late. She rubbed on some lotion to repel the no-see-ums. She'd thought northern mosquitoes were bad, but at least you could see and kill them. No-see-ums were horrid and their bites were sharp. She pulled out her phone, wondering why she hadn't thought to do this before.

She scrolled through her contacts until she found Kim's phone. Kim was one of Gwen's friends from Hamline; they'd both started teaching there at the same time.

Hey, kim. billie here. hope u r well. gotta ask—any good jobs for a history prof in Cities? G won't admit but not happy here. did she burn any bridges? any jobs at Hamline or elsewhere? plz don't tell her i'm reaching out on her behalf.

Kim went to bed ridiculously early as a technique to get her kids to bed, so Billie didn't expect an answer before morning.

Eventually, she heard Gwen go to bed, but Billie was feeling too restless, too angry, too tired to try tearing down Gwen's invisible walls tonight. How did you reach someone who didn't want to be reached? Billie ended up wandering back into the kitchen where the sketchbook lay open to the unfinished drawing. She leaned on one arm, studying the sketch. It appeared to be two people facing each other, a woman with shoulder-length black hair with her back to the viewer, possibly holding something like a sword that was only visible over her left shoulder. The person facing her also held a sword. Hmmm. The more she looked, the clearer the scene became.

Billie picked up the pencil. The underlying structure of the one visible face was there. Maybe she could coax out the image with a few pencil strokes. Hair-short. Face—wide with well-defined chin. Clothing—nondescript, cargo pants maybe? Boxy shirt?

Lost in her work, Billie sketched for an hour, hyper focused on each mark she made, determined to read and follow the ghost's guidelines. It was quiet in the house, the only sound her pencil moving across the paper. She'd loved pencils ever since she learned that the friction of moving the pencil across the paper created enough heat that the graphite melted into the tiny hills and valleys of the paper's surface. Pencils sacrificed themselves for words and images.

She finally put the pencil down, removed her glasses, and rubbed her eyes. She might need to get bifocals one of these days, but to do so was to admit she was aging, and there just wasn't room in her basket of anxieties for that. Agoraphobia took up most of the oxygen in the room.

Billie looked down at the drawing and gasped. She jammed her glasses back on. What the hell? Then she covered her mouth and moaned. Oh. My. God. What had she done?

There must not have been enough direction from the original drawing, so Billie had guessed and interpreted and ended up... sketching her own face.

She'd wanted to help Gwen but had ended up drawing herself weirdly engaged in a swordfight, of all things, with a black-haired woman. Billie banged her head softly on the table.

Sighing, she wrote a short note in the corner of the page. *So, so sorry. Thought I could help, but thanks to previously unknown but now apparent narcissistic tendencies, I drew myself. Gaack.*

Feeling foolish, Billie finally went to bed.

CHAPTER ELEVEN
Gwen, November 12

Gwen woke up early enough that it was still dark outside. She lay there imagining that they were still at home, in their 1930s St. Paul brick bungalow with the original woodwork and cute working fireplace, with fresh snow blanketing the city in clean white sparkles. The air would bite when she stepped outside, but Gwen loved the change in the air that fall brought, along with the insistence that it was time to start something new, to turn over a new leaf, gather your nuts for winter. Time to stock up on fresh wax for her skis, maybe buy a new winter coat, take a class, learn to play the ukulele.

Sadly, fall had always seemed to ramp up Mom's ghost obsession. For some people Halloween was all about trick-or-treating, neighborhood haunted houses, or carving pumpkins. For her mom, fall brought out the Ouija board as a way to communicate with the spirits of her dead ancestors, none of whom she knew because she'd been adopted. One October when Gwen was in high school, her mom had scheduled a séance for herself and friends at the house. Gwen, small and slender at the time, decided to hide behind the living room drapes to prove the séance was fake. And she did.

Earlier that afternoon, the woman conducting the séance had insisted on being alone in the living room to better clear the "psychic space" for the spirits, but what she'd actually done was install three speakers, one of them on the floor behind the drapes. Gwen tripped over it as she'd slid behind the drapes while the woman used the bathroom and before everyone arrived. Somehow, during the séance, the woman triggered a knocking sound from the speaker she'd hidden in the front closet, a sad sobbing from the speaker in the fireplace, and a moaning from the speaker at Gwen's feet. The woman had also triggered some sort of mist that filled the room with the scent of old socks. Who decided that visiting spirits smelled like a locker room?

At the height of the performance, as Mom's dead relatives were "present and telling her they loved her," Gwen had jumped out waving the speaker as evidence of fraud. Mom had been so angry that she couldn't speak for hours. Now, at age fifty-four, Gwen wondered why she hadn't just let her mom have what she'd needed—a connection to a family she'd never known.

Shaking off the past, Gwen rolled out of bed and opened the blinds. Palm-like bushes surrounded their St. Augustine house. The lawn was made of thick, stiff grass that they both found painful to walk on without shoes—the blades were like little knives. But they loved the house, and the area. According to their neighbor Sassy, over the years, the neighborhood had fallen into disrepair, the houses' paint entirely weathered off, their windows blinded by rotting sheets of plywood. But then, house by house, windows were replaced, paint reapplied, and the neighborhood came back. It was a tight area, with narrow streets, narrow driveways, and almost no lawns, but it thrummed with life. And of course, there was that tree in the middle of the street. Where else would a person see that?

"G'morning."

Gwen turned. Billie, still half asleep, reached out her hand so Gwen dropped back onto the bed and gave her a quick hug, inhaling the comforting smells of Billie's white musk soap and shampoo. She appreciated that no matter how hard the previous day had been, they could, in their hearts, forgive each other overnight and get on with things the next day.

"I'm meeting Kylie and Austin at the fort," Gwen said. "You want to come?"

"I have to work at nine. But I thought you've been banned."

Gwen shrugged. "I did too, but Kylie says they have a plan, so we'll see."

As Gwen parked in the fort's lot, she was grateful to be out of winter, but everything was still so new—it had only been two months—that homesickness often crept over her. She resolved to shake it off so she could figure out what this ghost wanted.

"Gwen!" Kylie wore a skirt made entirely of leather belts lashed together with the flattened plastic lace Gwen had used to make lanyards at summer camp.

Gwen waved, trying for enthusiasm but failing. Ghostly possession was too exhausting for excitement. "I thought Austin was coming."

Kylie smiled. "He's already where he needs to be. C'mon." She pulled Gwen off the blacktop, past the ticket booth, and down onto the sandy area next to the sea wall. The wall was so high she couldn't see the river.

"Where are we going?"

"We're heading for the northwest bastion, the one farthest from the entrance." Eventually, they followed the sandy path around the first bastion and through the grassy moat to the northwest bastion, where Austin stood against the fort wall, or rather, *curtain* as Jeremy had lectured her.

The sheer size of the fort towering above her weighed down her spirit. She watched as Austin picked up an aluminum ladder and clanked it loudly against the sloping wall.

"Quiet, honey. We don't want the rangers to know we're here." Kylie smiled at Gwen. "We dropped this off this morning before the sun came up, and Austin's been guarding it."

Gwen stared up the ladder. "This is how we're getting into the fort? But it doesn't reach high enough."

Kylie grabbed Gwen's hands and squeezed. "That's the best part. We don't need to get inside the fort, we just need to get as close to it as we can. We're hoping the ghost will come to you."

"Through the walls?"

Austin nodded. "Ghosts can pass through solid matter, but these walls are really, really thick. We're thinking that the higher you are, the better chance your ghost will be able to reach you." His face flushed with excitement. "That's our theory, anyway. The ghost is clearly trapped by the boundaries of the fort so we don't know how far it can reach through the walls or if it can come down the outside."

Kylie adjusted the ladder. "The thinnest part of the fort is clearly the front door, but the rangers will see us there. So this is our best option."

"You want me to climb way up there, balance on the ladder, and draw at the same time?" She knew aluminum was strong, but it looked flimsy when you were about to climb it.

Kylie moved one of the ladder's feet. "I'll be on the ladder right behind you, arms around your legs to stabilize you."

Gwen shook her head. "This is crazy." The wall was at least thirty feet high, the ladder, fully extended, a dizzying twenty feet, according to its yellow label.

"We have to try. Disguises to get us inside will only work until you start drawing, then all hell will break loose again." Kylie caught Gwen's gaze and held it. "The only way to figure out what's going on is to let the ghost continue to draw."

Gwen unpacked her sketchbook and jammed the pencil into her pocket. She stuck the sketchbook into the back of her jeans. "I still don't get how or why it's drawing things that haven't happened, that may never happen."

Austin almost hopped with barely contained excitement. "It could be a time-traveling ghost."

Gwen bent over with a groan. "No, God, please. There is only so much paranormal shit a rational person can take in a day." She looked at her companions. "No insult intended."

"None taken," they said in unison.

"It's just that my entire life, I've believed that...ghosts aren't real, time travel isn't possible, and aliens don't live among us."

When Austin snorted in disgust, Kylie shushed him. "Everyone lands in different locations along the paranormal comfort continuum." She shook the ladder once more. "Okay, up you go."

As a kid, whenever Gwen had been worried about a test or scared of doing something new in swimming lessons like jumping off the high board, her dad had always squeezed her hand and said "Courage, kiddo." Decades later, when he was only hours from dying and they'd both known it, he'd squeezed her hand and whispered through parched lips, "Courage, kiddo."

Standing at the base of the ladder, Gwen blinked hard to stop the tears. It had been four years but still, the thought that her father was no longer in the world made it hard to breathe. She blew out a few deep breaths, heard his voice saying *Courage, kiddo*, then she grabbed the cool metal and began to climb. The ladder was at enough of an angle that climbing wasn't difficult, but she could feel it bowing slightly under her weight as she climbed. She felt oddly exposed even though the traffic on Avenida Menendez couldn't see her. Directly behind her was a small, tree-lined neighborhood, and to the left was the river where a boat might see her, but that was it.

The ladder rattled as she climbed high enough to use the ladder's top step as an easel. She felt a little queasy when she looked down.

"Don't look down," Kylie said as she climbed up behind her until she was at Gwen's waist, her hands firmly grasping the ladder. "I got you."

With one hand, Gwen propped up the sketchbook on the ladder and leaned it against the fort, then pulled out her pencil.

"Everyone okay up there?" called Austin.

"I'm good," Gwen said, her left hand gripping the ladder. "But I'm not letting go of this ladder for anything." She stared at her right hand. "But nothing is happening."

"We'll wait," Kylie said.

Gwen felt herself mentally reaching out, trying to connect with the ghost. Could it feel her? Lordy, if her mother could see her now, she'd be freaking proud, which wasn't a happy thought. Gwen shook her head, which made her a little dizzy so she gripped the ladder tighter with her now sweaty left hand.

"Wait, something's…here we go."

Somehow the ghost was able to penetrate the wall enough that Gwen's hand began to move. Not fast, not firmly, but she was drawing. The ghost's possession was only a shadow of what it'd been inside the fort. Her hand stopped a few minutes later. "Done."

"Turn the page before it leaves."

Feeling too wobbly to take both hands off the ladder, Gwen managed to flip to a fresh page with just one hand and the ghost began again.

"I'm impressed," Kylie said. "This is one determined spirit."

Gwen's hold on the ladder slipped and her thighs trembled from holding herself in one place. She waited a few more minutes but nothing more happened. "Finally. We're done."

"Hand me the sketchbook. Austin, catch."

Slowly, Gwen followed Kylie down the ladder then sort of collapsed against the wall, her legs unwilling to hold her up.

Kylie dropped to the grass and stretched out her legs. "Gwen, you did great! How many people have been possessed by a ghost and made two drawings all while standing at the top of a ladder?"

Gwen let herself smile. "I'm guessing not many."

"Well, this is freaky." Austin had opened the sketchbook.

"What did I draw?"

"Here's the first one." He held the book open so they could both see.

Gwen pushed off the wall. What the hell? Two people sat against a stone wall, likely coquina, talking. One of them was a man dressed in the same baggy uniform as the guard from another drawing, but with opaque, cloudy eyes. The other person, dressed in cargo pants, a long-sleeved shirt, and Hoka sneakers, was Billie.

"Isn't that…?" Kylie looked at Gwen.

"It's Billie."

Austin turned the page. "Here's the second one…Ooh, this is not good."

They all three gasped at the image. "What the actual fuck is happening here?" Gwen glared up the fort wall and shook her fist. "What are you trying to tell me?" She rested her forehead against the rough stone and sighed. "Listen to me. Talking to a ghost, as if it could answer my questions. As if it could even hear me."

The drawing was of Gwen, collapsed on the ground, her chest and stomach stained with something dark. A pool of that same dark liquid gathered beneath her. They didn't need color to know the dark liquid was blood.

"You've been shot," Austin breathed.

The three of them stared at the drawing. "This is another warning," Kylie whispered.

Gwen forced herself to breathe in through her nose and out through her mouth, a technique Billie sometimes used to find calm. She looked at the drawing, determined not to freak out. No one knew the future, especially not the ghost of someone who'd been dead for who knew how long. This wasn't her future; this was a puzzle to solve. She flipped back a few pages to show them Billie's work. "Yesterday when I got kicked out of the fort, the ghost wasn't able to finish the last drawing. Last night Billie thought she might be able to coax out more details and ended up drawing herself."

Kylie laughed. "You're kidding me, right? There are two drawings of Billie?"

Gwen shrugged. "Can we really count the first one, since Billie drew that herself?"

It made no sense that Billie was showing up in these drawings. She began to pace. Was it because Billie was on her mind? Was Gwen somehow influencing what the ghost drew? "The ghost has obviously seen Billie because she came with me the day we all met. But then it shows me threatened by a gun, which hasn't happened, and then there's my fifty-fifth birthday party, which hasn't happened." She held up a hand to stop them both. "A time-traveling ghost is just not an option. Neither is a time-traveling *alien* ghost," she said with a smile.

Kylie helped Austin retract the ladder, all of them wincing at the loud metallic ringing. But no one came to stare down at them from the gun deck. "Gwen, paranormal activity is hard to prove, hard to study, and hard to understand. I've been doing this for twenty-five years, since I was ten, and my mom did it for forty-five years."

"Your mom?"

"She started SAPS. I literally grew up on St. Augustine ghosts. And we've never had the experience that you're having now."

"Is your mom…"

"Died two years ago. I've been trying since then to connect, but nothing." Kylie's eyes filled.

Gwen reached for anything to help but came up with little that would be of use. "I'm so sorry…but wouldn't that mean she didn't need to linger, that she was free to go…wherever?"

"Perhaps. I just wish I could talk to her one more time, or see her smile once more."

Gwen didn't believe in a literal heaven and hell, but she understood Kylie's need to imagine her mother somewhere. Gwen imagined her father reading in a library.

Gwen wanted to talk more about mothers and paranormal activity, but she was hit with such a wave of exhaustion that all she wanted to do was get back home and show Billie the new drawings. "It's just so hard to believe all this is real." She grabbed an end of the ladder and helped Austin carry it back toward the sea wall. Then Austin shouldered the entire thing and headed for a set of wooden stairs that led to a higher level of the moat. Kylie explained that Austin would hide the ladder under the stairs so they could use it again.

As they began walking toward their cars, slowly so Austin could catch up with them, Kylie stopped and rested a hand on Gwen's arm. "Remember this: the inexplicable can still be real. Things can still exist even if humans don't understand them."

After Austin rejoined them at the cars, Kylie cocked her head. "Let me try something." She opened the sketchbook. "I don't know about the drawing of your birthday, or the two with Billie, but look at these four drawings. Two men exchanging money, possibly for a 'hit'? Then this night scene, which looks like the Nights of Lights that starts in about a week. Maybe that's when the 'hit' happens? Then two men hold you at gunpoint here." She flipped to another page. "And here is the result of that 'hit.' You've been shot."

"Aunt Kylie, you're brilliant."

Gwen pursed her lips. "It makes sense when you lay it out like that. But who are the men? Why do they want to harm me?" Gwen sighed. Would she ever figure out what was going on?

❖

Gwen texted her TA, who'd finally recovered from his food poisoning, and he agreed to take her afternoon classes. Gwen then headed home, trying not to worry about the new images, but failing.

"Billie," she called as she hurried into the house, letting the screen door bang shut behind her. "I need to show you these—"

"I know what you did." The expression on Billie's face chilled Gwen to the bone. She'd never seen such a harsh, cold look in her eyes or the hard set of her mouth.

"Billie, look, you are in one of my drawings from today. You and a blind man. And Kylie thinks two men are plotting to murder me during the Nights of Lights opening."

Billie barely looked at the drawings, then slammed the sketch-book shut. "I found out from Kim this morning that you *lied* to me."

"I what?" Gwen stopped. Shit. Kim had sworn she would never tell.

"You told me that you *didn't* get an offer from the history center. You said someone else got the job."

"Well, I…" Gwen didn't know what to say. She'd kept the secret so well that she couldn't actually say the truth out loud.

"Your dream job, director of the Minnesota History Center, the job we both agreed was *made* for you. You got an offer and you turned it down without telling me." Billie's voice quavered with the same hot anger that was coming off her body in waves.

Gwen swallowed. "You needed to get out of winter. If I'd taken that job, you'd still be stuck in winter, stuck in the house, stuck in your agoraphobia." Her brain spun like a carnival wheel trying to land on the best way to explain.

"This is why you're angry with me, why you resent me."

"I'm not angry—"

"You are on edge all the time. You lash out at me nearly every day. We've fought more during the last year than we've fought in the previous twenty-four. You're punishing me for a decision that *you* made all by yourself."

"I'm not mad...I'm not punishing..." Gwen threw up her hands. "Okay, I might be a little frustrated. I hate teaching. I don't want to teach anymore."

"Then you should have taken the job you wanted. I would have figured it out."

Gwen felt the anger begin to rise through her chest. "No, you wouldn't have. You were a freaking mess. I thought you were going to harm yourself. You weren't getting enough out of therapy; you just gave up." She punched the air with her finger. "You just stopped trying. Our lives ended. We didn't see friends, didn't go anywhere. And eventually, our friends moved on. Why do you think that last year in St. Paul was so quiet? Our friends had found other people to do things with. Even the Lauras got frustrated with us." She jammed her hands in her pockets in order to stop jabbing the air. "What else was I supposed to do? Your condition made it impossible to stay."

They had each retreated to opposite sides of the kitchen, fists clenched. "I should have been part of the decision," Billie growled. "You turned down the one job you've always wanted. We left our home, our friends—"

"You needed to leave!" The kitchen suddenly felt too small to hold their fury and she imagined the roof blowing off with its force.

"We should have decided together. You lied to me like I was a child unable to understand the truth. That was a betrayal of me, of our relationship. How are we—"

Gwen's anger filled her up. Finally, the truth was out, and Billie was blaming her for everything? "You're always going on about recommitting to the relationship. Well, you want proof of commitment? I gave up the *job* for you. I gave up our *house* for you. I gave up cross-country skiing and walks in the *snow* for you. How's that for fucking recommitment?"

She'd closed the distance and could feel the urge to punch a wall surging down her arms. She was breathing so hard she almost couldn't talk.

Billie was breathing just as hard. "I am beyond furious with you. How the fuck am I ever supposed to trust you again? I'm so angry that I cannot even speak right now. I'm leaving."

Gwen's jaw dropped as Billie scooped up the car keys and stormed out of the house. Gwen ran behind her out the door and yelled, "You're going to start driving again *now*? That's the stupidest thing…"

She watched as Billie gunned the engine then backed out of the carport and onto the street. "…you've ever done."

Shaking, Gwen poured herself a glass of wine, but left the glass and took the bottle to the porch. She spread out all the drawings, moved them repeatedly into different orders, but still could not find a narrative thread, a reason for each one. She took another swig from the bottle. She was getting nowhere, but she had to distract herself from what had just happened. Billie had a point, but so did Gwen. She really had done what she'd thought was best. How could Billie blame her for that?

CHAPTER TWELVE

Billie, November 12–13

Billie was so angry that she drove all the way through downtown, across the bridge to Anastasia Island, through quiet neighborhoods to the shore, then ten miles down the coast until she stopped at a little parking lot labeled *Butler Beach*. Only when she'd angle-parked and turned off the engine did it fully hit her that she'd driven a car for the first time in two years, and that she was farther from her safe zone than she'd been since the grueling trip from Minnesota to Florida.

Panic flooded through her as she gripped the steering wheel. Eyes squeezed shut, she slowed her breathing until she calmed down. Finally, she was able to open her eyes. The small gravel parking lot had a large beach house on either side. The boardwalk probably led to the beach. What was she going to do? Could she drive herself home? Did she need to call an Uber? Chuck would understand.

No. She could hear the distant sound of waves. She was almost to the ocean.

After a few more deep breaths, she left the car and crossed the long wooden boardwalk that protected the sand dunes, which were spotted with little yellow flowers, from damage. Now the waves were louder, and she hoped the sound would drown out her anguish, her shame. She felt so much that she couldn't really identify any specific feeling. Anger. Sadness. Disappointment. Betrayal. Shame.

Confusion. She should have been happy that Gwen had made such a sacrifice for her, but instead all she felt was rage—rage at Gwen for lying, and rage at herself for being such a mess that Gwen had felt forced to lie.

After they fought, one of them usually texted the other. Both the reason for the fight and the words said tended to fade quickly as a result, but this was a biggie, not easily forgotten or forgiven. Billie checked her phone and was glad there was nothing from Gwen because she had nothing to say to her. She jammed the phone back into her pocket without sending one of her own.

Soft sand was hard walking, but soon she reached the firmer stuff, still damp from the high tide. There it was. The Atlantic Ocean. Her pulse slowed and she inhaled the smells of salt and fish and sea.

Billie walked and walked, thinking of nothing, letting the waves wash away all thought. Shore birds peeped and skittered ahead of her, and several times a long line of brown pelicans flew overhead, silent but for the sound of air rushing over their wings. After several hours, Billie's feet began to hurt so she finally turned around. Ten steps later, she stopped at something white tumbling around in the surf. She chased it back into the inches-deep water and grabbed.

A lightning whelk—a complete one. She checked inside, relieved it was uninhabited and therefore collectible. Years ago she and Gwen used to collect shells, but it was tough on the Atlantic Coast because the waves rose higher and fell harder than on the Gulf side. Most shells quickly broke under such a beating, but somehow this one had survived intact long enough for Billie to rescue it. She caressed the smooth shell then dropped it into her pocket with her river rock. Gwen loved the Fibonacci spiral at the top of lightning whelks.

As she walked, Billie marveled at what she'd done: driven in a car fifteen miles to a beach. By herself. Agoraphobia was like living in a glass cage—you could see the world going on around you but were too anxious to fully engage. Yet she drove. She was on the beach without Gwen. Maybe she was finally starting to beat Fear's butt.

She stooped to snare another shell from the foamy surf. It was a broken moon snail, a soft tannish pink. Billie's thumb fit perfectly inside the shell's gentle curve, which was a creamy white. Billie stood there rubbing the broken shell. Drawn to it, she tucked into her pocket.

Dusk had caught up with Billie, turning everything on the beach to a warm, cozy blue. She lifted her eyes from her constant search for shells to observe the beach houses, most of them mansions. The houses didn't look familiar, but then she hadn't been paying attention. And every public access boardwalk she came to, which were few and far between, looked the same. Holy crap. She was lost.

Her breath came faster as she kept walking and the setting sun haloed one massive house, turning its walls and angles and windows a shimmery gold. In just minutes the sun slipped away and the house fell into shadow.

She looked around as the familiar panic clutched at her throat and her muscles began to tense. *Calm down. Calm down.* There were a few people strolling the beach as she had done, and none of them looked anxious to be out at dusk. The air was a little cool, but if she could get out of the wind sweeping off the ocean, she'd be just fine here all night.

She laughed out loud. Was this really happening? Was she considering finding a cozy spot between dunes to hunker down for the night? Yes, she was. She could do this. Excitement pulsed through her. She was getting better.

Knowing that she could was enough. She didn't actually need to do it, so she called Walt and explained her predicament.

"Child, you got lost on the beach?"

"Yeah, yeah, I know."

"Luckily, you called the right person, 'cause I'm a beach guy. Describe the houses in front of you."

"A three-story yellow house with two massive white decks and next to it is a blue stucco house with one, two, *three* turrets."

"I've always hated that house. Good news is I know where you are. You just keep on walking with the ocean on your right—that's heading north for you city folks. In five minutes the public access boardwalk is gonna be right there."

It was dark, but the sky was still a warm blue so she could see outlines of the houses, and then of the boardwalk. She felt calm and safe, even though she was walking on the edge of an ocean in the dark. The soft waves and salty smell felt like comfort. How could she hold it against Gwen for making this possible?

Using the railing to avoid stumbling in the dark, Billie crossed the dunes on the boardwalk and easily found her car. A moment of uncertainly tightened her shoulders when she started the car, but she shook it off. She could do this.

Going slowly, stopping the instant any stoplight turned yellow, Billie heaved a huge sigh when she pulled under the carport.

Gwen met her at the back door. "Jesus, Billie. Are you okay?"

Billie handed her the keys. Then she handed her the lightning whelk.

Gwen murmured her appreciation. "A whole shell. It's beautiful." She took a deep breath. "Does this mean you've forgiven me?"

Billie paused a beat. "No." She brushed past her. "I'm sleeping on the porch."

Sleep refused to come. When she closed her eyes, she could still hear the waves, and she could almost feel them, as if her blood had synced up with the waves. The thought did occur that if Gwen had taken the history center job, this never would have happened. But that didn't mean she could forgive her.

Finally, Billie gave up on sleep. The stack of Gwen's drawings sat on the table, so she turned on one of the small lamps on the porch and spread them out. It was a still evening, so a few no-see-ums nibbled on her legs, but she rubbed on some bug balm to keep them away. Maybe they should screen in the porch...if they had a future here, together.

She stared at the drawings. She could see the order Gwen had mentioned, but how the hell did the ghost know the future? And the fact that Billie was in two that the ghost had drawn—including the one she'd tried to finish but ended up drawing herself—was so odd that she was sure the ghost was just messing with them.

❖

Determined to avoid Gwen the next morning, Billie rose early, still dressed in yesterday's cargo pants and long-sleeved shirt, and left the house on foot. No more driving for a while. She stopped at the Blue Hen, the neighborhood restaurant, and ordered a bagel breakfast to go, with eggs, bacon, and sharp cheddar cheese.

Today was a Martha day, so Billie headed straight for the fort. This time she bought a ticket and entered rather than waiting outside. She climbed the worn stone steps to the gun deck and scanned the area. From the south side of the deck, she could see the approach to the fort's entrance, and most of the grounds. This was where she would wait. When Martha arrived, Billie would dash down the stairs and be waiting in the courtyard for her.

Making sure no park rangers were watching her violate the *No Eating in the Fort* rule, she nibbled on her bagel and thought about what Gwen had done. The only job Gwen had ever wanted these last ten years was to be the director of the Minnesota History Center. No teaching, lots of public speaking, exciting projects to oversee, funding to acquire. She'd love the building since it was first built in 1992. "Someday," she'd said the first time she and Billie had stepped into its beautiful, towering glass atrium. "Someday I'm going to be in charge here. And when I am…" She'd begun listing changes and Billie could see they were all brilliant ideas.

And Gwen could have done exactly that. She could have left teaching and run the whole show for—according to Kim—a salary that was twice what she made as a professor. Billie grimaced. It wasn't the loss of salary that bothered her—it was that Gwen had believed Billie to be so damaged that the only way she'd lose her fear of getting hurt, the fear that had caused the agoraphobia, was to trade the Midwest for a home without snow and ice. She leaned her elbows along the top of the wall, grateful her long sleeves protected her from the sharp tiny shells. Maybe Gwen was right, but on the other hand, Billie was sure she could have gotten better even if they'd stayed in Minnesota. The point was that Gwen cut Billie out of the decision. She sacrificed herself for Billie's sake, but how did a person ever repay that? How did a relationship recover from one person giving up everything for the sake of the other? Gwen was right—she didn't need to prove she'd re-committed. The move was proof.

Billie, on the other hand, felt as if all she'd done the last two years was take, take, take. And there was no way she could give back enough to replace what Gwen had lost. There was no way to recover that job offer, to rewind the clock so Gwen could call up the chair of the history center's board and say, "Yes, I would be honored to accept the position of the Minnesota History Center's director."

The morning passed slowly, with Billie pacing along the south wall, occasionally along the west or east wall for different scenery, but she always returned to her post within a minute or two. More tourists chattered as they strolled along the gun deck, but Billie ignored them. At one point, to avoid a crying baby, Billie fled to the southwest bastion and sat down in one of the cannon cutouts. All she heard was the traffic and the baby, but when the baby stopped, a man's voice drifted up from below her.

"No, I told you. You don't get the whole thing now."

The second voice was too low to hear, but the first man was getting agitated enough his voice had risen. "No deal. You take care of that bitch, then you get the rest."

Alarmed, she leaned forward, but the wall was just too wide, so she pulled out her phone, positioned her finger over the camera and held it over the edge of the wall, took the shot and immediately pulled her arm back as the men kept talking. She gasped when she looked at the photo. It was of two men standing close to the base of the fort, their faces turned toward each other, one man holding out money to the other. All Billie could see was the tops of their heads. Oh, my god. This was the exact image of one of Gwen's ghost drawings.

She held her breath and tried not to move, which was hard because the rough coquina dug into her hands and elbows as she got as close to the edge as she could. She started recording with her phone.

"Yes, you can trust me. I hate her and am willing to pay you to take care of it. Fucking *Gwendolyn* from Hicksville, Minnesota, thinks she can fucking take what's mine?"

Shit! He was talking about Gwen. Billie's whole body began to ache with the effort of keeping herself still. And the voice? Was it familiar?

"We'll do it the opening night of the Nights of Lights Festival. I'll get her to the ticket booth, then you take over. You know what to do, right?" Holy shit. The ghost had drawn something that had now happened.

Just then, she realized she couldn't see the fort's entrance from here, so she reluctantly stopped recording, left her spot and dashed across the bastion just as a familiar figure strode down the sidewalk. Damn it. *Martha.* She looked back at where she'd overheard the men talking. She couldn't deal with both at once. She had a photo; she had their voices. That should be enough to help Gwen figure this out.

Billie ran for the stairs. *That voice. That voice. Whose was it?* She had to play the recording for Gwen. To fight back her rising panic, she reminded herself that the Nights of Lights opening was still five days away. She and Gwen would have plenty of time to go to the cops and stop this before it happened.

Martha was already walking across the courtyard, two plastic bags of groceries in hand and the strap of her burlap bag sliding down her shoulder, when Billie reached the bottom of the steps. She fell in line right behind her as Martha marched with singular purpose across the grass and into a room in the far corner of the courtyard lit up by the afternoon sun. Billie recognized this as the nested series of three rooms. But Martha passed through this room and into the next room, which was darker with only a single window. Billie ran to catch up, confused. Where was Martha going? They were just going deeper into a part of the fort that had no exit. Martha was heading for the little powder magazine, a dead end.

Sure enough, Martha headed straight for the four-foot by four-foot tunnel.

"Martha," Billie snapped. "Stop." Martha jumped a foot into the air and whirled. "You and I need to have a chat. You've been selling Walt stolen goods and it's going to stop."

Martha shook her head, black braid whipping back and forth. "I am not stealing. Leave me alone." Stress thickened her accent to the point Billie struggled to catch all the words.

"Your items look brand new. Walt could get in big trouble when you get caught."

"I told you, nothing is stolen. I'm just doing what I must to take care of my nephew. I'm all he's got, so stop interfering. Go away." The woman shot a quick look at the tunnel entrance, then back to Billie. "Go, please."

"I don't think so. I need to see what's in your bag." Billie knew she was crossing a line here, but between what she'd just heard, and her sleepless night on the porch swing, she'd run out of energy to do the right thing.

"No!"

Billie stepped forward and grabbed the bag. Martha pulled it against her chest, then dropped to her knees and began crawling through the tunnel. Billie grabbed for Martha's leg and yelled, hoping one of the other tourists would come running. Scrabbling across the gritty floor, Billie managed to keep hold of both Martha's foot and the burlap bag as they emerged from the tunnel into the cramped barrel room. Martha lurched to her feet, trying to kick Billie free, then they were both on their feet.

"Let go of the bag," Billie yelled. Martha's desperation had to mean the bag contained stolen goods. Martha pulled her across the narrow room to the end wall, her teeth clenched, eyes blazing and in a tangle of legs and arms they both fell toward the wall. Billie realized at the last minute that Martha was *throwing* herself at the wall and Billie was along for the ride. Just before she hit the graying, chipped coquina, Billie braced herself, but she didn't hit anything. Instead she was falling, falling, down a black pit. "What the hell?" she yelled.

"You idiot!" yelled Martha as they fell as a writhing ball of limbs.

There was no light, only a loud rushing sound, and an almost overwhelming earthy smell, then a high, piercing tone so sharp that Billie covered her ears. She rolled out of the wall and slammed onto the floor, her shins smacking against something hard. She lay on her back and stared at the ceiling. What the *fuck*? Did she just roll *out* of the wall?

Martha was struggling to her feet and gathering up fruit and other groceries that had fallen out of the now-split plastic bags. "You stupid, stupid woman," Martha hissed as she jammed everything into the burlap bag. "You are going to be so sorry you did that."

Billie struggled to sit up, shaking her head. They were in the same room, but now it was half-filled with crates marked *Powder* and reeked of wet mold infected with more wet mold. "I'm going to be sorry I did *what*? We aren't done here yet."

Martha leaned in close, and her grin made Billie uneasy. "Yes, we are. You will never see me again. I learned how to live in your world. Now you must learn to live in mine. I stole nothing. I bought things to sell in your time and I used the money to buy food for my family."

"My time?"

"Most of those damned Cubans are gone, Praise God, so only English is spoken here, but I managed to pick up a few words before we sent them all packing. Bienvenidos a mil ochocientos treinta y siete. Good luck."

Billie rubbed her aching shin, struggling to remember numbers in Spanish. What was Martha babbling on about, and what did 1,837 mean? "I don't understand—" was all Billie managed to get out before Martha's hand came out of nowhere with something hard in it and smashed against Billie's head. Pain zapped her like a taser and down she went.

❖

When Billie came to, she gingerly touched the side of her head and came away with blood, no longer the bright red of fresh blood, but darker, as if she'd been out for a while. God, what a mess. She tangled with Martha, something weird happened, then she let her guard down and got clobbered by a woman half her size. The Lauras were never going to let her hear the last of this. When the wooziness subsided, Billie got to her feet and crawled back through the tunnel. But this wasn't the same almost-empty room she'd run through minutes ago. This one held crates, barrels, tools, tents, and baskets of food. At least there wasn't any gunpowder. She crossed through to the first room, which was just as full, then stepped out into the courtyard.

This wasn't the right courtyard. Instead of neat grass and a handful of benches, this courtyard was full of ugly little pup tents, some held up with poles, others with old-fashioned rifles. The smell of men and feet and urine rose up all around her, so she backed into the room and looked around. Huh?

"Hey, soldier, out here." An angry voice yelled at someone, then that angry voice became a man standing in front of her, shaking his fist. "Why in God's Holy Balls are you out of uniform? Demerits for you, whatever your name is. But there's no time to change. You're up for guard duty. Winston's come down with the grippe, so you need to cover." The man tossed Billie a rifle which she managed to catch without dropping. "Southeast bastion. Go. We don't expect those savages to come for their buddies locked up here, but we gotta be ready just in case. Now go."

Billie opened her mouth to explain that she had no idea what he was talking about, but instead nodded and hurried for the stairs. She appeared to be the only woman among a tent forest of men, so keeping quiet seemed smart. The stone steps were gone, replaced with a steep, wooden ramp. She ran up the ramp, struggling the last five feet against gravity. What the hell was going on?

At the top she stopped. Southeast bastion. South meant the side close to the city, east meant the side close to the river. She hurried to that bastion and surveyed the horizon. Her mouth dropped open. Where were the downtown trees? It was just buildings packed together. In fact, the city seemed to have spread closer to the fort and was made up of many small, ramshackle buildings. And the bridge to Anastasia Island was gone, the beautiful Bridge of Lions. A small raft crossed the river where the bridge once stood. There was no marina filled with its forest of sailboat masts. There were no power boats on the river, only a handful of rowboats and the single raft.

Billie whirled in a circle. The butt-ugly Ripley's Believe It or Not building to the west? Gone. The long, high A1A bridge north of the city that led to Vilano Beach? Gone.

She turned again. Castillo Drive. Gone. In fact, she heard no cars. A stream of horse-drawn wagons and buggies passed by the fort. Somewhere, a horse whinnied. No ticket booth. No park rangers. She looked at the ground below between the fort and the river. The hot shot oven was there, but only half-constructed, a stack of coquina blocks resting beside it. And there was no neat concrete seawall along the river, just rocks and dirt.

Billie began to tremble and her heart raced, all signs that a panic attack was imminent. She needed to hide from whatever was happening to her.

The sun sank in the west as the noises in the fort quieted. A few torches lit up the nearest edge of St. Augustine, but otherwise the world around the fort was blacker than ink. Shaking now, she gasped at the thick blanket of stars spread out above her.

Lightheaded with fear and panic, Billie stepped inside the skinny guard tower, the penis-shaped structure Gwen said she'd been trying to draw when the ghost instead drew the "Hamlet" Coacoochee. Billie dropped the rifle against the wall and hugged herself, squeezing as hard as she could to focus on the physical rather than the panic. *Check the facts.* Martha had said a number, 1,837, which made no sense. 1,837. 1,837.

When the truth hit, Billie collapsed against the guard tower's inner wall and then sat down hard. Martha's 1,837 could just be a number, but it could also mean something else. In Spanish they didn't say the year as two numbers like they did in English: 18 and 37. Instead, in Spanish the year was said as 1,837.

Was that what Martha had meant? Had Billie somehow fallen through a portal to 1837? *No, no, no. That would be crazy.* She curled up on the gritty floor of the tower and squeezed her eyes shut. She might not be *miles* from home, but *years* from home. How was an agoraphobe to deal with *that*?

Snores and snuffles came from the courtyard below. A few men talked quietly from the next bastion. Shaking violently now, Billie curled up into a ball and burrowed down into her shirt, eyes squeezed shut yet again. She would sleep, and everything would be back to normal when she woke up.

But sleep was impossible. Billie's heart raced as Gwen's mantra filled her head. *Ghosts aren't real.* Gwen had learned this wasn't true. *Time travel isn't possible.* Billie rubbed her face and clutched at her hair, squeezing so hard it hurt. All she'd wanted to do was protect Walt and look where she was now. Was this real? Could she even get *back*?

If she did, Gwen was going to be really, *really* pissed to learn that time travel was, in fact, possible.

CHAPTER THIRTEEN

Gwen, November 13

The fact that Billie had already left the house by the time Gwen woke up meant she was *really* angry. Lately, Gwen had been the one quick to anger, but now it was Billie's turn. As Gwen got dressed, she fought with herself. Was Billie right? Should she have involved Billie in the decision? Should she have taken the history center job? Confusion roiled her gut. Had she really screwed up?

No. She'd had no other choice. She had done the only thing she could to help Billie. She was there for Billie's dislocated elbow, the first painful experience. She was there when Billie fell on the ice and broke both wrists. Then Billie was rear-ended by another car, giving her neck and back pain that lasted for months. Then she blew out her knee and needed knee replacement surgery. The recovery and physical therapy had been incredibly painful. Gwen had been there when the algophobia had quickly morphed into agoraphobia and Billie had stood by the front door shaking, tears streaming down her face, unable to step outside. Gwen had driven her to doctors' appointments, physical therapy appointments, to psychotherapy appointments, all within a few miles of the house.

And when the pandemic had hit, Gwen had been happy to stay home with her, but she almost turned into an agoraphobic herself. She'd struggled to leave the house once most people had been vaccinated, but she did leave, slowly starting to see friends again while Billie stayed at home, trapped by her fears. That's when they'd begun to have trouble—when Gwen was tired of staying home, tired of Billie being afraid to leave the house. As the worst of the pandemic faded, and Billie still refused to leave, their friends, much as they loved them, moved on. Soon, Gwen felt as stuck as Billie.

Taking the Flagler College job was the only way she could see to help Billie recover. What had been her dad's self-help quote about relationships? *Love is a willingness to sacrifice*. Well, that's what she did. Frustrated, she slammed the back door even though Billie wasn't home to hear it. Damn it. She'd done the right thing, hadn't she?

By the time she reached the fort, Kylie was already waiting for her. "I set the ladder up earlier this morning so we're good to go."

Gwen felt a little more comfortable and was able to ignore all the city noises as she climbed the ladder, so the experience was easier than the first one. The ghost drew quickly as Gwen relaxed, watching her hand move across the page without hesitation.

After they'd returned the ladder to its hiding place under the wooden stairs north of the fort, they found a shady spot on the grass and examined the two new drawings. Gwen made a face. "Christ, it's Billie again."

"What's she doing?" Kylie leaned closer. "Looks like maybe she and another woman are fighting over a bag or something. And it's in a really small room. Look how low that concave ceiling is."

The woman looked familiar, so Gwen grabbed her phone and scrolled to the photo of Martha that Billie had sent her. "She's fighting with Martha, a woman she believes is selling her boss stolen goods. Maybe that's what's in the bag."

Gwen turned the page. The second drawing was of Coacoochee, dressed in the same drab prison garb as in the earlier drawing, but instead of being behind bars, the man was in the courtyard, bending over to pick up what appeared to be a sword. "What's he doing?"

"He's arming himself. Is he escaping?"

"Walt said he and the others escaped through a small window high up on their cell wall. Besides, who'd leave a sword around for a prisoner to pick up?" With a groan, Gwen checked the time. "I have to get to work."

On the long walk back to the parking lot, Gwen finally took the plunge. "You said that your mom started SAPS, and that you grew up with all this paranormal stuff."

Kylie nodded. "My mom and I were two peas in a pod. Both loved it."

"But you were a child. Didn't all the ghost stuff frighten you? Didn't you have nightmares about aliens abducting you?"

Kylie was the sort of person who thought for a minute before answering, so Gwen was learning to relax into the silence. "I wasn't afraid. I guess because Mom made it seem so normal, and she always explained what she was doing, and why."

"I wonder what was different about our childhoods that you weren't afraid, and I was." She explained her mom's fascination with all things paranormal, but instead of being interested in it, Gwen had just been terrified. "I didn't have a good night's sleep from about age six until I went away to college."

Kylie shook her head. "I don't know. Maybe it's an ability to accept the unknown, to be okay with ambiguity?"

Gwen snorted. "I am sort of a black-and-white person. It's either one thing or another—can't quite get comfortable with something in the middle."

"You want some advice?"

"Sure."

Kylie pulled out her keychain. Dangling on the end was a small black ball. Gwen laughed. "Seriously? A Magic 8 Ball?"

"Just ask a question."

"The Magic 8 Ball is worse than a Ouija board or tarot cards." She rolled her eyes but shook the ball. "Okay, was my mom right about everything?" She turned it upside down. "It says, *Without a doubt*."

Gwen found herself laughing along with Kylie. "The important thing isn't the answer you're given," Kylie said, "but what you do with it."

They reached the lot and Kylie leaned against her car. "I'm hoping your experience with your ghost is helping shift your perspective, to see that the 8 ball and Ouija and tarot and astrology and everything else are just tools we humans can use to thrive during our time on this earth."

Gwen smiled as she handed back the keychain. "I'm working on it. But it's hard to forgive my mom for not paying attention when I told her I was scared, for not finding a way to make me feel safe in the middle of all her paranormal obsessions."

Kylie gave her a wave before climbing into her car. "No one escapes childhood unscathed."

Except for her colleague Jeremy crowing about how many drawings he'd done every time he passed her open office door, work went well. She had lunch with Amy from the art department, the one who'd cooked up the competition. Gwen was pleased to hear that the art professors were struggling with their personal essays. When Amy asked how the drawing was going, Gwen laughed and realized that she'd almost burst out with the truth, that a ghost was doing most of her drawing. "Let's just say I'm not going to win any awards, but I am improving."

Back in her office, Gwen checked her phone. Billie must be terribly angry because usually, by now, they would have connected and apologized. Gwen went cold with the sudden thought that something bad had happened. She made herself some Market Spice tea, calming herself with the familiar deep citrus scent. There was no reason to start catastrophizing here. That was Billie's thing.

But when there still was no text from Billie by midafternoon, Gwen finally broke down. *Where r u? Ok?*

By the end of the afternoon, Billie still had not responded, so Gwen hit *Find My* to see where Billie and her phone were. *No data available* appeared instead of the map with the friendly red dot. She tried again. *No data available*. Well, that was just weird.

She called the antique store and asked Walt if he'd seen Billie. "No, I haven't. She was on the schedule for this afternoon but didn't show up. I've been worrying a bit since she never cancels, never seems to get sick. I mean, other than her, well, you know, her *problem*."

The old guy clearly didn't want to say *emotional breakdown due to algophobia and agoraphobia*. "Thanks, Walt. I'm sure she's fine. Probably her phone went dead, or she lost it somewhere."

Gwen stood in her open office window watching students head home for the day, laughing and teasing each other. It would have been fun to attend college here, with the great weather, the exotic buildings, the ocean fifteen minutes away. She knew she couldn't turn back the clock, but if she could, she'd go here. If time travel were possible, she might return to her eighteen-year-old self and whisper "Flagler College, St. Augustine" into her ear.

Where the hell was Billie? Why couldn't the phone app track her? Then a horrible thought occurred to her. What if the ghost wasn't trying to warn Gwen about something bad that was going to happen to Gwen? What if it instead was trying to warn her that something bad might happen to *Billie*? What if it already had, and Gwen had missed it?

Unable to focus on the papers she was supposed to be grading, Gwen sat down and made a list of the eleven drawings she'd done so far: Coacoochee in velvet, her fifty-fifth birthday, two Native men in a fort cell, two men pointing guns at Gwen, Nights of Lights, two men exchanging money, Billie in a swordfight with a black-haired woman, Gwen bleeding on the ground, Billie sitting next to a blind man, Billie fighting over a bag with Martha, and Coacoochee picking up a sword.

Gobbledygook. The only threads were Coacoochee, Gwen, and Billie.

As she pulled into their driveway, she could see a figure reclining on the porch swing. Oh, thank God. She parked, then dashed around to the front of the house, ready to be angry at Billie for disappearing, but staggered to a halt when she reached the porch. "Oh!"

Mason stood up, grinning, and threw his arms wide open. "Surprise!" Her stepbrother's heavy eyebrows danced above dark brown eyes, and his crew cut was now blond instead of brown.

"Mason! What are you doing here?" She was oddly pleased he'd arrived early since she was feeling a little unsure of what to do about Billie.

He gave her a long hug that made her almost think he missed her. "I decided to come a few days early. Took an Uber for the first time. The guy drove me all the way down here! Couldn't believe it. I've been here for a few hours. Luckily, your porch doesn't have a door."

Gwen extracted herself from his arms. "I thought you were going to stay in a hotel."

Mason dropped back onto the swing, arms stretched out along the back. "Decided to save Mom some money. Hope it's okay." For a second, she could see in him the uncertain fifteen-year-old Mason the first day they'd met.

She forced a smile. "It's fine, but I need to be honest with you. Billie and I had a huge fight last night and she hasn't come home yet."

Mason straightened. "Do we need to call the cops?"

"They won't do anything until the person's been missing for twenty-four hours, and I know she was here this morning because I heard her moving around in the kitchen."

"What do we do?"

Gwen joined him on the swing. "I don't know."

He pulled out his phone. "I suggest pizza delivery. It's on me… Or rather, it's on Mom."

Gwen was too worried about Billie to confront Mason with his lie about Faye's will, so she tuned him out as he began telling her about his latest financial venture. Where was Billie? Had she left town? Neither of them had *ever* been angry enough to actually leave. They'd always stayed to face each other.

This time something was different. Something was wrong.

CHAPTER FOURTEEN
Billie, November 14

illie woke with a start. She'd shifted in her sleep and was now sprawled across the floor, still in the guard tower. She rolled onto her back and stared out the tower entrance, where the sky was tinged with pink. Dawn.

She stepped out of the penis-shaped tower and scanned. She was still here. It wasn't a dream. She closed her eyes. *Check the facts*. She was still in St. Augustine. She was only a few miles from where home would be…in about…she did the math…in about 187 years. She had to find the portal back. She had to warn Gwen. She had to keep the panic at bay.

Billie stepped up to the shallow wall and looked down into the courtyard. The men had begun to stir, coughing, clearing their throats, someone cursing over a lost sock. Shit, would she be safe once they realized she was a woman? She hunched a bit, which helped hide her breasts. Thank God she didn't have Gwen's chest.

Billie's head hurt. What was she supposed to do? Stay here and find another spot in the wall that would send her back to the present? Leave and look for Martha in the city? She realized she had to do both but decided to start with Martha. Moving as quietly as possible, she crept down the ramp, scooted around the edge of the courtyard, and slipped out the main entrance.

But then she froze. This new world, if it truly was 1837, seemed too large, too full of new dangers, too full of new sources of pain.

Trembling, she slipped her hand into her pocket, found the piece of moon snail and slid her thumb against the smooth inner chamber. The shell might be broken, but it still could play a role in her life. She felt a little broken some days, but she could still be useful. Inhaling deeply, she resolved to do what was necessary.

Heart pounding, Billie walked toward the city hoping she at least sort of blended in wearing pants and a shirt. She passed a man yelling at a horse that was apparently refusing to move, and two men arguing bitterly over a wagon of hay. She avoided making eye contact with anyone, terrified. It was not exciting to be back in the past at all. It was jarring, confusing, and everything smelled wrong. Was it less pollution? Things did smell fresher, at least until she passed a well-used outhouse and changed her mind. The buildings, the streets, the signs, everything *felt* wrong. Only when she reached Constitution Plaza, the oldest park still existing in the present, did she have any sense she was still in St. Augustine. In the park she was surprised to find a dramatic sculpture of a horse made entirely of old horseshoes, which lifted her spirits. At least art was valued in this time and place.

When she passed a group of women standing around a food stall laughing, Billie forced herself to stop. She needed to talk to them. Reluctantly, she approached, hunching over a bit. She cleared her throat, aiming for a lower voice. "Pardon me, ladies." They turned, scowling at the interruption. "I am…I am seeking a woman named Martha. About this tall, with long black braids."

The women looked at each other. "What do you want her for?" one asked.

"Ahh, because I owe her money and need to pay her."

A full-sized woman held out her hand. "Give it to me, hon, and I'll make sure she gets it." She waggled her eyebrows and the others burst into laughter.

Billie frowned to play the part of a severe man. "Where would I find her?"

They all shrugged. "We don't know any Martha. But lots of new people have moved in since the Spanish gave up the fort."

Sweating profusely, with tremors shuddering through her muscles, Billie kept moving. She walked up and down the streets, getting lost because nothing looked the same, none of the streets were labeled, and there were no traffic sounds to orient her, no boat engines to help her identify east. For hours, she walked, up and down the blocks, stopping to talk to anyone she saw. A few knew Martha but couldn't remember where she lived.

Billie kept her eyes on the ground to ensure she knew exactly where she was stepping. If she fell and broke something, there would be nothing in this world for pain relief, nothing to reduce inflammation. She could die of an infection without ever finding her way home.

In the afternoon, Billie returned to the fort, relieved the horrible symptoms of agoraphobia hadn't kicked in, but she was now unsure how to proceed. Did she sneak in and steal a uniform so she'd blend in more? Did she pretend she was a merchant or something? Inhaling deeply for courage, she entered the fort. Just inside, a broom and a mop leaned against the wall, a bucket nearby. Billie scooped up the mop and bucket. Perfect. She began in the first room she passed, pretending to mop but really pushing the mop against the wall, first at the base then again higher up. She figured if the mop disappeared, she'd found the return portal.

Miraculously, the men in the fort, both those clearly in charge and the minions in the baggy pants and tunic uniforms, left her alone. She was just the "guy who cleaned," someone too lowly to acknowledge. She worked her way through the rooms, skipping the cells. She couldn't get in those, but then neither could Martha. As she passed, she noticed the small, barred window high in the wall of the first cell. No wonder Walt had doubted Coacoochee had escaped that way. It looked like a ridiculously tight squeeze. The natives in the dank cell were scattered across the floor, sleeping only on blankets.

At one point the fort emptied out and judging from the comments made by the passing men, they were headed to eat somewhere. Dinner time. Billie's stomach rumbled, and she realized she was probably dehydrated, but she didn't dare stop until she found the portal. The empty courtyard meant she could move more freely, tapping the walls with the end of the mop. She did stop at a small table with an empty plate and a mug of water, but before she swallowed the liquid she spit it out. It wasn't water. Ale? She took another drink, this time swallowing it anyway for the liquid. At least it was wet.

The sun had passed well overhead and was starting to sink down where the Ripley's Believe It or Not building would someday appear. Billie stood shivering in the shade at the edge of the courtyard. She'd tried every wall, but she hadn't found it, not even in the powder magazine. The wall she and Martha had come through was solid as rock, every inch of it.

She started again, ignoring the men as they returned and gathered in small groups on the gun deck laughing and singing. Each time she passed the crowded cells, the men inside each totally ignored her, speaking quietly in their native tongue. The smell of that many men imprisoned with nothing but buckets for toilets was eye-watering.

As she worked, she thought about Martha. The woman hadn't been stealing items from museums. She'd been bringing them from the past.

Billie realized how brave Martha had been to have one foot in the nineteenth century and one in the twenty-first. She probably traveled back and forth three or four times a week, likely a jarring experience, but it showed her devotion to her nephew.

Would Martha have told her the truth if Billie hadn't grabbed her bag? Probably not. Who would believe a fantastical story like that?

It was dark by the time she made it through the first floor of the fort again. Someone had lit torches around the courtyard, and in a few of the rooms. Otherwise, the place was dark.

While some of the fort's rooms held wooden beds so not all the men had to sleep in tents, most rooms were filled with barrels and wooden crates. Like a salmon swimming upstream to where life had started, Billie returned to the series of rooms that led to the powder magazine and in the second, more secluded room, she felt her way behind a massive stack of crates until she was well-hidden against one wall. The day's weirdness caught up with her and she was so exhausted from fighting off panic attacks she could barely keep her eyes open. She lowered herself to the floor, hoping she wasn't sharing the room with rats or mice. She had stolen two blankets from one of the tents, so she rolled up one for a pillow and spread the other one over her legs. God, it was dark in here, the sole window too dirty to let in any light. Only a faint outline of the open door broke the black.

She put her head down and allowed herself to close her eyes. She'd never in her life felt so alone. She did not belong here, in this place, in this time. *Gwen, I'm sorry. You have no idea where I am. You've got to be worried by now.* Billie was worried as well. If she couldn't find her way back, she was screwed. This was a hell of a way to test out the "Movie Theater Theory of Time Travel."

She pulled out her phone and scrolled through her photos. She and Gwen on a North Carolina beach ten years ago. Gwen at the house in St. Paul. The two of them on their bikes, pre-agoraphobia. She squeezed her eyes shut as hot tears threatened, but she refused to cry. She couldn't afford to be distracted. She played a few videos of Gwen at the beach, the light from the phone warming her hiding place, the sound of Gwen's laughter closing her throat. She wanted to watch them over and over again but shut off the phone to save the battery so she'd have the flashlight if needed.

"You are not from around here."

Billie shot up, clutching the scratchy blanket. The voice had come from the nearest corner of the room. Her heart raced so fast she felt dizzy.

"I can tell because you smell different. You are a stranger from a strange, faraway place."

Hand to chest, she forced herself to calm down. The man sounded kind, not threatening. She strained to see who was speaking. "Who are you?"

"Name's Brush, Nathaniel Brush. And you?"

"Billie. My name's Billie."

"Well, Billie, welcome to my corner of Fort Marion. I'm happy to have the company."

Fort Marion? Oh yeah, that was what the Americans renamed the Castillo when they took possession. Determined to be brave, Billie got to her knees and crawled forward until she bumped into someone's arm. "Shit. Sorry." She settled back against the wall, weirdly happy to have company. "You sleep here?"

"Yes, I do. But the officers aren't to know, so I would appreciate you keeping my secret."

"Of course, but why not sleep in the barracks with the others?"

Nathaniel sighed. "I am no longer in the Army. Two months ago, when I lost enough sight that I could no longer fire a weapon or shoe a horse, I was released."

"That's cruel."

"That's life. My friends hide me in here at night and share their food with me. Without them I would be dead." There was a little rustling, and she felt his arm come closer. "I have some bread left. Would you like some?"

Billie's mouth watered. "I have not eaten all day."

"Please, eat."

Billie bit off a hunk and mumbled her thanks through the large mouthful. The bread had little taste, but it was food.

They sat in silence as Billie ate, finally swallowing the last of the bread. "Nathaniel, thank you so much. I never realized how much I take food for granted."

"I was serious when I said you smell different. Everything about you is unfamiliar to me."

"I am…I am from very far away, that is true."

"And you are a woman."

Shit. *Shit.*

"My sense of smell became very strong as my vision dimmed. Also, I can still see well enough to know that a few moments ago you just held a unique item in your hands. It made sounds like a person laughing, and I could see there were images, moving images."

Billie dropped her head into her hands. Christ. What the hell was she supposed to say now? Cameras—still or video---wouldn't be invented for decades. "You saw that."

"Enough of it to suspect that few in this world have seen such a thing before." He shifted against the wall. "Are you from the moon, or one of the other celestial bodies in the night sky?" She detected no laughter or any sign that he was joking.

She chuckled anyway. "You're asking if I'm an alien."

"Alien? Is that what you are called? Are you a visitor from the sky?"

"No, I'm not an alien. I am from the United States of America, just as you are."

He shifted against the wall, and she could feel his gaze, not threatening, but deeply curious. "No, you are too different, and that object with the moving images is not from this world."

Billie considered her options. Should she tell him the truth? She'd either gain a friend who'd be totally in awe of her very existence, or she'd be reported as a danger to the world and put in front of a firing squad. She'd come out as a lesbian hundreds of times.

But as a time traveler? Not once.

Chapter Fifteen

Gwen, November 15

Gwen woke up early and reached for the other side of the bed, hoping against hope that Billie had snuck in during the night without waking her. She touched nothing but a smooth, cold sheet.

She went through the motions of getting dressed, but everything felt wrong, as if she'd been transported to a wrong place, a wrong time. That Billie wasn't here just didn't make sense. And she knew she was overreacting—Billie had only been gone twenty-four hours without communicating, but that was long enough to tilt Gwen's world. She still didn't know whether to be angry or frightened, but when Billie finally showed up, she'd better be ready for some fury.

"No word?" Mason called from the living room.

Gwen stood there, unsure of herself. "No. I don't know what to do."

"First thing is we go to the police." He found the St. Augustine Police Station on his phone. "C'mon, I'll drive. You look like a walking coma."

Gwen called in sick while he drove, then stared at every person they passed walking the sidewalk or even biking. Billie used to love to bike; maybe she'd gotten back on that "horse."

The police station smelled like old coffee, which turned her stomach a little, but she didn't care. Billie was missing.

The policewoman was very attentive and polite, not blinking an eye when Gwen said her *wife* had gone missing. Maybe it wasn't Floridians who hated gays, but just their elected representatives. She watched the woman's competent fingers fly over the keyboard as she interviewed Gwen.

"Do you have a photo?"

Gwen showed her one on her phone, and the officer took a photo of it.

"Okay, has your wife been the subject of threats or acts of violence?"

"No."

"Any pattern of disappearing?"

"No."

"Mentally impaired?"

"No, but she has intermittent agoraphobia."

The policewoman looked up. "She doesn't leave the house?"

"Her safe zone is about two miles. She rarely voluntarily goes beyond that."

The policewoman typed for a long time, then retrieved sheets from the printer. She handed Gwen the printout. "This is what I've entered into the system, and what will go out to the squad cars. Should anything on this sheet change, call me at this number."

"So that's it?" Mason said. "No one's going to start looking for her?"

The policewoman scowled. "We take disappearances seriously, but it will take us awhile to get the information out to everyone. Officers will be assigned immediately to canvass the neighborhood. We'll relay the known details to all on-duty personnel as well as county and state law enforcement agencies. I know it's hard, but you need to be patient."

Mason grumbled as he drove them back to the house. "Be patient? Hasn't she ever been concerned about someone she loves? And what does this mean for our plans to attend the opening night of Nights of Lights? That's only a handful of days away. Can we still go if Billie hasn't come home yet?"

Gwen glared at him. "Seriously? My wife is missing, and you still want to play tourist? Why are you so hot to trot for the opening night?"

Mason shrugged. "I just thought it sounded like a cool moment when someone flips a switch and the whole city lights up like a Christmas tree."

"Mason, what the hell is going on with you? Why are you even here?"

"I told you why. And I needed a vacation, okay? I've had some investments go sour so I just need to forget for a while." He hunched over the wheel, defensive.

"Mase, I'm glad you're here, but Faye said—" Her phone rang; it was Jeremy. Damn it. If she didn't answer he'd just keep calling. The man had never heard of a text. "Hey, Jeremy."

"Sorry you're sick, boss, but I hope you'll be able to keep drawing. We are getting close, and actually have a shot at this. Turns out artists aren't very good at writing personal essays." He chuckled. "If you're feeling okay, how about we try some night drawing? The opening night of Nights of Lights is fun…lots of people to draw."

"You know I can't draw faces."

"We'll just draw their backs, so no faces required. How about if I meet you there, say six thirty p.m.?"

Gwen pursed her lips. How much should she tell him? "Jer, I have some things going on. My brother Mason is here visiting, for one, and he wants to attend opening night as well. But more importantly, Billie has gone missing."

"*What?*"

Gwen explained in as few words as possible, knowing that Jeremy would spread the word across the entire campus. While she was embarrassed to admit they'd had such a huge fight, the more people who knew to look for Billie, the better.

"God, Gwen, I'm really sorry. Is there anything I can do?"

"Not now, but thanks."

"Well, let's see how you feel in a few days. It might be good for you to get out and be with people at the event. I'll be in touch."

Gwen shut off her phone. What was it with the men in her life and their obsession with the Nights of Lights opening ceremony?

Mason parked in the driveway. "Okay, maybe we should make a list of the places Billie liked to go or hang out. We could check those places."

"Because of her…condition, she didn't drive, didn't bike, and was just very cautious about going anywhere she'd never been before. Walt told me that the other night, after our fight, she fled to the beach, but got lost and couldn't find her car. He had to help her figure out where she was."

Mason stopped. "What if she got lost on the beach again and her phone's dead?"

"The beach isn't isolated. People live there, so she'd either stop someone and ask to use their phone or knock on someone's door and ask for help." She sighed. "But what if she's hurt and out of sight?"

"How much beach is there?"

"Fifteen miles."

"Yikes. Can people drive on the beach?"

"Yeah, but not in this car. We'd need something with better traction."

"We need a four-wheeler or something. Hey, I noticed your neighbor across the street has one under a tarp. I'll go ask him."

"No, that's not a good idea." Gwen started to explain about Clayton, but Mason being Mason, shot out of the car without listening and was halfway across the street.

"Hey, bro!" he called. "Got a minute to help out a neighbor?" While the two of them talked, Gwen worried that Clayton would punch Mason or flip him off. The man just had that "back off" vibe. But instead, Clayton nodded, then headed for the four-wheeler.

Mason returned, triumphant. "Nice guy. Gonna help us. He'll load the four-wheeler into his truck, then you two will travel the beach, and I'll drive his pickup to the south end and pick you up. Hope there's a bar nearby."

Gwen couldn't believe it when, a few minutes later, she was standing next to Clayton, the freaky, staring guy with the tattooed neck. "Ah, hi. I'm Gwen." The guy was even scarier up close because his eyes landed everywhere but on her.

"Clayton." He looked at the ground and shuffled his feet.

"I really appreciate your helping us." The neck tattoos were snakes and roses of all things. Maybe this guy wasn't as tough as he'd seemed.

"It's nothing. Ready to go if you are."

She sat between Clayton and Mason as they drove to St. Augustine Beach, the northernmost beach in a string of beaches. Not surprisingly, country western music blared out of the left speaker; nothing came out of the right. Every time she tried to start a conversation with Clayton, she got a grunt or a nod or a "Yup." He smelled of peppermint, not of cigarette smoke as she'd expected.

She gave up and turned to Mason. "I talked to Faye the other day."

"Did you?"

"Mase, why are you here? Faye didn't send you to talk about the will. That was a total bullshit story."

He looked at his hands. "Memory issues. She's starting to forget. Really sad."

Gwen snorted. "She's fine and you know it. Your mother is as sharp as ever."

When Mason folded his arms and stared out the side window, she stopped pushing. He'd been a touchy kid, and had turned into a touchy adult.

The breeze coming off the Atlantic Ocean at St. Augustine Beach was brisk, but the sun heated up both the sand and Gwen. They parked and unloaded the ATV, using the sandy public access to reach the beach. Once they started south, most of remaining beach accesses would be private—pedestrian boardwalks that stretched from each house across the delicate sand dunes to the beach.

Not really wanting to but seeing no other choice, she climbed onto the back of the four-wheeler behind Clayton and off they went, leaving Mason with the truck. She gripped the edge of the seat for balance. The beach was busy, so she felt safer than if she and Clayton had been alone.

"I'm gonna keep us next to the dunes," Clayton shouted over his shoulder to be heard above the waves, the wind, and the engine. "If something happened to her there, it may take a while for someone to see her."

The next three hours yielded Gwen nothing but an aching neck and eyes that burned from the salt spray. But as they stopped a few times to stretch their legs, Gwen was able to get Clayton talking about his job as a carpenter for a local contractor. He even smiled once. By the time they reached the southern end of the beaches and could go no farther, he was clearly more comfortable with her. Gwen texted Mason, then squinting against the brilliant sun sparkles shooting off the ocean, finally found the courage to ask the question. "Clayton, why is this the first time you've talked to me? You just stare at us but never smile or wave or anything."

He jammed his fists into his pockets and flushed red. "Couldn't get up the nerve."

Gwen waited, wanting more.

"When I found out you were from Minnesota I wanted to talk to you so bad, but I couldn't. Just couldn't. I wanted to ask if you've ever been to the Lost Forty."

"Yes, it's amazing." Gwen stooped to pick up a shell, disappointed it was only the top of a lightning whelk.

"My family vacationed in Minnesota once, and when I heard the story about a logging surveyor mistakenly marking that area as a lake, I just thought it was so cool, you know? We're told that mistakes are bad, but because of that guy's mistake those forty acres were never logged so the trees are huge."

Gwen nodded. It was a special place, a giant, never-logged forest in the middle of a normal, Minnesota-sized forest that had been logged down to stubs one hundred years ago.

"Me and my brother and my parents tried to hold hands around one tree. Couldn't do it. Can you *imagine?*"

Gwen smiled, seeing Clayton as a child discovering the Lost Forty. "Thank you, Clayton, for helping me this afternoon. Do you mind if I ask you something else?"

Clayton draped one knee across the four-wheeler's seat. "Ask away."

"Sassy told us that you grew up in the house that Billie and I bought. Because you are constantly staring at the house, we wondered if you resent us for buying it."

Clayton rubbed his head. "No, not at all. I have so many good memories of that house, living there with my parents and little brother. After they were killed in a car accident when I was ten, I was put in foster home after foster home. I hated it." He sighed, his chest heaving. "I was going to buy the house until one day I realized how happy it made me to *look* at it, almost like a photo from the past. I guess that's what I'm doing when you see me staring...I'm just lost in a happy past." He swallowed a few times. "Life's been shitty ever since they died, so I need a few 'happys' every now and then."

Blinking hard, Gwen gave him a quick hug that turned him red again. "I'm so sorry you had such a difficult childhood. You can gaze at the house all you want, and we'll understand."

Gwen stopped. *We.* She was not a *we* without Billie. "Clayton, thank you again. We didn't find anything, but I really appreciate you taking the time to help people you don't know."

He ducked his head then looked her in the eye. "I'm sorry Billie has gone missing, but I really had fun."

"And the fun can continue!" shouted Mason from the boardwalk. "Let's go."

After loading up the four-wheeler, Clayton mentioned there was a hole-in-the wall restaurant just up the A1A a few miles. Hungry herself, Gwen offered to pay, so they soon were sitting on a rustic outdoor patio with a view of the ocean, the fresh breeze rippling their tablecloth, menus in their hands and drinks on the way. As she watched Mason and Clayton bond over some sports story that was in the current news but that she'd ignored, she realized she was glad Mason was here, and she was glad she'd finally met Clayton. Both seemed to be supportive and trustworthy, so she decided it was time to totally come clean.

After they'd placed their orders and the beers had arrived, Gwen cleared her throat, feeling like she had when she'd come out to her parents forty years ago. "There's another wrinkle to the story of me and Billie. It has to do with…with a ghost."

Mason threw back his head and laughed. "Yeah, right. You don't believe in ghosts."

"I do now." She proceeded to explain everything, including showing them photos of some of the drawings.

"I am freaking jealous," Clayton said. "I've lived here my entire life and have never had a ghost experience but look at you. An actual possession."

Mason kept flicking back and forth through the photos. "So is the ghost trying to warn you of something that might happen to you, or something that might happen to Billie?" She could almost see the gears turning in that head. Billie used to call Mason a visual savant. Maybe he could find some sort of pattern.

"I don't know," she replied. "Maybe both. But I've been banned from the fort for causing a disturbance and upsetting people." She grinned. "When I close my eyes as the ghost draws, it freaks people out. But if I leave them open, then people can see my entire eyeballs have gone black."

"Awesome," Clayton breathed.

"Look at this one of Billie," Gwen said. "She finished the drawing herself, but it looks like she's in a swordfight with what looks like, at least from the back, a black-haired woman. And here she is struggling with Martha, and there she's talking with a blind man."

Mason flipped back and forth between the pages. "Are they supposed to be connected?"

"No idea, but we are assuming so. Do you see any sort of link? Any pattern?"

As Mason studied them again, Clayton gave a nervous laugh. "What are you, some sort of detective?"

"No, I just love patterns," Mason said. "Our brains hate randomness so we're constantly struggling to impose order by connecting unrelated facts or ideas. My brain's just a little more obsessed than most. Drives me crazy." He looked at Gwen. "Apparently, I'm pretty good at it, and my aunts wanted me to head in that direction."

"Why didn't you?" Clayton sifted through the drawings as well. Gwen waited, very interested in the answer.

Mason smiled sadly. "Because I lacked the balls to do something that scared me."

Gwen wanted to tell him it was okay, but the opportunity passed when Mason sat back in his chair and folded his arms. "I'm sorry, G, but these just look random and unrelated."

Gwen's heart sank a bit that Mason had no answers.

"But who's this dude in this one, picking up a sword?" Clayton asked.

"That's Coacoochee." She shared what she knew of the Seminole's story.

"Is the ghost done drawing?" Clayton asked. "Maybe you could get more clues if you keep drawing."

Mason snorted. "She got kicked out of the fort so she can't draw anymore."

Gwen drained her beer. "Yes, but my friends Kylie and Austin figured out the ghost could maybe reach me through the wall, so they brought a ladder that got me most of the way up the wall, but it's freaking scary to be that high. The ghost can sort of get through, but I can feel it's struggling to reach me."

Clayton checked the time. "The fort's closed now. We should go see if the ghost will draw more."

"Yes!" Mason slapped the table. "Let's do it." Both Mason and Clayton looked far too excited about the idea.

"I don't know. I'm really worried about Billie."

Mason leaned across the table. "But what if the ghost has more clues for you, more drawings with Billie in them?"

When she hesitated, Clayton snapped his fingers. "I have a long construction ladder. We'll get you all the way to the top so the ghost can more easily reach you."

Despite Gwen's protests about not wanting to climb so high, they were soon back at Clayton's carport adding the ladder to the pickup while she'd retrieved her sketchbook.

Even though it was now dark, downtown was hopping, as usual, with lots of traffic and a constant stream of headlights, but the fort itself was quiet, lit only by the floodlights. Clayton unloaded the four-wheeler and strapped the ladder across the front basket. "Kind of tippy, but I'll go slow."

When Clayton and Mason put the ladder against the fort wall and began extending it, the ladder went up and up and up until it almost reached the top of the wall. Thirty-three feet, higher than Kylie's ladder. Gwen felt a little queasy. "Ah, guys, I don't think so."

Mason was already stuffing the sketchbook into the back of his pants. "I'll be up there right behind you."

Clayton held the ladder and nodded for her to start. "And I'll come up half way so my weight will stabilize the ladder."

Gwen stared up into the dark. Stars were visible beyond the tip of the ladder. "I—"

"Gwen, what did your dad always say when you were afraid of something?"

"Okay, okay." And she was climbing, Mason right behind her.

"Don't look down," he said. "Just look up. And remember this is to help Billie."

Breathing heavily now, Gwen reached the top of the ladder. "Shit," she muttered. "Too high. I can see right into the gun deck." It was so eerie, nothing there but a few benches, the cannons, shifting shadows, and silence. If she'd had the flexibility and strength she used to, she would have just climbed across the wall and dropped down onto the deck. "Okay, sketchbook."

She could feel Mason move up higher and settle right behind her, his arms around her, his head near her shoulder. She opened the book, rested it on top of the wall, and almost before she had a good grip on the pencil, the drawing began.

"You doing that?" Mason whispered.

"No."

"Holy shit." He called down to Clayton. "It's working."

At one point, Mason shone his phone's light onto the paper, but she didn't need the light. He just wanted to watch. "Damn, this is crazy. So fast. So accurate. Like the ghost knows exactly what to do."

"It's had a few years to think about this, I'm guessing."

"Ghosts think?"

After she'd finished the second drawing, she was about to close the book when her hand turned the page and began again. "More! It's drawing more."

By the time the ghost left, Gwen had made four drawings. Once again, her legs shook with the effort and she wondered if she could climb down safely, but both Mason and Clayton kept encouraging her until she touched the ground with a relieved groan. God, she just wanted to fall into bed. Where the hell was Billie and why was Gwen having to go through all of this without her?

Not until both four-wheeler and ladder were loaded up and they were back in the pickup cab did she open the book. Clayton turned on the overhead light. The first drawing was of Billie standing next to an open coffin that contained a woman. Gwen shuddered when she realized the dead woman was Martha. At least Billie wasn't in the coffin. The second drawing was of Billie bent next to an iron gate, trying to insert a key.

"What does this even mean?" Clayton muttered. "This ghost is totally obsessed with Billie."

"Let's look at the third one." She turned the page and snorted at the image of herself sitting on a fort bench drawing, with Kylie at her feet, and Billie and Austin off to the side. "This is obviously me, mid-possession."

"You look almost happy," Clayton said.

"Not to be inappropriate," Mason said, "but you look like you're *really* enjoying it, if you get my drift."

Gwen glared at him. "Don't be ridiculous." But as Gwen studied the drawing, she could almost see what Mason was saying.

Her eyes were that horrible black as Billie had described them, but soft and unfocused. And she wore a half-smile.

"Let's see the last one." Mason turned the page for her.

Gwen's heart nearly stopped. *Oh no. Oh no.* She covered her mouth to stop herself from crying out. This was another drawing of Billie and the woman with the black hair having a sword fight just like the unfinished drawing Billie had completed on her own late one night. But in this version, Billie had opened her arms wide, closed her eyes, and dropped her sword. The black-haired woman's sword was raised and she was about to run Billie through.

CHAPTER SIXTEEN
Billie, November 15–17

Billie and Nathaniel talked through the night. She shared the truth, and rather than being freaked out or disbelieving, he accepted the news that she was from the future with remarkable calm, something Billie wasn't sure she'd have been able to manage if she'd been in his situation, but it helped that her phone was obvious proof she was from a different time, or a different world. Nathaniel was quite disappointed she wasn't from the stars and repeatedly asked her, "You're sure you're not an alien?"

He shared details of his life as an Army blacksmith in charge of shoeing horses and repairing tools. "You can't work with fire, hot metal, and horses if you can't see what you are doing," he said, his voice flat with sadness.

"I saw an amazing sculpture in the city plaza yesterday, a horse made out of horseshoes."

"That was mine," Nathaniel said with undisguised pride.

He told her about the war with the Seminoles, which was going poorly for the US Army. "The officers are too arrogant to take the Natives seriously, so are constantly getting men killed. I've lost a whole heap of friends." Because the current fighting was farther south, Fort Marion was used to warehouse supplies, house about one hundred soldiers, and serve as a prison for captured Seminoles. "Their chief, Osceola, is here, but he's not going to last much longer because he's elderly and sick. Wild Cat and his bunch were brought in a few weeks ago."

Wild Cat. Coacoochee. He must be in one of those cells full of Native Americans.

"You'll probably see them in the afternoons when they're let out into the courtyard for exercise."

The next morning, enough weak daylight filtered through their single window that she could see Nathaniel was a broad-shouldered man with dark brown hair, a wide smile, and deep-set eyes that were opaque and cloudy. She'd learned during the night that he was twenty-five, but he looked forty-five, his skin lined, his eyes punctuated with crows' feet. His long arms certainly looked capable of wrestling the foot of a reluctant horse into shoeing position. Nothing about Nathaniel was very clean but Billie had noticed yesterday that very few people she met were twenty-first-century clean. She herself had begun longing for a hot shower and a bar of soap.

"Shall we sneak out before we're found?" she asked.

Nathaniel nodded and they got to their feet. "I try not to look blind walking through the fort. If you could walk directly in front of me, then I can focus on you and not wander into a wall."

They managed to leave the fort without incident, probably because the officers were on the gun deck screaming at some poor soldier for breaking some stupid rule. But things were surprisingly lax with a war going on. Once outside, Billie breathed a sigh of relief. "Okay, the first thing I need help with is selling my watch. We need money for food."

Grateful she'd never succumbed to the Apple watch craze, Billie allowed Nathaniel to explore the watch with his hands. "It doesn't feel or look too strange, too futuristic, so we should be able to do that."

Billie had become accustomed to the fort and the nearby streets, so now all of that was in her safe space, which helped keep the agoraphobic symptoms at bay. Her heart no longer raced as she and Nathaniel walked the narrow streets. She led them, with Nathaniel's directions, to a small shop at the south end of what would one day be

St. George Street. He negotiated for her, and the result was a handful of soiled coins she didn't recognize. Upon examination they turned out to be twenty-five- and fifty-cent pieces. Then they went to a small market in Constitution Plaza, the park that in her present was filled with lush grass, flower beds and a gazebo. Walt had explained it also once held a statue honoring Confederate soldiers but that had been removed a few years earlier, which was a relief. Billie never understood why so many people insisted on honoring Confederates, who were all basically traitors to the United States.

In this time the Plaza was nothing but dirt, some vendor stalls, and Nathaniel's horse statue. They purchased more bread, some sort of dried meat, and a small bag of boiled eggs.

The whole time Billie kept her eyes out for Martha and asked about her whenever possible. Nothing.

She and Nathaniel ended up breakfasting nearby on the bank of the river, which wasn't a bad place to be. A bevy of ducks floated by, quacking for no obvious reason.

"So, tell me again. You think someone is planning to harm Gwen during this night light."

"Nights of Lights, yes. One of the drawings showed two men pointing guns at her just outside the fort, and I overheard two men planning it. I even recorded it on my phone."

"Recorded it?"

Billie blew out a long breath. How to explain technology she herself didn't understand? "It is a record of the conversation that you can listen to over and over again."

"I *love* your phony."

"Phone."

"Yes, phone. Could you play it for me?"

Miraculously, there was still some charge left, so she looked around. No one stood nearby, and the river noises were low so she wouldn't have to turn it up too high. She played it for him. "I know the voice, but I just can't see the face that goes with it."

"Again, please." When the short recording ended, Nathaniel stretched out his long legs. "Your record is a miraculous thing, but

I have an idea. Why don't you listen again, but this time, close your eyes. Don't let your vision interfere with your hearing."

"Interfere?"

"Sometimes vision is so strong that it grabs our mind's attention and lets nothing else in."

Billie settled her body on the grass and sat up straight like she was in yoga class. She touched *play* and closed her eyes. "Wow, this is different."

"Again."

She played it three more times then her eyes flew open. "Holy shit. It's *him*." She leapt to her feet. "I know who this is. It's a person Gwen trusts! She will have no warning, no idea that he's going to harm her." She paced in agitation. "I must get back. I must stop him."

"Beg pardon?"

Billie whirled to face a skinny teenager with pale skin and a gangly frame draped in a ragged shirt and pants. "Someone said you were looking for Martha?"

Billie's heart soared. "Yes, yes. Do you know where she is?"

The boy nodded, clearly sad. "Follow me."

With Nathaniel on her arm, Billie followed the boy down a few streets and into a small white church that had seen better days.

The church was empty and stuffy, with barely enough light coming through filthy windows to show that a pine coffin rested at the front of the church.

"No," Billie whispered.

The boy led them down the center aisle, their feet scuffing the building's sandy floor. "She was my aunt, the one who's kept me alive since Ma and Pa died."

Unable to breathe, Billie stepped up to the coffin. Martha lay there, face bruised but still recognizable. "No, no, no," Billie moaned.

"T'was a horse and wagon coming down the road too fast and she fell and they run her over like a dog." The boy's voice broke, and Nathaniel reached out to pat him on the shoulder.

"Do you have any other family, boy?" he asked.

"No. My…my woman got sent away, but I stayed behind to help Aunt Martha."

Billie struggled against the lump in her throat and wiped away her tears. This boy had lost his support, and she had lost the only person who knew how to travel back to her present. Bleary-eyed, she dug out the money from her watch. "She worked hard to support you, so I'd like you to have this." She thrust the handful of coins at him, and fled the church, forgetting about Nathaniel entirely. By the time she remembered and turned around, he'd felt his way out using the pews and was at the door.

"Why did you do that?" he asked.

She tucked Nathaniel's hand under her arm and started down the street. "I interrupted her routine. She was trying to avoid me. For all I know, I could have caused the accident. I just feel responsible. The kid needs the money more than I do."

Late that afternoon, just after Billie and Nathaniel had snuck back into "their" storeroom, iron cell doors clanged open. She peeked out to see army soldiers at the sally port, the stairs, at each vault entrance, and lined up along the gun deck, rifles aimed into the courtyard. At least one hundred Seminole prisoners, all with their black hair blunt cut at their shoulders, poured from the cells into the courtyard. Most ambled and chatted among themselves, while a few ran in place. Billie studied each face until she found him: Coacoochee. He didn't look much like a wild cat now, thin and stooped, but she remembered Walt's history lesson. Coacoochee and nineteen men in his cell would soon escape and breathe new life into the Seminole resistance. While his body looked weak, she could see when he turned in her direction that his eyes blazed with furious resolve.

The next two days passed in much the same way. Billie and Nathaniel would sneak into their storeroom at night, then wander the town during the day. Between support from Nathaniel's friends, and Billie helping unload a boat for one man, and stacking wood for another, they had enough to eat and drink. But Billie moved through the days in a fog. Now and then she was able to mentally step back and, for a moment, appreciate the magnificence of time travel, the privilege—almost—of experiencing a time and place no one but she and Martha had seen. But then concern for Gwen would chase that all away.

Both nights, while Nathaniel and the others slept, Billie crept around the fort with the mop handle. Was there some sort of incantation needed? A particular material or rock or stone that opened the portal? Because she'd read or watched dozens of time travel stories, she searched her memory for all the methods: time machine, temporal anomalies, slingshotting around the sun in a spaceship, and going through a wormhole. Number one, none of that helped. And number two, time travel was science fiction, fantasy. It wasn't supposed to be real, and yet, here she was, trapped in 1837. She didn't even have any idea what went on in the United States in 1837. Who was president? What were the issues? Slavery was still legal. Was Florida even a state? Her fingers itched to Google all those questions, but that obviously wasn't going to work.

The third night Billie was too tired to search for the portal, so just sat in the dark with Nathaniel. "Do you think time runs simultaneously?" she asked, thinking of her "Movie Theater Theory of Time Travel."

"What do you mean?"

"It's November 17, 1837, right?"

She felt him nod. "Okay, so do you think it could currently be November 17 in my time, in the future?"

"Instead of Christmas Day, or the middle of June?"

"Yeah. No one that I know of other than Martha has traveled through time. She could have answered this question."

"Was Martha dressed for this weather? It's cooler now."

"Yes, she was."

"Well, I'm obviously no expert on time travel, or on much of anything for that matter, but it seems that God would have set things up to be orderly."

Billie chuckled at the thought of the Christian god having anything to do with time travel, but it made about as much sense as her movie theater theory. "Let's say Martha left here at six a.m. on November first, she'd arrive at six a.m. on November first in the future. If she left the future on November second at three p.m., she'd arrive back here, in 1837, at three p.m. on November second. You wouldn't lose or gain days or hours, but time would just continue at the same rate."

"I think, to avoid chaos, that would be the way things would go."

Billie gently banged her head against the coquina wall because the pain of her helplessness was almost unbearable, and because her "Movie Theater Theory of Time Travel" was likely true. She was stuck in the 1837 movie theater without any way to reach Gwen in the "future" movie theater.

"That's what I was afraid of." She could feel Nathaniel waiting in the dark. "Tomorrow night is November eighteenth, both here and in the future. That's the opening night for Nights of Lights, when Gwen will be attacked by two men, one of whom Gwen knows and trusts." She banged her head harder until Nathaniel hissed at her to stop. "I am here, unable to do anything. I cannot get back. I cannot get a message to her. I am helpless. Gwen is twenty-four hours away from death and I can't do a thing to stop it."

"What about leaving a note in the structure of the fort somehow? You know that it survives."

"But it undergoes too much renovation over the decades. Some of the interior walls change location, the coquina crumbles and needs to be repaired. And very few of the buildings in town will survive until my time."

"I cannot help but think that things would be easier if you'd been an alien."

She smiled in the dark. "So sorry to disappoint."

They sat in silence until Nathaniel laughed softly. "As you say, life is going on simultaneously for those people who can travel through time. But neither you nor I can do that, so for us, time is linear. The future will only arrive one year at a time, year by year, so here's a bizarre idea. Remember that this is St. Augustine, city of ghosts. You could always get yourself murdered, haunt the fort, then possess Gwen's drawing hand when she arrives in your time and warn her then."

Billie gasped. "What?"

"We never know why ghosts haunt the places they do, but one theory is that the souls of the murdered are too troubled by the violence to move on." He patted her knee. "Of course I am kidding. I would never want you to be murdered. I like having you around. It's like having a mother again, only one who's from the future and who could possibly be an alien."

Billie closed her eyes and replayed all the drawings Gwen had done, and in a startling flash of insight they fell into an order that felt right: the two men exchanging money, the same two men pointing a gun at Gwen, Gwen dead on the ground. Those drawings could only have been done by someone who'd overheard the men, who knew what they were planning. Then the drawings of Coacoochee in his cell, and Gwen at fifty-five, alive but without Billie.

The rest of the images jumbled in her brain as she leaned over, face in her hands. Holy shit. Holy fucking shit. She was the only person who knew the "future." She was the only person who was back in the past with Coacoochee. She had the knowledge. She had the artistic skills.

The ghost at the fort? The ghost who could draw as well as Billie? The ghost who loved Gwen enough to haunt the fort for decades in order to warn her? Billie moaned in anguish.

She was the ghost.

After a long silence, Nathaniel touched her knee. "What's going on?"

Billie bit back a sob. "It's me. I'm the ghost."

He gasped. "No, that can't…"

Billie spelled it out, describing every drawing. "There might even be more drawings since I've left, so who knows what they show. But the first one was Coacoochee dressed as Hamlet. This was smart because it established what the man looked like, so when Gwen drew the Natives imprisoned at the fort in 1837, we recognized him." She went through the ones she remembered. "Then the series ends with me sword fighting with someone. Given the chopped off black hair, it is probably one of the imprisoned Natives, maybe even Coacoochee."

"Why would you think that? He's locked up on the other side of the courtyard. He can't hurt you, can't get his hands on a sword."

Billie pressed her lips together, feeling sick. "One of the benefits of being from the future is knowing when certain things happen. Thanks to my friend Walt, I know that Coacoochee, in fact, escapes from the fort on November 22. That's five nights from now."

"But I still don't get how you are connected."

"I need to become a ghost that haunts the fort. That means someone needs to murder me. Will you do it?"

She felt Nate's recoil. "Gods no! To murder someone, you need to be angry or threatened or afraid."

"Exactly." Billie rubbed both hands down her face. The solution was obvious. "Who would be more angry or threatened than a Seminole whose entire family, whose entire *tribe* has been ripped from their home and sent to the Oklahoma Territory? Who has been imprisoned in the fort's dark cells for weeks?" She placed a hand over her pounding heart. Her head throbbed with the harsh reality of it all. "Nathaniel, I'm afraid. I'm so very afraid. How do you handle being blind? It's got to be hard. How do you handle the fear?" Her agoraphobia had dimmed in 1837, but now the algophobia, the fear of pain, came flooding back.

She felt him grope for her hand, and let him hold it when he found it, his warmth spreading up her arm. "Giving in to fear is a choice. I can't control *feeling* fear. I can't make it go away. But I can recognize that I can either let it control my life, or I can make my own choices. Yes, I'm often afraid, but I don't let that stop me from doing what I need to do, from getting up every morning and finding food and talking to people and doing what I can to help others. I control my actions. I don't give fear that power."

Billie closed her eyes. Life could be hard and cruel, yet somehow people managed to find the strength, like Nathaniel, to do what needed to be done. She was living in 1837. From this moment on, time would march in a straight line, day after day, year after year, until Gwen would be born, the two of them meet, move to Florida, and Billie would fall back in time.

But just as in the Cineplex, no matter which movie Billie and Laura had watched, all the movies continued at the same pace. Martha knew the secret to jumping from theater to theater, moving from the 1837 movie to the present movie, but that secret had died with her. Billie was stuck in the 1837 theater, unable to help. If Gwen didn't know about the men plotting to harm her, she was doomed.

Billie's heart skipped with such force she clutched at her chest. Gwen dead. The horror of that made her shake with anger and frustration and deep despair.

No. No. No. She had no way to travel to the "future" movie theater to save Gwen. All she could do was act here, in 1837, to stop the attack, no matter how risky or unlikely…or deadly the action. She straightened her spine as resolve flowed through her veins like liquid steel. Nathaniel was right. She had the ability to choose even if fear gnawed at her insides. Coacoochee was going to escape through his window on November 22. But if someone unlocked his cell, left a sword nearby, then blocked the only exit, also armed with a sword, Coacoochee would not hesitate to rush that person and slash her in two with the sword. It would not be his fault—the man needed to escape to continue leading his people—but it would still be murder, and that's what she needed.

It was the only way she could save Gwen, and she would do it, no matter her fear.

Billie was resolved, but her body still clenched at what awaited her. Fuck. Becoming a ghost was really, *really* going to hurt.

CHAPTER SEVENTEEN

Gwen, November 17

Gwen called the detective to whom she'd first reported Billie's disappearance.

"Nothing? Still?"

"We've checked the bus station, checked in with Uber and Lyft drivers, checked flights out of Jacksonville. Gone to every hotel in St. Augustine in case she's being held against her will, but nothing. No one remembers seeing anyone who meets Ms. Norton's description. We've entered her in the registry so police throughout the United States know she's missing."

Gwen struggled to speak around the tightness in her throat. "Okay. I'd appreciate it if you could keep looking."

"Absolutely. And if you hear from her, please let us know."

Gwen called in sick again and sent an email to her boss explaining that her spouse had gone missing and this needed to take priority over work.

But what could she do, really? She finally went for a long walk, and by the time she returned, a small crowd waited for her.

"Hey, Gwen," Mason called. "We've got reinforcements. I called Clayton for help, and he called Kylie and Austin. I say we work the problem until we figure it out." Clayton nodded, as did Kylie and Austin.

Gwen forced a smile, then pulled out all the drawings. Mason dropped them onto the kitchen floor and everyone grabbed a chair and began to discuss, but Gwen held back, exhausted. She'd already stared at the images so much they were burned onto her retinas.

The four of them discussed, reshuffled, argued, pointed, and then shuffled again. Gwen watched them. If anyone could figure this out, it was Mason with his freakish ability to see patterns. Maybe there were enough drawings now to make sense of whatever the ghost was trying to tell her.

Mason got down on his knees. "Let me try something." He scratched his head, muttering to himself, and rearranged the drawings for nearly fifteen minutes while they watched. Finally, he sat back on his heels. "There. This is it. While I'm not sure I can say I've found a *pattern*, I think I've found a *story*."

Gwen's heart skipped a beat. Could he have done it? She looked over Mason's shoulder. It was an order of the images she hadn't tried yet, basically because it made no sense.

"I start out strong," he said, "but I'm going to need some help as we get further into these drawings. Everyone needs to use their imagination, but here's my take on what could have happened. It's not important the order in which the drawings came to Gwen. Kylie has said the ghost has been waiting a long time, so may have lost the ability to craft a cohesive story and is just throwing images at us hoping we can connect the dots." He pointed to the drawing looking down the fort wall to two men exchanging money. "We know from your VISA bill that Billie was in the fort the day she disappeared, probably waiting for Martha to show up. What if she overhears these two men plotting to kill Gwen? Everything bad starts here, when she knows someone wants to harm you." Everyone but Gwen nodded so he kept going. "Second drawing: Nights of Lights, when the murder will take place."

"My murder."

"Yes," Mason said, shooting her an apologetic smile. "Third drawing: the men pointing guns at Gwen. Fourth drawing: Gwen is down, clearly bleeding from several gunshot wounds. Now these two drawings are less detailed, as if the ghost is trying to *create* something rather than report something. This isn't something the ghost has witnessed because it hasn't happened, at least not yet."

Her friends nodded. "Keep going," Austin said.

"Fifth drawing: Martha and Billie are struggling in a small room in the fort. I don't know the room, however, because I've never been inside the fort."

"It's the powder magazine," Austin offered. "That's the only room small enough to match the drawing. The concave ceiling is low, and it's almost like being inside a barrel. Only the two end walls are flat."

Kylie squeezed Austin's shoulder. "This kid knows more about that fort than the park rangers who run it."

"Notice anything else?" Mason asked.

Austin bit his lip and tapped the drawing. "Billie's shoulder and Martha's arm aren't just pressed against the wall but actually seem to be disappearing into it?" Austin and Mason exchanged a look, so Mason took over.

"Gwen, you're going to hate this, but I think that wall is a portal through time."

Clayton whistled. "Holy moly. I could see that."

"*What*?" Gwen made a face. "Now you're just making things up."

"No, no," Clayton said. "It's totally possible. They fall back in time and land in Martha's real time. Maybe she knows how to move back and forth so she brings items from her time into our present, sells them to antique dealers like Walt for cash, uses the cash to buy food, then takes the food back through the portal to her time. Can you imagine tasting Oreos or Cheetos in her time?"

"But when is her time?" Kylie asked, gazing at the drawings as if they were moving.

Mason straightened the next image. "That's the easiest part. Sixth drawing: Indians locked in a cell at the fort. According to Walt, it would either be the 1830s when Seminoles were imprisoned, or the 1880s when Apache and Comanche were imprisoned. Walt thinks the guard's uniform is early to mid 1800s. But that's not enough for us to place the drawing." He pointed to the next drawing. "Seventh drawing is Coacoochee in his Hamlet getup, which identifies him. So when we go back to the drawing of the Natives in the cell, we can see one of them is Coacoochee, which places us in November, 1837."

"God damn, this is complex, but I'm with you." Clayton shot Mason an encouraging look. "Keep going."

"Drawing number eight, Billie's back in 1837 and is talking to a man with obvious vision issues. Don't know what role he plays, but he's in the 1830s uniform. By now we have to assume that Billie is trying to find her way back. Maybe the way she arrived is not the way home. She throws herself against the wall, but nothing happens."

"She had to have been going out of her mind worrying about Gwen," Kylie said softly.

"No doubt," Mason agreed. "Next drawing, number nine, Martha in a coffin." He stopped, then cleared his throat. "If Martha was the only one who knew the way back and forth between times, then now that she's dead, Billie has no one to ask for help. Maybe she's tried all the walls. Or maybe the soldiers make it impossible for her to do that. Or maybe she's not safe in the fort. I don't know. But either way, with Martha dead, Billie is good and stuck in 1837."

Mason was sweating now, so stopped to wipe his upper lip. "God, I really hate this part."

Gwen glared at her brother. "I'm starting to hate *you*."

"Billie's stuck back in 1837 now, but let's go back to the drawing of the men exchanging money. I know it's a stretch, but Billie could have overheard this in our present time but didn't get the chance to tell you this before falling *back* in time. Like Kylie said, she must have been going crazy not being able to get back here and warn you."

Gwen could imagine Billie's panic, her desperation to find a way home. And how was her agoraphobic wife handling being that far from home?

Kylie cleared her throat. "I think I can see what happened next. After contacting us at SAPS, Billie learned that the spirits of people who are murdered tend to hang around and haunt their murder site. And she already knows that a ghost has been trying to warn you about some danger."

"Murder?" Gwen shouted. "Now you've all gone too far."

Mason held up a hand. "Think about it. Billie knows that Coacoochee is going to escape the night of November 22, 1837. He's going to escape out the window. But…" He tapped the tenth drawing. "Let's say Billie somehow manages to steal the key and unlock the cell so he and the others can use that easier route instead." He touched the next drawing. "Not sure about this one. A Native and a sword?"

Clayton leaned forward. "How about this? Coacoochee has left his cell and picks up a sword. Where'd the sword come from? It's not likely that one of the soldiers would have just left his sword lying about, so someone probably put it right there where he could find it. I'll bet my truck that someone was Billie."

"Holy shit," Austin breathed.

"Here's the hardest image." Mason took over the narrative again. "What if, when Coacoochee races around the corner and heads for the exit, that exit is blocked by someone with a sword? Coacoochee's desperate. He's angry. He's hungry. He's got to get free. These two drawings of Billie in a swordfight with a woman with black hair? We can't see that person's face or chest. What if *she* is really a *he*, one of the Seminole men who'd had their braids chopped off? What if this is really *Coacoochee*?"

Gwen realized that both Kylie and Austin had tears streaming down their cheeks. Her own eyes filled as well.

Clayton heaved a massive sigh. "From what you've all told me, Billie is one smart woman. She probably realized that if she were to be murdered in order to become a ghost that could warn Gwen, she needed to arrange for that murder. An escaping Seminole was the perfect vehicle. She pretends to be a threat, but at the last minute opens her arms and exposes herself to…to the assault." All eyes fell on the drawing of Billie about to be slashed by a sword.

"Jesus...I don't know how anyone could do that. It would be freaking terrifying." Austin had gone pale and his hands trembled a little.

Gwen couldn't speak. This was ridiculous. Billie never would have allowed herself to be...sliced open... She stopped, unable to continue the thought.

"My theory," Mason said, his eyes red, "is the sword attack by Coacoochee kills Billie. Her spirit becomes a ghost with a mission, a ghost whose sole purpose is to await the day Gwen enters the fort with her sketchbook and pencil." He points to the second to the last drawing. "The ghost witnessed this scene, with Kylie and Austin helping while Gwen drew. The last image, one that's sort of fuzzy like the earlier ones where the ghost was guessing, shows the happy ending. Gwen figures out the warning, avoids being shot, and lives to celebrate her fifty-fifth birthday." He sighs. "Billie is not in the image, of course. She's gone wherever...wherever ghosts go. So... so that's about it."

By now everyone sat with their heads or faces in their hands, sad and crying or just sad.

Gwen glared at each of them, then burst out laughing. All eyes riveted toward her. "You should write fiction, Mase. You're good at it."

The four of them looked at each other as if Gwen was too dense to get it. "Let me get this straight," she said. "You are saying that Billie has disappeared because she fought with Martha and fell *into* a wall in the fort which took her back to 1837. She knows who has been or who will be threatening me, but because Billie's unable to find her way "back to the future," if you will, she decides to plan her own murder. She unlocks Coacoochee's cell and leaves him a sword. Then she runs around the corner to the entrance, the *sally port* to be exact, and waits, holding another sword and looking like a soldier trying to stop the escape.

"Coacoochee and his men realize the cell is unlocked so they sneak out, discover that miraculously someone's left a sword lying about, and now armed, they quietly head for the exit, only to find the way blocked by Billie and her sword, which she has no idea how to use, by the way."

Gwen swallowed. She was saying the words, repeating Mason's ridiculous story, but she didn't believe it. She couldn't. "After a few parries and thrusts, or maybe none at all, Billie drops her sword and lets Coacoochee run her through or slice her open, causing a devastating wound that will create unimaginable pain and then she dies. She becomes a ghost and hangs around the fort for 187 years until I show up."

Mason had the good grace to look uncertain. "That's about it."

Gwen paused for a second to appreciate what a volcano must feel like before it erupts. "Are you fucking *kidding* me? For your stupid scenario to make sense, Billie has to be dead. *Dead*, Mason, dead. Gone. Never coming back." Her voice broke at the horror of her words. "That cannot be. It's wrong. Billie is *not* the ghost. She calls you a visual savant, but I think you're just *stupid*."

As that last word echoed through the kitchen, Kylie stood and faced Gwen. "If she were the ghost, it would explain everything."

"What?"

"How did it feel to be possessed once you stopped fighting it?"

Gwen exhaled, unwilling to share but knowing it was important. "It felt...safe, warm...like I was loved."

"Your body or your mind sensed the ghost was someone you could trust, so you let it in. That's why I agree with Mason that the ghost is...is what is left of Billie's spirit, her essence. She has clung to this existence for decades just to warn you. You need to *listen*."

Gwen stomped a foot. "Warn me? That's just it. I have no idea who is threatening me, who wants to harm me. None. For all I know it could be one of you!" She waved a hand at Mason and Clayton.

"What? I'm your brother," Mason squeaked.

"Who stands to inherit everything if I'm out of the picture, and you arrived the day Billie disappeared. Coincidence?"

Mason cursed and got to his feet. "Are you—"

"And you, Clayton, the neighbor who didn't speak to either of us but just lurked? You've been freaking us out since we moved in."

He held up both hands. "I get it."

Austin looked uncertain, as if Gwen would accuse him next.

"And besides, Billie and the ghost were together at the fort while I drew. Isn't that some sort of time travel no-no, meeting yourself in a different time?"

They exchanged a glance she didn't understand so she glared at Mason. He made a face. "Well, normally, yes, that would mess up the space-time continuum—"

"That's not a real thing! That's from *Star Trek* or some other fantasy show!"

"But Billie from the past wasn't actually alive, Gwen, she was just a spirit, so—"

Gwen leapt to her feet, growling in her throat. "I think you should all leave," she said, hating that her voice trembled. "You've ceased being helpful. I want Billie back. I want some idea of who the bad guy is. The ghost never showed me. If the ghost was Billie, she would have found some way, silly or otherwise, to reach me, to tell me."

"Maybe she didn't see who it was, like Mason surmised," Kylie said. "If she didn't see it, she can't draw it, so needs to find another way."

"Don't say 'she.' We don't know who the ghost is. But where's this 'another way?' I got nothing."

Austin suddenly began rocking back and forth, hugging himself. "I might," he said softly, watching Gwen. "You'd better sit back down."

Now what, Gwen wanted to growl. She wanted to break something, to howl at the ocean, to make this horrid story stop. Lost, she sat back down.

Austin reached into his back pocket. "After you got thrown out of the fort, and the ladder thing was so hard for both you and the ghost, I went to the fort yesterday." He winced and looked at Kylie.

"I skipped class. Sorry." She waved him on. "I was hoping that the ghost might draw through me and finish all the clues, but it didn't. I sat there long enough, though, that I did feel a presence near me— Aunt Kylie, it was amazing, like I was vibrating or something."

"Focus, honey."

"Yeah, right. Anyway, pretty soon an image came to me. It didn't make any sense, and was kind of silly, but in case the image was the ghost trying to communicate, I drew it."

Austin hesitated. "I didn't show anyone because it's weird, and just looks like I was doodling or messing around or something." He unfolded the paper and handed it to Kylie, who passed it to Clayton, then Mason, until the paper ended up in Gwen's hands.

She looked down, stared at the image, and *got* it, as if sucker-punched in the gut. She couldn't breathe. She struggled to get air, but the sucker-punch happened again and again. Finally, she was able to gasp a few times, then fell back against her chair. A mad buzzing started in her ears until it filled her entire head. Her vision blurred, but she blinked enough to finally clear it.

"This means something to you," Mason whispered. "What?"

The drawing was of a car, the sort of boxy thing a kid might draw. The car's driver had one arm out of the window and was almost too big for the car. The driver had massive black eyes, thin arms, and sort-of hands that ended in three fingers. The driver was clearly the culture's idea of an alien, a little green man. And the alien wore a massive watch.

Seriously, Gwen, anyone could be an alien. Take your friend Jeremy out there, all fake tan and big white teeth and obnoxiously expensive watch. For all we know he could be an alien from Alpha Centauri wearing a Jeremy suit.

Billie had said those words just a few weeks ago. The ghost knew things that only Billie and Gwen knew.

"I need to be alone," Gwen whispered. She felt the four of them look at each other, then decide as a group to give her what she needed.

"Beers at my place, but not for you," Clayton said, waggling his finger at Austin, and they left.

The house was now quiet, far too quiet.

No Billie laughing at her own silly jokes or sharing the newest meme about cats or dogs or squirrels. No Billie here to give her another anniversary card like the one for their twentieth, which read: *Love at first sight is easy to understand. It's when two people have been looking at each other for years that it becomes a miracle.*

No one else had known about the Jeremy-as-alien joke. No one else knew how much they made fun of his grandfather's watch.

Ghosts were real.

Time travel was apparently possible.

Billie was very likely the ghost, which meant that Billie was dead.

CHAPTER EIGHTEEN

Gwen, November 17

Gwen sat in the aching silence left behind by her brother and the others. The idea that Billie might be dead felt about as real as time travel or aliens. She just could not wrap her mind around it. There was no body, no accident, nothing. Just poof—she was gone. And according to Mason, her disappearance involved both ghosts and time travel. Gwen's heart raced to think that Billie was no longer alive; she didn't want to go through the rest of her life without her. She didn't want to face mornings, or long afternoons, or lonely nights without Billie at her side, teasing her, encouraging her, loving her. How had she lost sight of how much she needed Billie? So what if Gwen hadn't "fallen in love" with her recently? What a stupid and unrealistic romantic notion. She still loved Billie. She still didn't want to be with anyone else.

Gwen looked back down at the drawing of the two men exchanging money. Both wore jackets, but something...what was that? Gwen leaned closer. The edge of a large wristwatch peeked out from one man's sleeve. Jeremy's watch. This just confirmed what the ghost—Billie?—had been trying to communicate with the drawing of the alien. Jeremy Wilkinson. Upstanding citizen. Concerned father. Devoted student of history. How could he hate her so much after only two months?

She considered the drawing of her with the Lauras celebrating her fifty-fifth birthday. Her face was worn and her eyes sad, as if she were trying to be happy for her friends' sake but was failing. Billie wasn't in the picture…because Billie was gone.

Gwen sat down hard on the nearest chair. *Oh, Billie. What have I done?* She buried her face in her hands. She'd wasted so much time being angry with Billie, for choosing to turn down the dream job at the history center, for needing to leave winter, a season Gwen loved. Yet Billie was the person who every night before bed would fill a hot water bottle and slide it under the sheets so Gwen's icy feet would find it at bedtime. She was the person who made Gwen laugh every single day even when a job or a colleague or a family member had made Gwen's day dreary and exhausting. Billie had loved her without reserve or judgment or regret, and what had Gwen done? Blamed her for things beyond her control. Blamed her for her fear of pain. Blamed her for the terror she felt whenever she left the house.

Gwen jumped when her phone beeped. She checked. It was a text from Jeremy. *Nights of Lights tomorrow night! Let's meet at the fort's ticket booth. 6:30 pm. Be there or be square.*

Her jaw tightened. Of course he hadn't asked about Billie. He didn't care. All he wanted was to get her to the ticket booth at six thirty so the hired gun could kill her.

Gwen needed a plan. She could call the police but had absolutely zero evidence that Jeremy might be planning to harm her. Images drawn by a ghost would be unlikely to convince the police to take action.

She could enlist the help of her friends, but if Jeremy and his friend were armed, it would be too dangerous for anyone else to get involved.

She could refuse to meet Jeremy, just blowing him off. But if he were determined to harm her, he'd just plot something else, and the next time she wouldn't have any warning. At least the ghost was able to warn her about tomorrow night.

The ghost.

Billie.

No, her only choice was to see this through herself and end it, otherwise Billie's sacrifice would be in vain. The only way to honor the woman she loved was to stay alive, even though without Billie in the world, life held little appeal.

She sat there quietly, trying on different scenarios in her head, as if watching many versions of the same TV episode, seeking a plan that had the best chance of succeeding.

An hour later, she finally drew in a huge breath for courage and walked over to Clayton's, where everyone sat around a fire pit in the small backyard. When she pulled up an empty chair all conversation ceased. "I want to thank you for your help. I don't know if Billie is the ghost, but I've decided to stop trying to figure it out. I'm going to bed now. Tomorrow night Mason and I will attend the Nights of Lights opening, then I'm going to find a way to move on from this horrible experience."

"But what about the drawings—"

"I need to let go," she said. "I'm done. If Billie really is gone, I'm going to need some time to grieve."

Kylie stood and gave her a hug. Austin did as well, too shy to look her in the eye.

Mason remained seated. "Gonna have another beer with Clayton."

Gwen lightly touched his knee. "I need a few minutes alone with Clayton, if that's okay."

Mason's forehead wrinkled. "I can't stay?"

She shook her head.

Mumbling, Mason stood and waved to Clayton. "Thanks for the beer, man." He followed Kylie and Austin across the street to their car.

When they were finally alone, Gwen turned to the large man waiting patiently. "I need a gun, preferably one not traceable to you."

"What makes you—"

"This is Florida. You're a young man. You have a gun. I need to borrow it."

"Well, I—"

"Please."

Her plan was ridiculous and likely to fail. Only with a gun did she have any chance of success.

CHAPTER NINETEEN

Gwen, November 18

Grief crawled into bed with Gwen and poked her each time she came close to falling asleep. *How can you sleep if Billie is dead? Why are you just lying there? Why aren't you screaming or running or throwing something?*

Gwen wanted to do all those things. She wanted to close her eyes, wish really hard, and open them to find Billie's hazel eyes gazing into hers. She wanted to reach out with a foot or a hand and feel Billie's warmth and safety. Gwen rolled over. How had she taken all that for granted for so long? *Live each day as if it were your last,* was the ridiculous advice always plastered across posters and art from the big box stores, yet if she'd done that, she would have been eating coconut cake every day, in bed, naked with Billie, an old k.d. lang CD playing in the background.

Gwen rolled over again. Sun peeked around the edges of the curtain. She had to get up. Nights of Lights was tonight. She had to put a stop to all of Jeremy's nonsense in order to honor Billie's sacrifice.

"You okay?" Mason asked from the sofa as she shuffled past.

"No, not really, but I'm going to get through this day." She owed it to Billie. She owed everything to Billie.

❖

The opening night for Nights of Lights turned St. Augustine from a busy tourist town into an *insanely* busy tourist town. Jeremy had warned her, again via text, that parking would be impossible so she either needed to park somewhere early or walk to the event. All day she'd found herself thinking of every interaction she'd had with Jeremy and not once had she felt any sort of animosity. Sure, his "Hey, boss" schtick wore thin quickly, but otherwise, she'd seen nothing but a happy, jocular guy. That he'd buried his hatred so deep felt more threatening than if he'd been the type of person unable to hide it.

"C'mon, Mase," she called, checking the time. "We gotta go."

Dusk had settled over the city as they walked toward Constitution Plaza. She could hear an orchestra playing, so knew they were getting close. They finally reached the edges of the crowd, which had spilled over into the next block. Casually, she led Mason around the crowd to the start of St. George St.

"Mason?"

"Yeah?" He was scanning the crowd like a Secret Service agent, clearly on the lookout for anyone who might burst out of the crowd and point a gun at her.

"I need to use the restroom. There's a public one just thirty steps up St. George." She pointed. "See, there's the sign right there."

"I'll come with you."

She stopped him. "I'll be fine. I'll be back in five minutes. Stay and watch the crowd. You love watching people."

He started to follow but she pushed him back. "Stay here."

She looked over her shoulder a few times to make sure he wasn't following or watching her, but he'd turned back to watch the orchestra so she zipped into a side street and began to jog. She had fifteen minutes to get to the fort so she'd be there, in place, thirty minutes before she and Jeremy were to meet.

Not being a jogger, she soon had to slow to a fast walk, which was hard because the sidewalks and side streets were packed with people. She got a text from Mason: *Where r u*. Then another. She silenced her phone and kept going, sending him a silent apology. Finally, she crossed Avenida Menendez onto the fort grounds and left most of the crowds behind. The fort's floodlights lit up the bastions, but along the curtains there were dark spots, and it was these she was counting on. Just before the ticket booth, she turned right and followed the sloping sidewalk down to the sandy ground between the sea wall and the fort. Here she could access the dry moat. Heart racing, she doubled back along the moat's shallow wall until she was even with the ticket booth. When Jeremy and his "friend" arrived, they'd hopefully stand there talking. She was close enough that her phone should be able to pick up and record the voices. She dropped down and huddled against the wall with her back to the river, making sure all of her was in the shadow of the moat wall and wiping her perspiring hands on her pants. What the hell was she doing? This might be the stupidest idea ever, hiding eight feet from someone with a gun who wanted to hurt her. She pulled herself in tighter, forcing herself to breathe slower. They'd hear her gasping if she didn't.

The river was alive with boats all waiting to watch the bridge and the city light up at six thirty. Some blared music, others throbbed with laughter and conversation. It was jarring to know that most people in this city were having a wonderful evening. She was just trying not to get killed.

Gwen checked the time. Six fifteen. Jeremy should be here soon. As she waited, she could feel the heavy fort beside her and now understood why she'd hated it from the moment she'd seen it. If Mason's story had come anywhere close to what had actually happened, Billie had died here 187 years ago.

An idea came to her. Jeremy had said ghosts were sometimes visible along the top of the wall. What if she were to look up? Would Billie be able to sense her presence? Would she be there? Gwen longed to see her face one more time. Slowly, staying in the shadow, Gwen rotated her body enough that she was facing the fort...and looking into the barrel of a gun less than a foot from her face.

She gasped and froze.

A man she didn't recognize bent down and put the cold iron against her cheek. "Let me guess. You're Gwen."

She didn't move.

"Naughty girl. You were supposed to be up by the ticket booth. Good thing I came down here to take a piss." He grabbed her by the arm and yanked her to her feet. "Hey, Jeremy, your girl's down here." Jamming the gun into her side to hide it from the boaters, the man pulled her back up to the ticket booth. The gun was stuck so far between her ribs it hurt to breathe.

Jeremy stood in its shadows. "Parker, you fucking idiot," he hissed. "What part of 'keep me out of it' don't you understand?"

"*Why*, Jeremy?" Gwen found her voice. "What have I done to you? Why do you want me dead?"

Jeremy wore a black watch cap and a dark jacket. "How did you know that? You were hiding like you knew something was up. Did he tell you?" He jerked his head toward her captor.

Gwen smiled with more calm than she felt. "No, he didn't. A little ghost told me."

"Ha ha. Very funny. As for what you've done to me, you bitch, you fucking stole my job." He was so angry he was spitting out the words. "I've been busting my ass at Flagler for years. I should have been chair. I needed the raise. I can't go anywhere else to teach because this is my home. My family is here." His voice was low but trembled with emotion. "I applied. I interviewed. I did the video presentation. I taught the trial class. Everyone knew me, and yet they chose you, a total stranger, over me. It's disgusting how many asses I've kissed in this city and at the college, yet they still chose you."

"So leave. You could have gotten a job anywhere."

"I can't leave, don't you get it? Pa called me a coward my entire life, but I'm not, I'm *not*. Taking risks isn't for everyone, you know." His voice lifted an octave. "He called me the Wizard of Oz Trilogy—no brain, no heart, no balls!" He poked a furious finger at her. "I'm not, I'm *not*. That's why I'm taking back the job that should have been mine."

Gwen squirmed as Parker's hand tightened painfully around her arm. She tried to see if there were any boats near the fort's sea wall, but the wall was too high. Could she call for help? Out of options, she glared at Jeremy. "Killing me for a job is such a cliché, Jer. You've read too many bad mysteries or watched too many *CSI* episodes. And hiring someone to do your dirty work for you? I didn't think you were such a coward, but I guess your father was right. And here's an idea: If you're hurting that bad for money, why not sell that butt-ugly watch of yours?"

Jeremy thrust it into her face. "Shut your fucking mouth or I'll use the watch to shut it for you."

His threats helped her remember a specific move from a self-defense course she'd taken thirty years ago. She just needed Parker to hold her across the chest instead of by her arm, so she started pulling away, twisting, anything to make it hard for him to maintain his grip.

"Gwen, stop," Jeremy growled. "You're not getting out of this."

Parker finally pulled her back against his chest. Shaking, she took a deep breath for courage then bent over, pulling the man down with her. She jammed her elbow back into his groin, then as he doubled over howling with pain, she did the same to his face. Free, Gwen ran back down toward the sea wall. There were boats everywhere. When she reached a cannon cutout, she began jumping up and down and screaming and waving her arms at the very second that the city and the bridge lit up the sky. Someone had just flipped the switch to officially start Nights of Lights. Cars honked, spectators hooted and clapped, boats tooted their horns, boaters cheered. There was so much noise that Gwen's voice was lost in the cacophony. "No! Here! Help!" She ran farther down the path to the next cutout, waving her arms. "Help!"

A gun pressed against her waist. "Take a good look at the lights, *boss*." Jeremy's voice was right in her ear. "Wouldn't want you to die without having the Nights of Lights experience." He grabbed the base of her neck. "You try that self-defense shit with me and you're dead right here, right now. Got it?"

Gwen nodded, confused as hell about what she should hope for. Should she hope that Billie could somehow help her? Or should she hope that Billie's ghost had gone wherever ghosts go so it wouldn't witness Gwen's failure? Gwen was going to die in the next few minutes, making Billie's sacrifice meaningless.

CHAPTER TWENTY

Gwen, November 18

Gwen stumbled as Jeremy dragged her along the sea wall. "Let's find a more private spot, shall we? Then it's into the river for you."

"You're drowning me? I knew you didn't have the nerve to shoot me, so go ahead. I can swim."

"Not with a few bullets in you."

Gwen was starting to feel more anger than fear. This was Jeremy, the goofy "alien" with the big white teeth and a man not savvy enough understand his watch was ostentatious and ugly. "This is so short-sighted. People on the river have seen us. And besides, what makes you think you'll get the chair position when I'm gone?"

"Because I was first on the list until one of the board of trustees thought it was a good idea to bring in new blood." He gave a nervous laugh. "Sadly, Parker here is going to spill that 'new blood' all over the ground." Parker caught up with them but was walking awkwardly. He spit at Gwen but missed.

They took her to a spot against the fort's northern wall that was mostly in shadow, but to make sure, Parker kicked out the nearest floodlight and now they were entirely in the dark.

"Jeremy, this really isn't necessary. I'm moving back to Minnesota anyway. I won't tell anyone about this."

"Your little girlfriend ever show up?"

"Wife, and no. I don't suppose you had anything to do with that."

"Wish I did, but no and I don't believe you won't tell. If I let you go, the first thing you'll do is call the cops and call the college president. I'd never be chair, I'd lose my job, a job that I love, and end up in jail. No, it's neater if we do it my way." He threw her against the fort wall, the coquina digging into her back and elbows, then motioned to Parker. That's when Gwen pulled out Clayton's unregistered gun, stepped up to Jeremy and jammed the gun into his chest.

Jeremy laughed, then moved so swiftly he had the gun before she even knew what had happened. Her mouth dropped open as she stared at her empty hands. As Billie would have said, *That went well.*

"Pretty cool trick, huh? I saw it on a TV show and practiced until I could do it myself."

Parker chuckled. "I'm impressed, asshole. Didn't think you had any skills."

"Okay, *Gwendolyn*, you are now officially a Dead Woman Walking," Jeremy said, laughing at his joke. "Get over here, up against the wall."

"That's a *curtain*, you fucking moron."

Flustered, Jeremy shoved her into the corner where the bastion connected to the curtain, then he moved against the bastion wall and Parker took up his position along the curtain. They had her cornered.

"Your stupid watch is butt-ugly," she snarled. "And your kid is spoiled, obnoxious, and will end up a drug addict stealing for a hit."

Jeremy raised his gun and used both hands to steady it. "Insulting the guy about to kill you. Interesting tactic."

Gwen closed her eyes. *I'm sorry, Billie. The gun was stupid. Coming here alone was stupid, but I couldn't endanger anyone else. So, so sorry. I love you.*

A bizarre calm settled over her. They were armed, she was not. They were intent on killing her; she realized she probably wouldn't have been able to pull the trigger even if she still had Clayton's gun. Hidden in the fort's cold shadow, she might as well have been on the top of Mount Everest or deep in the Marianas Trench. No one was coming for her. Her life would end tonight.

Oddly, this new reality was less upsetting than she'd thought it would be. Billie was gone. Dad was gone. It was her turn now.

Waiting the few seconds it would take to end her life felt like hours. Why didn't they shoot her? Were they waiting for her to open her eyes? Finally, she opened one eye, then the other. Even with both eyes open she struggled to understand what she was seeing.

"What the fuck?" whispered Parker. His gun was no longer pointing at Gwen, but at a point between Gwen and Jeremy.

"Shit, fuck everything." Jeremy's voice was tight with strain and confusion and his bald head glistened in the dusky shadows. He was no longer pointing his gun at her but was moving it toward Parker. Gwen gaped at the scene. Both men seemed to be in a battle for control of their arms, and of the guns. They had now both pivoted and were aiming directly at each other.

"Holy shit!" Gwen leapt forward when she finally got it. "Billie! Billie!" She looked up the fort wall but could see nothing. "Billie, don't do this," she whispered. "I know you're trying to protect me, and I love you for that, but not this way."

"Don't you dare shoot me, you piss-head motherfucker!" Jeremy's voice shook with fear.

"Something's moving my finger. I can't…" Parker winced with the effort, sweat visible even in the dark. "I can't…I can't…"

Time stopped as both men trembled with the effort *not* to shoot each other. Gwen tried pushing Jeremy's arms in another direction, but he was locked in place. Billie's ghost was just too strong.

After something gently pushed her back against the wall, the guns fired. Gwen screamed.

Parker staggered back, clutching his throat as blood poured through his fingers. His eyes went dead before he hit the ground with a heavy thud, his head bouncing twice.

"No, no," Gwen moaned.

Jeremy lay on his back, blood spurting from a hole in his chest, eyes open. She held a trembling hand over his mouth to feel one long exhale, then nothing.

"Holy shit," Gwen breathed as she sagged against the wall, horrified and relieved at the same time. "Billie," she said. "You shouldn't have done that…but thank you." Her knees were so weak she knew she'd be unable to go for help until she recovered. The men were dead, her fingerprints were on one of the guns, and the fact that the two men shot each other was going to be hard to explain.

As she puzzled out what to do next, the air near her feet grew cold, then slowly moved up her body. The same thing had happened at the old military hospital when the ghostly hands wanted her to look up. On wobbly legs, she stepped back from the fort far enough she could look up, shielding her eyes from the bright lights on the river. There was nothing but the top edge of the fort silhouetted against the dark blue sky.

But when Gwen sighed then looked again, a thread of white smoke swirled above the fort. It grew in strength until it began to take human form. "Billie?"

And there she was, her own Billie, her shape still shifting but enough of her face formed that Gwen could see it was her.

An anguished sob slipped from Gwen's lips as she forced herself to remember that this wasn't Billie. It was her essence, her spirit, all that was left of her. Gwen reached up as if to catch her. "Billie, I love you."

Billie's ghost shaped its wavering hands into a small heart that began to glow a soft red, and Gwen's heart cracked into a million pieces.

As Gwen's heart broke apart, Billie's ghost began to loosen and spread. Then it swirled into a shimmering ball and slowly descended the wall.

Gwen held her hands up, crying out as the now crimson swirls formed a perfect heart almost resting in her hands. Almost too gutted to speak, Gwen managed to croak out, "Thank you."

And just in case her mom had been right about ghosts needing to be released, Gwen whispered, "Time for you to leave, my love. Be at peace."

She held the cool essence of her beloved for another second or two, then through her tears, Gwen watched as the heart loosened, unfurled, then stretched up into slender threads that slowly danced their way higher and higher until they disappeared into the night sky.

CHAPTER TWENTY-ONE

Gwen, November 21–22

Gwen swung the porch swing back and forth with her toe, listening to the sounds of Mason making lunch. She had to admit that it had been helpful having him here, especially during these three days after her "Nights of Lights" experience. He was with her the whole time she was being interviewed by the police. He reminded her that her fingerprints would be found on the gun, so she needed to explain how that came about. He held her at two in the morning when reality slammed into her and she couldn't stop crying. He hadn't, however, forgiven her for ditching him that night. She knew that because at least three times she'd asked him if he'd forgiven her. "Nope, might never happen."

He did, however, admit that he also struggled to forgive himself. After she gave him the slip during the festival, it took him about fifteen minutes to figure out that she'd probably gone to the fort. By the time he jogged over there, the police and ambulance had already arrived.

The police had returned her backpack, which held her sketchbook. Luckily, the afternoon of the Nights of Lights she'd removed all the drawings Billie's ghost had made. On the outside chance that she survived the encounter with Jeremy, the cops would look through her pack and at the sketchbook, and many of the drawings would have been hard to explain.

Sleep had eluded her the last three nights. Every time she closed her eyes she'd seen either Billie's ghost above her on the fort wall, or the swirling heart she'd held in her hands. Sometimes she saw Jeremy's body, or the blood gushing from Parker's throat.

Gwen shuddered and replaced the image with one of Billie laughing. It had been nine days since she'd seen her, and three days since her ghost had "dematerialized," as Kylie had called it, reassuring Gwen that Billie was finally gone, and at peace.

Gwen knew she needed to tell the Lauras about Billie, as well as their other friends, but she had no idea what she would say. She needed to call her stepmother Faye and tell her the news; she'd asked Mason to let her do it, but she kept putting it off.

Mason came in with two plates and put them on the little table. "Lunch is served," he said. "I make a mean grilled cheese sandwich."

Gwen forced herself to swallow a few bites for his sake, but then gave up and leaned back in the uncomfortable chair, the hard wooden slats digging into her back. This discomfort was nothing compared to what Billie had gone through to save her.

"You going in to work tomorrow?" Mason asked.

She gave him a sad smile. "I resigned this morning."

Mason groaned. "C'mon, no. After a loss you aren't supposed to make any big decisions or big changes for a year. You're the one who told me that after Dad died."

She shrugged. Mason was right, but this was different. She'd taken the wrong job and brought Billie down here thinking it would be best for her. Instead, it got her killed. Gwen swallowed and wiped her eyes.

"Those eyes leaking again?" Mason said in his attempt to combine both humor and empathy.

"I should never have taken the job. I'm so done with teaching and I knew that."

"You going to move back to St. Paul?"

Gwen nodded. "Our friends are there. You and Faye aren't far away." She took another bite. "But I am going to wait until spring.

I need to be here for a while, need to spend time at the fort to make sure she's really and truly gone."

"What are you going to do for money?"

"Walt needs someone to fill in for Billie, so I'm going to do that." She exhaled sadly. "Boy, that was hard explaining the whole story to Walt."

"Did you tell him the truth, or the version you told to the cops, that Billie left you and moved to Mexico?"

"I didn't want him to think badly of Billie, so I told him the truth. But how can people take the news of time travel so calmly?" She put down her sandwich, unable to eat. "Mase, why did you come here? I'm glad you did, but your 'will' story was a lie. Are you in some sort of trouble?"

Mason pressed his lips together then shook his head.

"Then why?"

He rubbed the top of his crew cut so hard the bristles stood at attention. He sighed. "I missed you...both of you."

"But—"

He held up one hand. "I know I sort of disappeared after college, but I was excited about being out on my own without Mom and your dad helping me, without you and Billie keeping me company. I was also ashamed about dropping out, but nothing at school felt right. I *still* don't know what I want to be when I grow up, so it's been a hard ten years. But I'm okay. I just really missed hanging out with you guys...but I was too embarrassed to admit that, so I came up with the will thing. Totally lame, right?"

Gwen stood and pulled him onto his feet and into a hug. They clung to each other for a long time. "Not lame at all. I'm so glad you are here." Gwen gave him a quick squeeze then stepped back, wiping her eyes as another wave of missing Billie hit her.

She returned to the porch swing while Mason bussed the dishes, then curled up under Billie's favorite blanket and let another day slip away.

❖

The next morning, she was back on the swing. In fact, she'd never left it other than to relieve herself a few times. She had slept some, off and on, during the night so was feeling a little more human. Mason joined her on the swing. "So, look. I don't know what to do. Should I stay? Would that be helpful? Should I leave? Would you rather be alone?" She loved that he knew to give her options.

She reached for his hand. "Could you stay for a while? If I'm alone I'm just going to drown in my sadness."

Mason nodded, then squeezed her hand. "Seems like you're already doing that."

They sat there in silence, watching a few cars go by, then two kids on little pink bikes. Earl and Sassy got into their car, waving sadly as they drove by. She'd told them the "official" version, that Billie had left her.

Clayton's screen door slammed as he left his house, a huge whiteboard under one arm. Mason stood to call him over, but Clayton was already walking toward them.

"Hey, bro," Mason said, motioning him up onto the porch.

"Dude," Clayton replied.

Gwen rolled her eyes. Men.

Clayton looked at her and blushed pink with shyness. "Do you have a minute?" When she nodded, he pulled over one of the wooden chairs, set it up in front of the swing and carefully placed his white board on the chair. Then he pulled over a chair for himself.

Mason laughed. "I feel like I'm in high school again."

Clayton ignored him and gave Gwen a funny look, half excited, half terrified. "I need to talk to you about time."

She smiled. "I have plenty of that."

He uncapped a black marker and drew a long horizontal line. "Time moves in a line, right? We live one day, then we live the next, and then the next, right?"

"Except for Groundhog Day," she said, thinking of one of Billie's favorite movies about a time loop. "Bill Murray had to live the same day over and over again."

"Right, exactly. But without a Groundhog Day time loop, life is linear, right?"

She nodded, wondering where Clayton was going and what it had to do with her.

"I've read hundreds of books on time travel and watched every movie and TV show that involved time travel and one thing seems to be constant...except for the movie *Time Trap*. That was disturbing as hell." He inhaled, then blew out a huge breath. "Sorry, I gotta focus. Other than *that* stupid movie, time in the past and time in the present move at the same rate. Take Martha, that woman Billie was following." He made a few marks on the whiteboard. "She travels to the present, sells stuff, then goes back to 1837. Time there passes at the same rate that it does here. I talked to Walt and the other antique store owners yesterday. They said Martha wore different clothing each time, so it's not like she was stuck in a time loop. And she was the same age, so hadn't aged from week to week, just like we wouldn't appear to age from week to week."

"Okaaay."

"We don't have proof that time moves at the same rate, but it makes sense, right? Same sun, same planet, same length of days."

Mason chuckled and tapped Gwen's knee. "Sounds like Billie's 'Movie Theater Theory of Time Travel,' doesn't it?"

"Oh, God, not that," Gwen said. "It always made my head hurt."

Clayton kept going, erasing the marks he'd made for Martha. "Okay. Today is November 22." He marked that on the line. "What date did Billie likely go back in time?"

"November 13."

He drew that on the present timeline, then drew an arc reaching back in time. "So that means she landed here, on November 13, 1837, right?"

"That makes sense," Mason agreed.

Clayton tapped his chin with the marker. "She's stuck there, knowing that on November 18, the opening of the light festival, someone is going to harm you. She can't find the portal back, so November 18 passes in 1837 just as it did here. For all she knows, you were murdered that night." He swallowed hard. "Imagine how devastating that would have been."

Gwen blinked fast, determined to not start crying again. "It would have killed her."

"Exactly. But while Billie doesn't know much about 1837, she does have one piece of information."

Mason nodded. "She knows Coacoochee's escape happens on November 22, which is today." His eyes widened so fast Gwen thought he was in pain, but he leapt to his feet. "Holy fucking shit! Oh, my god! Oh, my god! Dude, you're brilliant!" He threw his arms around Clayton and they laughed and jumped up and down as Mason explained Billie's movie theater time travel theory using jargon she didn't understand.

"Hey, guys, you've left me behind."

Clayton, so excited he was almost giggling, sat back down. "I *love* this 'Movie Theater Theory of Time Travel.' It's the perfect metaphor. We are pretty sure that Billie arranges things so Coacoochee kills her the night of November 22." He tapped today's date. "Today is November 22. That means the murder hasn't happened yet. The 1837 movie is still running, but the murder hasn't happened yet."

Gwen's stomach cramped. "You mean that she hasn't been killed yet? That doesn't make any sense. She was killed over one hundred and eighty years ago."

Mason waved his arms in frustration. "You have to stop thinking so linearly. Don't you remember Billie and Laura B's theory? When a person has access to time travel, that basically means that all time periods happen simultaneously, like the Cineplex movies all running at the same time. That means she won't be murdered until *tonight*." Mason grabbed her hands and started jumping up and down. "Gwen, Gwen! Don't you get it? We can go back in time and stop the murder. We can save Billie."

"But if we stop Coacoochee from killing her, then Billie won't be able to become a ghost and save me." Her head hurt.

"She's already saved you. You survived that night. That part of the movie's over."

"I still don't get it."

Mason paced the small porch, which proved to be too confining so they all three poured down the steps and both Clayton and Mason paced the driveway. Gwen stood, her arms wrapped around her chest, struggling to understand.

Mason ran through Billie and Laura's theory again, which served to confuse her and charge up Clayton, who started hopping around the yard. "Yes! Yes! You're fucking brilliant, man!" Laughing, Mason defended himself from Clayton's ecstatic punches.

Clayton stopped and checked the time. "It's ten a.m. now and it gets dark around five. This means you have seven hours to get back there, find Billie, and get her out of harm's way."

Gwen buried her face in her hands. "My brain is going to explode, right here, right now, all over both of you."

Mason pulled her hands down and squeezed them. "I know, I know. Let's try one more time. The events of 1837 happened. Billie died. Her ghost waited for you. The two of you defeated Jeremy. He's gone. Dead."

Gwen nodded so he continued. "But time travel means you get to switch theaters and return to the 1837 movie. You can go back there, find Billie and bring her back to the present, to this very moment. The movies don't run backwards, only forwards. Jeremy will still. Be. *Dead*."

Something warm and bubbly began working its way up Gwen's chest and throat. "We could save Billie? She doesn't have to die?"

"We pull her out of the 1837 movie before she dies. We switch movie theaters."

The bubbly feeling blossomed into a fountain of hope. Gwen yanked him into her arms then they jumped up and down together like little kids. "Billie could live! We could save her! Holy shit! Holy fucking shit! Oh, my god! My god!"

Clayton was grinning and crying at the same time. "Let's do this!"

But then Mason pulled back and folded himself in half with an anguished groan. He straightened, his face white with grief. "We don't know where the portal is for returning to the present. Anyone who goes back to save Billie will have to stay there with her." He straightened. "I'll go. I'm kind of a fuck-up in the twenty-first century. Maybe I'll have better luck back in the nineteenth."

Gwen's mind spun with all that Clayton and Mason had laid out. She could save Billie, just as Billie had saved her. They could keep going, keep loving each other, keep supporting and entertaining and needing each other. She held up a hand to stop Mason. "So I could go to the fort right now, throw myself against the time portal in the wall, and be back in 1837? I could stop Coacoochee from killing her?"

Clayton was so excited he bounced on his toes. "Yes. You can save Billie."

"But once I do, we're both stuck back there. We cannot get back to the present, so we'll have to leave the fort and find some place to live in that time period?"

Clayton nodded. "Yup. But you don't want to interrupt things with Coacoochee too early. That just allows too much time for things to go wrong. You should go back, find a place to hide, then interrupt things just in time. That way you won't interfere with Coacoochee and his men escaping. Their escape is necessary for the original history to remain intact. He plays a huge role in eluding the US Army and keeping some of the Seminoles in Florida."

"I'll go with you," Mason said.

She smiled at him. "No, your mom needs you. I'm going to do this alone." She looked at them. "But I am going to need some help."

CHAPTER TWENTY-TWO

Gwen, November 22

Kylie came over as soon as Clayton called. She was so excited that Gwen might be able to save Billie that she was shaking. "You are so brave," she said. "I'm not sure I'd be able to do what you're doing."

Gwen's throat tightened. She wasn't sure *herself* if she could do it. "You're sure you don't need this skirt?" She held up a long, black skirt that Kylie was insisting she wear to blend in better.

"To be blunt, it's an ugly skirt, so I'm sure."

"Okay, thanks." Gwen had a gray and black tunic she could wear that looked sort of retro…not 1837 retro, but it was the best she could do. She would bring a heavy wool sweater, some underwear for both of them, and warm socks. Florida winter nights were cool.

"Before you leave, as the president of SAPS, I just have to ask. Since Billie's ghost ascended, have you seen any ghosts like you did on the ghost tour?"

Gwen closed her eyes against the pain of those last moments with the ghost. If she couldn't save Billie from death by sword tonight, then Billie would be truly gone…and Gwen would be stuck back in 1837 all alone. "No, I haven't seen any more ghosts. I think they may be done with me."

Kylie gave her a quick hug. "I'm glad to hear it."

Clayton interrupted to hand her two prescription bottles. "Antibiotics," he said. "You'll need these in case of infections."

Gwen bit back a smile when she noticed that Clayton couldn't stop blushing whenever Kylie was in the room. Now if the guy would just get over his shyness enough to *say* something.

"Is Austin in school?" Gwen asked.

"Yes, I haven't told him what you're planning. He was devastated enough when Billie disappeared. He's going to be very sad when he learns that you have followed her…back to 1837." She laughed, her eyes crinkling in the corners. "So weird to be talking about time travel as if it's normal and real and done every day."

"No kidding." First ghosts, now time travel. She was living in the Upside Down.

Her brother and her friends kept her busy all day gathering things she might need for a better life in 1837. Soon her backpack was full of vitamins and protein bars and dried mangos and mixed nuts. At one point, when she noticed Earl and Sassy returning home, she excused herself and ran across the street. "I have a huge favor to ask," she said.

Sassy gave her a surprisingly vigorous hug given her age. "Anything, my dear."

"I need you to witness my will."

Earl's eyes widened behind his square black frames. "Now?"

"Could we step inside for a minute? I don't want my brother to see this."

Inside, Gwen pulled out a folded piece of paper from her back pocket and asked for a pen. Then she wrote *Last Will and Testament of Gwendolyn Sarah Tucker. I leave all my possessions, including my home in St. Augustine, all my bank accounts, investments, and my car, to my stepbrother, Mason J. Henderson of Winona, Minnesota. Signed today, November 22, 2025, and witnessed by Earl Washington and Sassy Washington.*

"Now if you could both sign this and put your contact information below your name, I'd appreciate it."

Sassy scowled at the paper. "You going somewhere?"

Gwen chuckled. "No, but now that…now that Billie has…left me, I'm just trying to be prepared in case anything happens." She hadn't told them that Billie had died instead of leaving her…but now she realized what a good choice that had been. No one needed to know the truth. Gwen and Billie would just disappear and be a mystery forever.

Both Earl and Sassy signed the paper, but when Sassy tried to give it back to her, Gwen held up her hand. "Would you mind hanging on to it…in case something happens?"

Earl rested a heavy hand on her shoulder. "I know you're sad that Billie left, but, kid, life is still worth living."

She looked into the man's concerned eyes. "No, no, Earl. Not to worry. I'm not going to do anything like that. I just want to make sure Mason gets my estate, small as it is."

After giving each of them a quick hug, Gwen hurried back across the street. Luckily, Mason didn't ask what she was up to. He would have protested if he'd known what she'd just done.

Gwen moved through the hours in a sort of fog, focusing on dealing with the items on her list rather than on the concept that she was about to travel back in time 187 years and would be living out the remainder of her life there. She could do it with Billie at her side. They would find jobs, a little house to rent. They would build a new life together in a new place and a new time. But if Gwen failed to find Billie in time to stop her from sacrificing herself, then Gwen would be doing all of that alone. She had a paralyzing flash of panic when she realized that no one in 1837 was going to need an expert on the American Civil War, which wouldn't happen for another twenty-four years. Did she even have enough knowledge of the 1830s to be able to invest or bet on events in order to have enough money to survive? She gave Mason the task of researching the time period and downloading relevant dates and events.

At four p.m., Clayton stood. "Okay, it's time. It'll be dark soon, and the fort closes at five."

Gwen's pulse raced and she wanted nothing more than to change her mind, to unpack her bags, return the skirt and the antibiotics, pour herself a glass of Merlot and watch *Kate and Leopold*, and all of Billie's other time travel favorites. She'd even watch *The Abyss* again; anything to delay things. This was crazy. Absolutely insane.

"Okay," she said. "Let's go." Billie didn't hesitate when it came to doing what was necessary to save Gwen, so Gwen sure as hell wasn't going to flinch once she realized she had the chance to save Billie. After they parked, Kylie handed Gwen a red wig with long flowing curls and a pair of purple reading glasses. "You're banned, so you need a disguise."

Laughing, Gwen jammed on the wig and traded her glasses for the readers, which blurred her vision instead of correcting it. She clung to Mason's elbow so she wouldn't fall.

The park ranger at the fort's ticket booth looked at them strangely when all four of them wanted the fifteen-dollar tickets. "But we close in twenty minutes."

"That's okay," Clayton said. "We just want to take a few pictures."

The man studied both Kylie and Gwen, then looked at something tacked up by his window. "Ah, forget the fees. But be back out in fifteen minutes." Relieved, they jogged for the entrance. The disguise had worked.

The fort was quiet that late in the afternoon. No groups of school children, no rangers giving guided tours, no men in period uniforms setting off the cannons. The sun had sunk so low in the sky that it was no longer visible. The twinkling lights on the bridge had already come on.

Gwen felt lightheaded as they entered the fort, and she returned the wig and glasses to Kylie. She had to save Billie. But time travel…would it hurt? Would she see anything or feel anything? She'd quizzed Clayton and Mason, but both had sadly shrugged. "All we know about time travel is what authors have made up," Clayton said. "But it can't be that painful or Martha wouldn't have done it several times a week."

Kylie led them around the edge of the courtyard, past the restrooms, and into the corner room. It was mostly empty except for a framed display about repairs done to the fort, and an old wagon. That room led to a smaller, darker room, which led to a tiny alcove with information about the powder magazine. A small opening, no more than four feet high and four feet wide, was actually a short tunnel that led into the final room. "We go through here," Kylie said. She immediately dropped into a crouch and crab-walked through the tunnel. Clayton, too tall for that, crawled on his knees. Mason swept his arm toward the opening. "After you."

Gwen crouched down and shuffled through, grimacing at her protesting muscles. She used the gray metal bar bolted to the tunnel for support. Once through the tunnel, she managed to unfold herself and stand without too much groaning. The small vault was built like a barrel, with two end walls and a low concave ceiling. "Austin thought the drawing shows this wall." Kylie pointed to the far wall. "If it had been the wall at this closer end, the tunnel entrance would have shown up in the ghost's drawing."

The room was hot, moist, and with the four of them, crowded. The blocks of coquina were dark and discolored and had been repaired many times with smears of concrete and plaster, which had fallen off in places to reveal bricks in one area, and a block of coquina in another.

They stared at the wall that Kylie had indicated. It looked like a normal, solid, hurt-if-you-threw-yourself-against-it wall. Mason pulled a small rock out of his pocket and threw it against the wall. It bounced back onto the floor.

"What?" Gwen moaned. "Why won't it work?"

Clayton picked up the rock, took a step back, and hurled it as hard as he could against the wall.

Without a sound, the rock disappeared into the wall.

"Shit," Mason said, his face drawn, his eyes red. "No, no. Gwen, I'm sorry. You can't do this. This is just too real, too scary, too much."

"We need to watch the time," Clayton said. "It's getting dark, so Coacoochee's escape could happen anytime. You need to find a place to hide near the entrance so you can pull Billie aside before Coacoochee and his sword come for her."

Gwen hugged Clayton, then Kylie, thanking them both for all their help. Then she threw her arms around Mason. He sobbed into her neck. "No, please don't go."

"I love you, little brother," she whispered in his ear.

Then she turned, and as if in a dream, before she gave in to the fear pounding through her body, Gwen backed up to give herself a running start. This was going to hurt if she wasn't moving fast enough to break into the portal. She hiked up the skirt and tucked it into her waistband so her legs were free. The others moved aside to clear her a path.

No. She couldn't do this. It was insane. Then she heard her father's voice in her head. *Courage, kiddo.*

She slowly inhaled then exhaled. She would never see her dad's grave again. And she should have made one phone call before taking this one-way trip to 1837, but it was too late now. If she hesitated, she might change her mind. *Courage, kiddo.*

"Thanks, Dad," Gwen whispered. "You're right. This is for Billie. She's worth the risk." Gwen dashed across the room, digging into the concrete floor with her sneakers. At the last moment, she wrapped her arms around her torso, twisted, then flung herself as hard as she could against the solid wall.

CHAPTER TWENTY-THREE
Billie, November 22

B illie opened her eyes but closed them immediately. If she was awake, that meant she had to get up, spend the day quivering in fear, then go through with her plan to be murdered tonight by a desperate and escaping Seminole man. She couldn't blame Coacoochee, since he'd actually be doing her a favor. She'd tried again to convince Nathaniel to murder her, but he refused. "I thought you were my friend," she snapped. He'd muttered a long string of obscure 1837 curse words and wouldn't talk to her for hours.

She also felt the weight of what might have happened four nights ago, November 18, in her own time. Had Jeremy lured Gwen to the fort? Had he and his accomplice murdered her as the drawings had shown?

She shook her head. No. She had the power to stop things, to change the timeline. Once she became a ghost, she would help Gwen draw images that would warn her about Jeremy. Billie would make sure there was a happy ending to the night of November 18, if it was the last thing she did...and it would be. She had to be murdered inside the fort to ensure she haunted it, but she had no knowledge of 1837 except that Coacoochee would escape tonight, November 22. She had no choice but to use what she knew.

Billie opened her eyes again.

"You awake?" Nathaniel asked, his voice gravelly with sleep.

"No." She felt oddly calm, at least in this moment. She was in charge now, not her algophobia, not her agoraphobia. She knew how this day had to end, and that ending was her choice and no one else's.

"You don't have to do this, you know."

Oh, but she did. The pain of being murdered would be nothing compared to the pain of a world without Gwen in it. She rolled onto her side and sat up. "Let's go find some breakfast."

The courtyard was blissfully empty, so they were able to walk through it unnoticed. The officers were either idiots who had no idea she and Nathaniel were squatting there or they didn't care. She suspected it was the latter. Even though the Army was actively fighting the Seminoles, the fort was nothing more than a storage closet for the Army since Seminoles weren't considered a threat to the fort or to St. Augustine. Other than the lovely weather, there was little to recommend life in St. Augustine in 1837 so she understood the officers' apathy.

The officers and their men were working outside on the north lawn rebuilding one of the defensive walls set into the grounds. Nathaniel had tried to explain the walls' purpose, but she'd waved him off. All she lived for was warning Gwen. Overhearing Jeremy and the other man plotting had been a gift, but one she'd been unable to share before falling back in time. Without those few moments of conversation, and Nathaniel's help in hearing the voice well enough to identify it, she wouldn't have had enough information to warn Gwen. But she did—she had the day, the place, the man. She had to get that information to Gwen.

Nathaniel had suggested one night as they were falling asleep that perhaps her attitude was wrong, that she should value her own life, accept she was here in this time, and go ahead and live her life.

She did stop a minute and think about that. Was Nathaniel right? Should she just let go of her life in the twenty-first century— now lost to her thanks to her inability to find the return portal—and embrace the present? She was in the south, which at this point in history was doubling down on its commitment to enslave as many people as possible. To get out of the region she'd have to pass as a man because women didn't and couldn't travel alone. She'd have to find a job, a place to stay. She'd have to hide who she was and never let her guard down. She'd have to become an abolitionist because it would be unethical not to. But she'd have to make sure she never stood out, never did anything that could alter the timeline.

The whole thing just made her tired. Billie was fifty-five years old and had lived a good life. She had no regrets, but also no clear goals for the future. The agoraphobia had pretty much taken care of any thoughts of a normal future. And if she chose not to face Coacoochee tonight but accepted life here, there were one thousand percent more sources of pain to fear. Her algophobia had taken a little vacation because life this last week had been so freaking strange that it took all her energy to feed herself and stay out of the way, but it was still there, living under her skin.

Besides, she owed Gwen so much, not only for the last few years of Billie's mental breakdown, but for the last twenty-five years. Those years had been rich with experiences and adventures and love. She wasn't going to turn her back on them, or on Gwen. No, she was doing the right thing. She would go through with it.

Billie spent her last day with Nathaniel. She did a few odd jobs in exchange for some bread and a hunk of dried beef. Nathaniel talked a storekeeper out of an old jug of ale so they had something almost drinkable to wash down the beef. They sat on a pile of logs next to the river and watched the soldiers digging around the fort.

"You haven't answered my question," Nathaniel said, taking another swig out of the jug.

Billie sighed. "No, you *can't* help. You need to stay hidden. I don't want Coacoochee to hurt you too." She closed her eyes for a second as memories of past pains made her skin crawl. "But when Coacoochee and his men have left...I would like some company.

I've never thought much about dying, but I always assumed I wouldn't die alone."

"You want me to watch you die."

"I want you to sit by me and talk to me and…" She inhaled deeply. "If I'm in a great deal of pain, I would like you to end it for me."

"How?"

"Cover my nose and mouth so I can't breathe. It would be the humane thing to do."

Nathaniel shook his shaggy head. "That's murder."

"Yes, but also compassion. In this time period, no one recovers from the type of wound Coacoochee will inflict with that sword. And besides, I don't want to recover, remember?"

He nodded. "I'll consider it."

At one point, as they sat by the river, a figure waved to them from a nearby street and jogged toward them. It was Martha's nephew.

"I've been looking for you," he said as he bent over, gasping for air. "I wanted to thank you for the money." He nodded at Billie. "Gonna use it to get to the Oklahoma Territory and find my woman. She's Seminole and had to leave the area."

Billie leapt to her feet. "What's your name?"

He shyly offered his hand. "Anthony Tucker, but you can call me Tony."

Anthony Tucker. Billie grinned. This was Gwen's ancestor from Oklahoma. "And what's your girlfriend's name?"

He rattled off a Seminole word then shrugged. "My aunt refused to learn the name, so she just called her Mary." With a shy wave, Anthony Tucker left them.

Billie shook her head, laughing. Gwen *did* have Seminole in her ancestry, but that no longer mattered since neither Coacoochee nor any of his tribe were the ghost.

She was the ghost and the idea terrified her. What if she failed? What if she couldn't last 187 years? What if she gave up? Then Jeremy Wilkinson would murder Gwen.

Evening came so quickly that Billie wondered if they'd leapt ahead in time sitting there on the logs. She mentally ran through her plan again. The pile of wooden crates stored outside the officers' barracks would be the perfect place for Nathaniel to hide during the…the confrontation. For the hundredth time, she rubbed the key in her pocket, the one Nathaniel had stolen from the coat an officer had carelessly left draped over a barrel. With this she would unlock Coacoochee's cell. She'd watched to make sure she knew which cell he entered after exercising in the courtyard.

They heard the officers yell to the soldiers working outside the fort that it was time for some "grub," which meant not a hot meal but bread and cold beef. As the food was distributed and the men sat down to eat, Billie straightened and tapped Nathaniel on the leg. "Once the men are done and go inside, that's our cue." She felt odd, as if watching a car crash but not being able to do anything about it. She was heading straight for her death, on purpose. Fear made her so light-headed that a few times she thought she might pass out.

She and Nathaniel brought up the rear as the last of the soldiers, some his friends, entered the fort. The friends hurried them into their usual hiding spot, then left. Billie didn't know exactly what time the Seminoles started their escape, but she had to unlock the cell door before they were committed to escaping through the window.

Dusk slid into evening, the darkness broken only by a handful of torches up on the gun deck and one at the entrance to the sally port. "Time to go," she whispered. She gathered up the two swords she'd stolen, also from the officers' barracks, and wrapped them in her blanket, which she would no longer need.

Most of the men were up on the gun deck, drinking and singing in the cool night air. A quick glance into the sally port showed Billie that the officers were in their barracks, the door closed, probably doing the same thing as their men, minus the singing. Light from an oil lamp leaked around the officers' door and illuminated the dirt floor. Billie put Nathaniel's hand on the stack of crates. "Hide yourself on the other side of these crates and *stay* there." She wished she could tuck him safely into their little room, but Billie needed to be at the entrance and Nathaniel insisted on being nearby.

After he was in place, Billie walked around the outer edge of the courtyard until she came to the cells. Until traveling back to a time without electricity, she hadn't known that the night wasn't totally black. With time, her eyes adjusted and she could see shapes and items and people, which was why Billie could see where she was going.

Gentle snores came from inside the first cell, her target. Billie unwrapped the swords and quietly placed one right next to the cell door. Her hands were now shaking so badly she almost couldn't insert the key into the lock, but she managed to get it in and turn it. The lock made such a loud clank she was sure someone would hear…but then she remembered she *needed* someone in the cell to hear it so they'd know that leaving through the door was an option.

She removed the key and whirled around, racing for the sally port where she dropped the key and ran to the entrance. Trembling, she raised the sword then turned to face the dark hallway. Determination kept her planted in place despite her fear. She was not turning back. This was for Gwen. Everything was for Gwen.

Unexpectedly, furious whispering broke out behind the stack of crates where Nathaniel was hiding. Then grunting and cursing and something fell against the crates. What the hell? He was alone back there. Nathaniel gasped and cursed under his breath, then moaned.

A figure stepped out from behind the crates. "Billie, you need to come here."

Billie's mouth dropped open. Was fear causing her to hallucinate? "Gwen?"

It was Gwen! Dressed in an ugly long skirt and the tunic she'd bought at an art fair years ago. Gwen was here? But how?

Gwen grabbed the sword's handle and pulled it out of Billie's hands. "Seriously, you're going to hurt someone with that. C'mon." She tugged on Billie's arm.

Billie locked her legs. "No, I can't. I have to do this so I can warn you."

"There's no time to explain." Gwen pulled harder.

"No, I have to do this." That Gwen was here, beside her, touching her, made no sense at all. She *must* be hallucinating.

Cursing, Gwen put the sword on the crates and grabbed Billie around the waist. "You've already saved me. The threat is over. I'm gonna be really pissed if I traveled back in time just to watch you die. *C'mon.* We're moving to a different movie theater."

"We're *what?*" Billie dug in her heels, but Gwen was strong enough to pull the much-taller Billie behind the crates, where Nathanial was on his knees, clutching his private parts. Gwen fell back against the wall and Billie collapsed on top of her. But before she could rise, she heard the Seminoles scuffing softly across the dirt floor.

"No, no!" Billie fought against Gwen and struggled to sit up, but Gwen's arms were like steel rods around her. The footsteps faded as the Seminoles fled the building. Billie shook with shock and fury. Gwen had just ruined *everything*, a destruction as earthshattering as if the walls of the fort had collapsed around them. If she caught up with Coacoochee maybe he'd still attack her. Billie twisted harder in Gwen's arms.

"Stop moving and listen," Gwen whispered into her ear. "You need to trust me. You went through with this in the original timeline. Coacoochee murdered you. You became a ghost that haunted the fort for 187 years until I showed up and you began drawing through me."

Billie's mind struggled to catch up. She wasn't dead. Gwen was holding her in her arms.

"Between your drawings and a message you gave Austin, I realized Jeremy was the one planning to harm me. Long story, but he didn't shoot me. Your ghost took care of things. But that happened three days ago."

Nathaniel stirred. "Sorry, Billie, I tried to stop her." His voice was strained. Gwen must have really bashed his balls.

"We need to get out of this fort," Gwen said. "At some point someone is going to realize Coacoochee and the others are gone, and all hell is going to break loose."

Billie sat up and changed her position so she was facing Gwen. "We can leave the fort, but we can't leave 1837." She stroked Gwen's cheek. "I couldn't find the return portal. We're stuck here."

Gwen nodded, then her smile lit up the darkness around them. "I only bought a one-way ticket so it works out just fine."

Billie sat back, stunned. "*Wait.* You knew you couldn't get back to the future, yet you still came?"

Gwen leaned her forehead against Billie's, her warm breath convincing Billie this was real. "Mason figured all this out, along with Clayton, our not-so-scary-anymore neighbor. Everyone wanted to help, but since it was one-way, I insisted on being the only one to travel through time. How could I not? You save me, then I save you. Pretty slick, huh?"

Billie kissed her. "You are, hands down, the bravest woman on the planet and I'm the smartest because I married you."

Gwen flushed with emotion, then smiled. "Oh, my god. I just fell again."

"What?"

Nathaniel leaned closer with a soft moan. "Sorry to interrupt, but Billie did not tell me that women in the future are so strong and aggressive. I may never walk normally again."

Billie heard the humor in his voice. "Gwen, meet my new best friend, Nathaniel Brush. Nathaniel, this is my wife, Gwendolyn Tucker, great-great-granddaughter of the young man we met this afternoon."

"Unbelievable," Nathaniel murmured as they shook hands at an awkward angle, both smiling.

"I'm sorry about your privates," Gwen said.

Billie shook her head with wonder. "I just can't believe you're here, and that you came back knowing there was no way to get back to the future."

"But there is!" someone whispered loudly.

The three of them looked at each other. None of them had spoken. Then a head poked around the corner of the crates. "Austin?"

Billie squeaked. "Jesus Christ, Gwen, you brought Austin back with you?"

"I didn't. What the hell are you doing here?"

"Let's save that for later. I found the portal. C'mon, it's right here. It's the door, the actual door of the fort. Freaky, huh?"

Billie and Gwen stood, as did Nathaniel. "Austin, you're serious? You know how to get home?"

The kid grinned like he'd found the cure for cancer. "Done it twice already today."

Billie grabbed Nathaniel by the shoulders. "Come with us."

"To the time of aggressive women?"

"Again, sorry," Gwen whispered.

"We know a doctor who can fix your eyes. You'll be able to see again. Blacksmiths are in great demand because few people have that skill in our time. You could create sculptures all day long." She shook him gently. "Come with us."

Nathaniel wiped his eyes and appeared to have trouble speaking. He finally managed. "I would be honored to accompany you."

Austin led them to the wooden door, which was open against the wall. "Same as with the portal to the past. You really have to throw yourself at the door. You'll land out there, on the bridge."

"Austin, you first,' Billie said. "Then Gwen, then Nathaniel, then me."

Billie felt lighter than goose down as she watched all three of them disappear into the door. She looked around, amazed she was still alive. That's when she realized the time here had changed her. She felt stronger, more capable, and sure of herself and what she could do. Anyone willing to be impaled on a sword for love was a pretty cool chick. Fuck algophobia. Fuck agoraphobia. Billie took a few steps back, then threw herself at the door.

CHAPTER TWENTY-FOUR

Gwen, November 22

By the time Billie landed on the bridge with a thump and a small groan, Gwen and Austin had Nathaniel on his feet. He was almost too excited to stand on his own, however. "The smells. All different. And look at the city. It's lit with a thousand torches, so many even *I* can see them."

Gwen felt a rush of affection for this total stranger, a man who had clearly helped Billie survive her time in the past. She also felt a nearly overwhelming sense of relief and happiness to be back in the twenty-first century. Yes, white supremacists had taken control of Congress, and democracy was under attack, but the world held cars and refrigerators and planes and pizza. It held diversity and marriage equality and peace treaties and Ted Lasso. Life just wasn't nearly as bad as she'd thought. Time to appreciate more, time to be grateful for the life she led.

Austin leaned over the railing of the bridge they were standing on, and looked down. "The gate at the end of this bridge is locked, so we can't exit that way. Instead we need to climb down from here into the dry moat." He reached into his backpack and pulled out a rope ladder, the kind people kept in their houses to escape from fires. He hooked it over the railing, then let it drop. "It's only about five feet down." He went over, then Billie. They stood below and steadied the ladder while Nathaniel, then Gwen, made their way down into the moat.

Pleased with himself, Austin packed up his ladder then led them along the grassy moat to the sandy area by the seawall, then up around the ticket booth. And just like that, they were walking down the sidewalk away from the fort, as if they'd just come from a tour instead of the nineteenth century.

Of course, Gwen hadn't driven to the fort, since she hadn't expected to return, so they had no way to get home. Austin called Kylie, holding the phone away from his face as she yelled at him. "Where are you? I've been looking for hours!"

"Aunt Kylie, I'm at the fort. Please come pick us up."

"Us?"

"Hey, Kylie," Billie and Gwen said at the same time.

"Oh, my lord! Don't anyone move."

When Kylie arrived ten minutes later, she tumbled out of the car and grabbed Austin into a hug, then started shaking him. "Why? What? And don't you ever do that again, whatever it was that you did!" When Austin started to explain, she held up her hand. "Let's save the full story for Clayton and Mason. They're waiting back at the house." She hugged Billie and Gwen together, then Billie introduced Nathaniel.

They all packed into Kylie's SUV, Nathaniel in the front seat, the rest of them in the back. Austin was so excited to show the twenty-first century to Nathaniel that he turned into a tour guide, leaning forward through the gap between the seats to point out landmarks the poor man couldn't see, explain stop lights and neon lights, and share all his favorite TV shows that Nathaniel must "absolutely binge-watch" with him. For his part, Nathaniel gripped the sides of his seat as the car went much faster than any horse and buggy. He murmured in surprise at Austin's explanations but seemed to grow calmer the more he witnessed. Gwen wasn't sure she'd be as accepting if she ended up 187 years in the future.

Gwen smiled as Austin talked. The one thing she couldn't stop doing was holding Billie's hand and gazing at her, safe, alive, and back where she belonged.

When Kylie parked in the driveway, Mason flew from the house and pulled both Gwen and Billie from the car, hugging them. "I can't believe this, I can't believe this."

Billie squeezed him tight. "Thanks for figuring all this out. I hear I have you to thank."

Mason was too choked up to answer, so Billie introduced Nathaniel, then said softly to both Nathaniel and Mason, "We need to hear everyone's story, but my new friend here hasn't had a bath in…how long?"

"Months."

Mason's nose wrinkled. "Never would have guessed it."

"Could you show him how the shower works, and maybe find something of yours he could wear?"

"C'mon, bro, let's get you cleaned up." Gwen threw a grateful look Mason's way and he grinned. "I'm just so freaking happy you're back."

They all ended up in Clayton's kitchen as he baked two Papa Murphy's pizzas he'd had in the freezer. Nathaniel now smelled like lavender soap and wore Mason's pants and T-shirt. They'd planned to eat outside around the campfire, but Nathaniel was so excited about the brightness of indoor lighting that they sat around the kitchen table instead so he could at least see some shapes. Clayton didn't take his eyes of Nathaniel, clearly enchanted that a man from almost two hundred years in the past sat in his kitchen. "I can't believe I live in a world where time travel is possible. It blows my mind?"

Nathaniel squinted at Clayton. "Blows your mind?"

They laughed at his confusion, but Clayton leaned forward. "I have *so* much to teach you."

"Me too," Austin chimed in.

"How are you liking this century so far?" Kylie asked.

Nathaniel had just taken his first bite of pepperoni pizza and chewed in amazement. After he swallowed, he said, "I'm not in the twenty-first century, I'm in heaven." He wolfed down the piece and reached for another.

Kylie turned to her nephew. "Okay, Austin, everyone's had time to adjust, and it's nearly midnight so way past your bedtime. Time to explain what you did, where you went, and why you have a goose egg on your forehead."

He sat up straighter and beamed. "I figured out yesterday that Coacoochee wasn't escaping until tonight, which meant there was still time to save Billie." He looked down at the table. "I thought I'd be the one to save her, but Gwen did that."

Kylie tapped the table. "You're skipping over the part where you went back in time without knowing where the return portal was."

Austin grinned. "Oh, yeah. I figured you'd be upset by that. But I knew the layout of the current fort. I knew the layout of the fort before each of its major renovations and restorations, so I was pretty sure I could figure it out. This morning instead of going to school I went to the fort, found the portal in the powder magazine, and just *fell* back in time. It was freaking awesome, but also a little scary. I started walking around, trying to look like I belonged there, trying to find the return portal.

"I finally realized that the only part of the fort that never changed, besides the outer walls, was the entrance, so I threw myself against the door, and pop! I'm back in my own time. I made the round trip a few more times, then went looking for Billie to stop her from getting skewered."

"What happened?" Kylie asked softly.

Austin flushed. He touched the raised bump on his forehead and grimaced. "By then it was dark and I was moving so fast I didn't see the shelf sticking out from one of the walls. Knocked myself out cold. When I finally came to, I stepped out into the courtyard and saw Coacoochee and his men escaping, but I was too far away to do anything." He winced, looking at Billie. "If Gwen hadn't been there, you would have been murdered."

Billie squeezed his shoulder. "But that didn't happen."

Austin nodded. "Once the Seminoles were gone, I snuck along the outside of the courtyard. I expected to find your body in the sally port, but then I heard all this whispering and recognized your voices. That's when I popped into the picture and brought everyone back through the portal in the door."

Kylie put down the pizza she was eating. "Two things: One, you're a hero, kid. Without you our friends would never have made it back. Two, you're grounded for a year." Her nostrils flared. "Maybe two."

Austin yelped, then relaxed when everyone laughed.

"Wait. One more thing, and this is serious." She pulled Austin to his feet and grabbed him by the shoulders. "You are not, under any circumstances, for any reason, for any person, to ever, ever again use that time portal."

"Oh, come on. *Really?*"

Kylie shook him and her knuckles were white. "Never, ever again."

The whole group held their breath, understanding that Kylie was right. A teenager moving through time? No. Just *no*.

Austin's shoulders dropped and he sighed. "I promise."

Gwen understood how Austin felt. Now that they knew the way back to the present, she could see how the portal could lure anyone interested in history.

"Hey!" Billie slapped the table in front of Gwen. "I know what you're thinking, you freaking history buff. I need the same promise from you. No using the portal."

Gwen sighed with happiness to have Billie back. "Oh, come on. *Really?*"

Even Austin laughed at that, but Gwen did promise not to become a time tourist. Then she turned to Mason and Clayton, insisting on the same promise. The two men exchanged a glance, clearly wanting to give time travel a try.

"Mason," Gwen said.

"Okay, I promise."

Gwen glared at Clayton until he ducked his head. "I promise," he said.

Satisfied, Gwen leaned back in her chair, basked in the warmth of her new friends, then sighed. "Well, I guess it's time for me to make a phone call." She looked at Nathaniel. "A phone is how we communicate with people who are far away." She showed him her list of contacts and how she just had to touch the screen.

Three rings and a familiar voice answered the phone.

"Hi, Mom," Gwen said.

"Great balls of fire. Gwendolyn. Been a minute since we've talked."

"You could say that." It had been at least a year. Gwen found that the less time they spent talking to each other, the better the relationship. "Two things, Mom. First, have you retired yet?"

"Nope, still at the clinic."

"Still doing surgeries?"

"Of course. My hands are steady as ever, my vision sharper than yours. Why?"

"I have a new friend in need of cataract surgery. His cataracts have gone untreated to the point he's almost completely blind."

"What sort of incompetent doctor lets things get that bad?"

"I'll explain when we see you. Could you squeeze us in next week?"

Gwen could feel her mom trying to tamp down her excitement to not frighten Gwen away. "Wednesday at ten work for you?"

"Perfect. We'll fly up on Monday." Poor Nathaniel wouldn't have much time to adjust to the twenty-first century before finding himself flying at thirty thousand feet, but they needed to fix his eyes.

"What's the second thing?"

Gwen snorted. "Well, this is going to come as surprise, but… well, ghosts are real."

Stunned, her mom said nothing, then burst out laughing. "There'd better be a good story behind that statement."

"And, well, time travel actually is possible."

"Wait, I need to sit down. This is almost too much." Her mom chuckled. "What about aliens?"

Gwen felt herself smile. "Jury's still out on that one. I'll see you next week, okay?" She said good-bye and tapped her phone.

Nathaniel watched her, then shook his head. "Will I ever learn all there is to know?"

"I'll help!" Austin cried.

Not until three a.m. was Nathaniel asleep on their couch, Mason asleep on Clayton's, and Kylie and Austin back home. Billie, freshly showered, sat on the porch swing with Gwen, their arms and legs entwined. "I can't believe how happy I am to be home and touching you."

Gwen nuzzled Billie's neck and sighed. "Me too."

"The History Department vs. the Art Department contest is over, right?"

Gwen nodded, and it finally hit her. Everything was over---the contest, her job, Billie's disappearance, Jeremy's plot.

"Who won? I've been…away."

It felt so good to laugh, something Gwen thought she'd never do again. "I'll say you were 'away.' But the college was so upset by Jeremy's death and the strange circumstances surrounding it that the dean called the whole thing off."

"Whew. You dodged that bullet."

"Why? I ended up with almost enough drawings."

"Yeah, but you would have been disqualified when they learned that I, while a dead person, had drawn many of them."

Gwen chuckled and hugged her tighter. "It's so good to have you back. Life without you was just so wrong."

The swing rocked them in silence until Gwen cleared her throat. "I'm sorry, Billie. This all happened because I made the decision to turn down the history center job without telling you. And then when we moved, I started feeling sorry for myself, and resenting you for a decision that I made."

Billie rested her head on Gwen's shoulder." I'm sorry, too. If I'd tried harder to fight back against the agoraphobia, you wouldn't have felt the need to get me out of winter."

"You can't control a mental illness."

"I know, but there was something in me that just gave up, that took comfort in staying home and disconnecting from the whole world." She pushed the floor with her toe to set them swinging again. "It was like being in the cocoon of the pandemic shutdown, only bigger and more satisfying. If you aren't part of the world then you don't have to worry about fixing it."

"That's a brilliant insight. Also, we were both focusing on the wrong things. You know how my dad used to constantly spout those self-help phrases like a self-help junkie?"

Billie nodded.

"He shared one of his sayings years ago that I didn't understand, but that struck me as something I might need someday so I remembered it. He said 'The grass is always greener...on the side you water the most.'"

Billie laughed. "Oh, my god. That's perfect. I've been watering my fear and my agoraphobia instead of watering our relationship."

"And I've been watering my resentment and anger over taking the wrong job instead of watering our relationship."

Billie sat back. "Well, I guess we need to start paying more attention to us."

"I'd like that."

"It's weird, but I feel like I'm seeing things more clearly than I have in a long time."

"Spending 187 years as a ghost will do that to a person."

"Good point." Billie said with a low chuckle. "Okay, let's summarize our current situation. You don't have a job. I work for minimum wage in an antique store. I'm doing better, as far as my phobias go, so I think we could move back to Minnesota if you wanted to."

Gwen started them swinging again. "I don't know what I want...except..." She reached for Billie's hand. "Except I know that I want *you*. At my fifty-fifth birthday party. At our twenty-fifth anniversary party. At my death bed."

"Yikes. Let's not leap that far ahead, shall we? We can just take this one day at a time."

"Sounds like a plan." Gwen still could not believe Billie was sitting next to her, alive. "I love you," she said.

"I love you too, but I'm afraid I must ask you a few questions." Billie leaned closer and wore her Serious Face.

"Okay." Gwen's heart fluttered at the mock stern look Billie gave her. How could she have ever doubted her love for Billie?

"Ghosts are...what?"

Gwen scowled, but she had no choice. "Ghosts are real."

"Time travel is...what?"

"Possible," Gwen said, laughing. "But I will maintain until the day I die that aliens do *not* live among us."

Billie made a sad face. "Oh, dear. I was just about to admit that I'm not really from North Dakota."

Gwen started giggling so loudly Billie had to hold her close and hush her so they wouldn't wake up Nathaniel, then they swung on the porch swing until the new day arrived.

About the Author

Catherine Friend is the author of the romantic adventures *The Spanish Pearl, The Crown of Valencia, A Pirate's Heart, The Copper Egg*, and *Spark*. She's won six Golden Crown Literary Society Awards and has been a Lambda Literary Award finalist twice. She's also won a Minnesota Book Award, a McKnight/Loft Fellowship, the Alice B. Readers Appreciation Award, and an Independent Book Publishers Association award. In addition to novels, she's written memoirs, nonfiction, and children's books.

She lives in small city on the Mississippi River with her wife and dogs. While she has retired from sheep farming, she doesn't plan to ever retire from writing. When not plotting her next novel, Catherine plays the ukulele, reads tarot cards, and loves swimming laps, although she does so more slowly than an asthmatic turtle.

Website: http://www.catherinefriend.com/

Books Available from Bold Strokes Books

Accidentally in Love by Kimberly Cooper Griffin. Nic and Lee have good reasons for keeping their distance. So why does their growing attraction seem more like a love-hate relationship? (978-1-63679-759-5)

Fatal Foul Play by David S. Pederson. After eight friends are stranded in an old lodge by a blinding snowstorm, a brutal murder leaves Mark Maddox to solve the crime as he discovers deadly secrets about people he thought he knew. (978-1-63679-794-6)

Frosted by the Girl Next Door by Aurora Rey and Jaime Clevenger. When heartbroken Casey Stevens opens a sex shop next door to uptight cupcake baker Tara McCoy, things get a little frosty. (978-1-63679-723-6)

Ghost of the Heart by Catherine Friend. Being possessed by a ghost was not on Gwen's bucket list, but she must admit that ghosts might be real, and one is obviously trying to send her a message. (978-1-63555-112-9)

Hot Honey Love by Nan Campbell. When chef Stef Lombardozzi puts her cooking career into the hands of filmmaker Mallory Radowski—the pickiest eater alive—she doesn't anticipate how hard she falls for her. (978-1-63679-743-4)

London by Patricia Evans. Jaq's and Bronwyn's lives become entwined as dangerous secrets emerge and Bronwyn's seemingly perfect life starts to unravel. (978-1-63679-778-6)

This Christmas by Georgia Beers. When Sam's grandmother rigs the Christmas parade to make Sam and Keegan queen and queen, sparks fly, but they can't forget the Big Embarrassing Thing that makes romance a total nope. (978-1-63679-729-8)

Unwrapped by D. Jackson Leigh. Asia du Muir is not going to let some party girl actress ruin her best chance to get noticed by a Broadway critic. Everyone knows you should never mix business and pleasure. (978-1-63679-667-3)

Language Lessons by Sage Donnell. Grace and Lenka never expected to fall in love. Is home really where the heart is if it means giving up your dreams? (978-1-63679-725-0)

New Horizons by Shia Woods. When Quinn Collins meets Alex Anders, Horizon Theater's enigmatic managing director, a passionate connection ignites, but amidst the complex backdrop of theater politics, their budding romance faces a formidable challenge. (978-1-63679-683-3)

Scrambled: A Tuesday Night Book Club Mystery by Jaime Maddox. Avery Hutchins makes a discovery about her father's death that will force her to face an impossible choice between doing what is right and finally finding a way to regain a part of herself she had lost. (978-1-63679-703-8)

Stolen Hearts by Michele Castleman. Finding the thief who stole a precious heirloom will become Ella's first move in a dangerous game of wits that exposes family secrets and could lead to her family's financial ruin. (978-1-63679-733-5)

Synchronicity by J.J. Hale. Dance, destiny, and undeniable passion collide at a summer camp as Haley and Cal navigate a love story that intertwines past scars with present desires. (978-1-63679-677-2)

The First Kiss by Patricia Evans. As the intrigue surrounding her latest case spins dangerously out of control, military police detective Parker Haven must choose between her career and the woman she's falling in love with. (978-1-63679-775-5)

Wild Fire by Radclyffe & Julie Cannon. When Olivia returns to the Red Sky Ranch, Riley's carefully crafted safe world goes up in flames. Can they take a risk and cross the fire line to find love? (978-1-63679-727-4)

Writ of Love by Cassidy Crane. Kelly and Jillian struggle to navigate the ruthless battleground of Big Law, grappling with desire, ambition, and the thin line between success and surrender. (978-1-63679-738-0)

Back to Belfast by Emma L. McGeown. Two colleagues are asked to trade jobs. Claire moves to Vancouver and Stacie moves to Belfast, and though they've never met in person, they can't seem to escape a growing attraction from afar. (978-1-63679-731-1)

Exposure by Nicole Disney and Kimberly Cooper Griffin. For photographer Jax Bailey and delivery driver Trace Logan, keeping it casual is a matter of perspective. (978-1-63679-697-0)

Hunt of Her Own by Elena Abbott. Finding forever won't be easy, but together Danaan's and Ashly's paths lead back to the supernatural sanctuary of Terabend. (978-1-63679-685-7)

Perfect by Kris Bryant. They say opposites attract, but Alix and Marianna have totally different dreams. No Hollywood love story is perfect, right? (978-1-63679-601-7)

Royal Expectations by Jenny Frame. When childhood sweethearts Princess Teddy Buckingham and Summer Fisher reunite, their feelings resurface and so does the public scrutiny that tore them apart. (978-1-63679-591-1)

Shadow Rider by Gina L. Dartt. In the Shadows, one can easily find death, but can Shay and Keagan find love as they fight to save the Five Nations? (978-1-63679-691-8)

The Breakdown by Ronica Black. Vaughn and Natalie have chemistry, but the outside world keeps knocking at the door, threatening more trouble, making the love and the life they want together impossible. (978-1-63679-675-8)

Tribute by L.M. Rose. To save her people, Fiona will be the tribute in a treaty marriage to the Tipruii princess, Simaala, and spend the rest of her days on the other side of the wall between their races. (978-1-63679-693-2)

Wild Wales by Patricia Evans. When Finn and Aisling fall in love, they must decide whether to return to the safety of the lives they had, or take a chance on wild love in windswept Wales. (978-1-63679-771-7)

Can't Buy Me Love by Georgia Beers. London and Kayla are perfect for one another, but if London reveals she's in a fake relationship with Kayla's ex, she risks not only the opportunity of her career, but Kayla's trust as well. (978-1-63679-665-9)

Chance Encounter by Renee Roman. Little did Sky Roberts know when she bought the raffle ticket for charity that she would also be taking a chance on love with the egotistical Drew Mitchell. (978-1-63679-619-2)

Comes in Waves by Ana Hartnett. For Tanya Brees, love in small-town Coral Bay comes in waves, but can she make it stay for good this time? (978-1-63679-597-3)

Dancing With Dahlia by Julia Underwood. How is Piper Fernley supposed to survive six weeks with the most controlling, uptight boss on earth? Because sometimes when you stop looking, your heart finds exactly what it needs. (978-1-63679-663-5)

Skyscraper by Gun Brooke. Attempting to save the life of an injured boy brings Rayne and Kaelyn together. As they strive for justice against corrupt Celestial authorities, they're unable to foresee how intertwined their fates will become. (978-1-63679-657-4)

The Curse by Alexandra Riley. Can Diana Dillon and her daughter, Ryder, survive the cursed farm with the help of Deputy Mel Defoe? Or will the land choose them to be the next victims? (978-1-63679-611-6)

The Heart Wants by Krystina Rivers. Fifteen years after they first meet, Army Major Reagan Jennings realizes she has one last chance to win the heart of the woman she's always loved. If only she can make Sydney see she's worth risking everything for. (978-1-63679-595-9)

Untethered by Shelley Thrasher. Helen Rogers, in her eighties, meets much-younger Grace on a lengthy cruise to Bali, and their intense relationship yields surprising insights and unexpected growth. (978-1-63679-636-9)

You Can't Go Home Again by Jeanette Bears. After their military career ends abruptly, Raegan Holcolm is forced back to their hometown to confront their past and discover where the road to recovery will lead them, or if it already led them home. (978-1-636790644-4)